D0867349

CAPRICE

A NOVEL

George Bowering

VIKING

Penguin Books Canada Limited, 2801 John Street, Markham, Ontario,
Canada L3R 1B4
Penguin Books, Harmondsworth, Middlesex, England
Viking Penguin Inc., 40 West 23rd Street, New York, New York
10010 U.S.A.
Penguin Books Australia Ltd., Ringwood, Victoria, Australia
Penguin Books (N.Z.) Ltd., Private Bag, Takapuna, Auckland 9,
New Zealand

First published by Penguin Books Canada Limited, 1987

Small portions of this story have been published, in earlier drafts, in the following magazines: *Brick*, *Descant*, *Epoch*, *The Malahat Review*, *Swift Current*, *Writing*; and in a pamphlet hand-printed by Robert Bringhurst and published by William Hoffer: *Spencer & Groulx*.

Printed in Canada

Canadian Cataloguing in Publication Data

Bowering, George, 1935–
Caprice
ISBN 0-670-81207-2
I. Title.
PS8503.O92C36 1987   C813'.54   C87-093117-2
PR9199.3.B69C36 1987

Library of Congress Catalog Card
Number 87-50383

This story is dedicated especially
to Manuel Louie and Windy Bone,
to their Lives
and my Dream.

If you just had ordinary English eyes, you would have seen late-morning sunlight flooding the light brown of the wide grassy valley and making giant knife shadows where the ridges slid down the hillsides, free of trees, wrinkles made in a wide land that didnt seem to be in that much of a hurry. As usual in the summer there wasnt a cloud in the sky, and you could not be sure where the sun was because you didnt dare look up at that half of the sky. You paid attention to shadows, to know what time it was, and because any animal with any sense was resting where it was darker.

But if you had those famous Indian eyes you could look down into the wide valley and see something moving, maybe a lot of things moving, but especially one black or at least dark horse, which meant probably a rider too, and in a little while a rider for certain. Coming from the east, walking so slowly that the puffs of dust rose no higher than the animal's knees.

There were two men halfway up one of those ridges, or rather the cleft between two of them, because there was a little stream that ran down the cleft, and once in a while a fish about the length of a baby's forearm would be seen lying still in a shadow where the stream found it possible to slow down for a while. These two men had long sticks with points on the end, and it was their job to stick fish whenever they could. Sometimes, when their families and friends were particularly insistent about fish, they would go down to the river and get wet while sinking nets on the ends of poles, but when the days were a little more relaxed, they liked to come here to the stream, because spearing was more enjoyable than netting, and the view was terrific. Sometimes you could be the first people to see someone new.

Actually one of the Indians could remember seeing a lot better than he could see, but he could also pretend he could see a lot better than he could see.

"Is it anyone we know?" he asked.

"I have never seen that horse before," said the second Indian.

"I was not enquiring about our familiarity with horses," said the first Indian. "Our familiarity with horses has not been in question for the past five generations at least."

"I know that it is customary for a young man to respect his elders," said the second Indian. "But that does not mean that I have to double over with laughter at your corny jokes."

The first Indian liked that. It made the joke worthwhile, and so he was still the season's master.

"All right," he said. "Can you tell me anything about the familiarity of the animal's rider?"

"Is the nature of your question a step in the education of a youth, or a confession that your eyes are not what they used to be?" asked the second Indian.

He was a proud athlete and of superior intelligence, or so said his family, and he had expressed the faith that he was destined to immortalize his people by application of his artistic predilections. That could get to be quite tiresome when one wanted to pass on a little lore, an old man's prerogative.

"Do tell an infirm old uncle what you think you see," he urged.

"I am not sure I can find the words," said the second Indian. "It is certainly no one we know, and perhaps something we have not seen among the white people who have been thoughtful enough to come and pursue their living among us."

"I hope you are not talking about magic again," said the first Indian. "You know how impatient I become when you get started on magic and the great spirit and all that."

"Not magic. Just a problem in words. Most of the white men around here call themselves cowboys, is that right?"

The first Indian was looking at a fish that was trying to decide whether to stick its front half out into the sunshine falling through the clear water of the stream. He thought he might let this one go.

"Cowboys."

"And their women. What are they called?"

"Some are called ranch wives. They fry dough and shake bedding on the back porch. They milk the milk cows and nail the house back together when it gets loose. They ride out and find lost animals. Others are called different things, the ones in town. I have heard one called Gert. Once I heard a cowboy refer to her as 'that fucking whore.' I thought that was rather redundant, but I imagine that you know more about the white man's language than I do, having worked with more informants. What would you call that creature on the dark horse?"

"Well, if the man who rides alone like that, with a rope and a weapon and some bags on the horse with him, is called a cowboy, what would you call a woman who rides a black horse west along the river valley, alone and in possession of all those things? Are you going to spear that fish? It's your turn."

The older man deliberately missed the fish and watched it scurry for the deepest shadows.

"What do you think? Could she be a ranch wife?"

"Not a chance. You should see her — "

Insolent kit!

"You should see her. She sits with her back straight and her hand on her upper leg. Not a bit of her bounces when the horse steps."

"Not a bit?"

"She rides just like a man."

The first Indian could see that the youngster would require a little more education in the area of his own language.

"She rides just like an Indian," said the second Indian.

"Is she an Indian?"

"No. She has red hair tied in two ropes that fall over the front part of her, where, as I said, she does not bounce."

The first Indian had not actually seen such a thing before, not such a thing riding alone with a weapon and bags. He didnt see her now, of course, though he could make out a rider and a horse, and he was willing to say now that the horse was black. He had never heard of such a thing. But it was not necessary to admit that. One could, and indeed, given his position, should allow his student to infer that such an apparition was riding out of the cache of his ancient knowledge as certainly as it was riding out of the east. If he were to continue to ask questions it would appear that he was doing so as part of his traditional role, and there could be no harm in that.

"What white man's word — "

"White man's word?"

"All right. What word used by the white man do you think should properly apply to such a phenomenon?" asked the first Indian.

"Well, she is not a ranch wife, or she would be up at the Double W or the Lazy 8, throwing scraps at the chickens. And she isnt a cowboy despite the clothes and weapon and bags, because though she does not bounce she is a woman or at least a girl — "

"Let us say woman, till we know for sure," said the old man.

He wasnt really that old, but the more time he spent with his protégé the older he felt. He was now thinking of himself as the old man rather than the full man of the tribe.

That was a white man's word. Tribe.

"So maybe we have to call her a cowgirl. I suppose that even though for the convenience we are calling her a woman, we can call her a cowgirl. That is, the white men call each other cowboys, and they dont seem to mind."

"We dont seem to mind being called Indians," said the first Indian.

"That's a different matter, surely," said the second Indian.

"It may be. It may be. But seeming is a different matter from being, too."

"Well, your fish seems to be back. Why dont you poke him?"

"Or her."

"I know your eyes are good enough to tell that much, old man."

The first Indian moved only the necessary part of his body, and in less time than it takes for a raven to turn in the air, the male fish was on his stick, already losing its colour in the late morning sun. The second Indian noticed that his teacher's eyes had not left his own during the operation. Every once in a while the old man would do something like that, and though it made the second Indian somehow a little embarrassed about some of the things he had been saying, it also assured him that he had been born among the right people.

"She might be called a bullgirl," he said.

He was a black horse. He was a beautiful horse, lucky and beautiful. Standing as he was now, without saddle and bags and weapon and rider, standing in the early summer evening sunlight, he was black, but when he moved his muscles under that black skin, there seemed to be dark purple lakes moving around on his surface. He stood, of course, with his long narrow neck reaching down, his lip curled up as he nipped the brown grass. Because of this his long black mane fell down one side of his neck, and if you were there you would have liked to feel that hair with your fingers. You would take your gloves off and let it fall over the back of your wrist and across the back of your thumb. If she let you.

It was because of her that he was lucky. She depended on him, and let him know that she did, whether silently or in the Spanish she spoke to him. That was the language he had been brought up on, and not in California. In Spain. She depended on him, but he was lucky. She treated him even better than his sire had been treated thousands of miles away in Spain, even better than he had been treated in the orange grove where he had first tasted grass of any colour.

In the evening sunlight the fire could not be seen, but there was a can of Chinese tea suspended over it. It was a small fire, made of greasewood and cow chips, and by the time it got dark there would be a small glow, and by the time it got light again a few pieces of sage would get it flaming again. Beside the fire she was sipping tea and reading. Her dark red hair was loose now, falling over the dark cloth on her shoulders. She was not reading Spanish. The only Spanish she knew was the language she spoke to the horse, including his name. She called him Cabayo.

She sat among her stuff, the bag of clothing, the bedding, the bag of books, the saddle, and her weapon. Her dark brown boots stood together by the fire, the soft leather falling to their sides. They were the kind of boots a snake could not or would not enter during the night. She had heard stories of snakes and scorpions in boots in the morning, but she had never seen such a thing. Some people back home said that the devil put scorpions on earth to vex the unwary. In the book she was reading the devil was more direct, or rather more personal.

The sun was almost always the same here. In the middle of the day it was so large and white that you didnt dare look up at the southern half of the sky. This time of night it spread lushly, like butter some poor poet would have said, all down through the valley and up the hillsides. It fetches small shadows behind every clump of sage and cactus, and inspires certain timid animals to hop from shadow to shadow. Grasshoppers shake their quick wings and start up their noise every child takes at first to be rattlesnakes.

If she had been a girl here she would have been instructed to hate rattlesnakes, to kill them whenever that was easy, to remember not to run away from them into the lair of another one. Boys she knew would have got together and held down each end of a rattlesnake with a forked stick, and turned the sticks in opposite directions, till the snake's skin snapped and rolled along its body. Usually one would simply bash its head with a rock. Snakes do not live till the sun goes down. They live till they die. Rattlesnakes have a reputation for speed, but they are especially fast when you dont know they are nearby. If you find one in front of you, coiled and with its head ready, you can wave your hand right past his face. She had done this a few times during the first days when she still thought about killing snakes. Now she just agreed with them, to stay out of each other's way. If one of them broke the agreement, very well, we would see who was faster, or who was paying attention. If the human hand held a snake, it might move faster than another human hand.

She poured another tin cup of tea out of the can. It was particularly strong now, and she was tempted to put sugar in it. Then she did put sugar in it. She drank a little of the tea and poured the rest out. Then she put on her blue knitted cap and got into bed. The still warm earth of the Thompson Valley was her mattress.

Everyday Luigi had tried a lot of places in his life. He wasnt all that old — he figured he must be about fifty-five, give or take a year or two. But time goes slower when you move around a lot. You can always remember what year something happened: oh yes, when I broke my leg, that must have been 1880, because I was living in Oregon that year. He noticed old folks around here always got into disputations about when things happened, ranch wives and their husbands unable to settle on whether their son Jesse got shot by one of the McLeans in 1877 or 1875. That was because they had spent their whole adult lives in the Thompson Valley, and time had just turned into a sluice of seasons. But Everyday Luigi had had a lot of different years in different climates, doing different jobs and wearing different names. Not to mention languages. Oh, 1872, that was the year I was speaking French.

He had been born, so his papers said, in Istria, and spent his childhood in Trieste, where it was not always a good idea to be Italian. So his first fourteen years were spent as Lause Martens rather than Luigi Martino. Now he could call himself whatever he wanted, but everyone called him Everday Luigi, except the people he spent most of his time with. They were Chinese, and generally called him something in a language he couldnt understand. The Chinamen who liked him tried to call him Lou.

"Risten, Roo, you get raundly outa big hotel. Boss mad as bull with foot in tlap."

"Hey, Soo Woo, how come you can say bull, and you cant say Lou?"

"You shake a fucking reg, Roo."

Everyday Luigi was a handyman for the boss and just about everyone else in the Chinese community as it would later be called. He delivered laundry, gathered firewood, swept the floor in the Canadian Cafe, and carried messages. They were written in a language that defeated him. All his life he had been learning languages to keep alive and get an edge. But he didnt even know which way to hold up the paper this time. For all he knew, when he carried a note from the laundry to the Nicola Hotel, he might have been carrying instructions to beat the messenger around the head with the spittoon.

He was the first person to see her riding into town on her beautiful black horse. Everyday Luigi hated getting onto a horse, and did so only when he had to, when he couldnt cadge a ride on somebody's wagon, when he had to get somewhere that was too far and too slow to walk, when there was danger of losing his job. That was how he lost his job at the Douglas Lake Ranch. He hadnt been doing anything that needed horsemanship, just cleaning out barns and corrals and mending rails and posts, but when they found out he had no sympathy for horses and no desire to sit on them, they fired him right off the ranch. They said it was like having a woman on board ship, nothing personal, just bad luck.

In Trieste the Austrians were fanatical about horses. They trained white ones to leap through the air at the end of a rope. They put up statues of old Hapsburgs on horses and hired Lause Martens, aged ten, to keep the pigeon shit and mulberries off them. Everyday Luigi could live without Austrians, though there were a few on ranches around here. And he could live without horses, but how could he? There were more horses than people around here, even counting the Chinamen.

But this was a beautiful horse, even for an eye that had turned away from an emperor's noble steed when he saw a pigeon land on its rump. In fact, this one had walked past four buildings before he remembered to look at its rider. When he did, he dropped a bundle of bedsheets in the dust.

That was probably an Italian response, that is, exaggerated and theatrical. But mouths often fell open when Caprice rode or walked past people who had the time to notice, which in a town like this was just about anybody.

Everyday Luigi was going to pick up the laundry, but first he thought he would look at the young woman for a while. She held her freckled face straight forward, but under the flat brim of her hat her grey eyes were turning left and right. Two dark red braids lay in front of her shoulders. Her skin was very white, with light freckles across the bridge of her nose and on her forehead. There was a small scar in the shape of the letter *C* on the skin over her left cheekbone.

If Luigi had been able to take his eyes from her he would have noticed that there were other people on the wooden sidewalk and in the dust of the street watching her. Whereas the main drag was generally characterized by movement, riders riding out of town, drinkers crashing in and out of doors, harassed children trying not to keep up with their shopping ranch folks. But right now there was no one moving except Caprice on her horse, slowly walking down the middle of the gravelly road.

Her back was straight, her right hand resting on the top of her thigh, elbow out. She was wearing clothes you werent likely to remember, some kind of grey sweater over a blue cotton shirt, a pair of dungarees, and dark brown riding boots with soft leather tight around her legs. She sat her horse as if he were a clothesline and she were a clothespeg, and the muscles of her thighs changed the colour of her dungarees.

Her boots had high riding heels, but no spurs. She was wearing a belt with a large silver buckle in the shape of a coiled snake, but she wore no gun-belt. She had a rifle in its scabbard hanging near her leg, but there was a cover on it, and a buckle that held it closed. She didnt seem to have a rope, but she had a whip. Luigi looked at the whip. Its stock was only about two inches thick. It was black, and shiny in the morning sun.

He watched her until she stopped her horse in front of the Nicola, and when she stepped off he remembered that he was fifty-five years old. This woman did not have a speck of Thompson Valley dust on her, and there he was, covered in a grey sift after walking halfway between the hotel and the laundry tubs.

He should have kicked the basket of sheets into the street and run after the vision, but he only picked up his load and headed toward the mocking voice of Soo Woo. Maybe he wasnt an Italian after all.

No one knew who she was or what she did or why she was here. Anyone who knew these things was either not here, or pretending not to know her. A lot of beautiful things are dangerous: weapons, animals, storm clouds. Even the dullest wits in town could see that this creature was dangerous in some way. Only a drunk or a materialist would miss that. There was no shortage of these in this country around this time. Once people find out that there is gold, or copper, or even coal in the country, and once the railroad has laid track through, there are going to be men arrive who are different in kind from the people who have been here since the ice drew back, or who came alone or in very small groups to see whether there were many animals with attractive pelts in the area. Once the mountain mines and the riverside placers got to be well known, and once expensive commodities were carried by rail from here to the coast or to the east, there were bound to be newcomers without ideals, a lot of them from across the medicine line a little over a hundred miles to the south.

One of these was a man named Frank Spencer, or so he said. No dangerous-sounding nickname, just that simple name anyone might have had, or used. He was, people said, from Tennessee, not an unusual beginning for people in the logging camps, tie-cutting camps, and ranches of British Columbia in the nineteenth century. People, some of whom were eager to see him stay north of the line, said that he had ridden with the Clantons, and that he had only ceased to do so when the Clantons made a date to meet the Earps at a corral in an Arizona town. After that he had travelled northward, making enemies in Colorado, Wyoming, and Montana, before crossing the medicine line to Alberta. Wherever he went people noticed that he had a blue mark on his hand, where, it was said, a lawman's bullet had passed through.

In Alberta he passed himself off as a cowboy, and if it had not been for the marvellous saloons in Calgary, and the presence of a number of his countrymen who knew him, he might have stayed there. As it was, he found it expedient to travel westward, and near the end of the 1880s he arrived in the Thompson Valley, where he seemed reconciled to tending cows instead of stealing them. Kamloops was not Tombstone. Since the arrival of the railroad, local citizens had been talking about the future. Spencer had heard this sort of thing before in several towns across the line. When people started talking about the future, that meant that things were going to be more difficult for individuals and groups who wished to live without the encumbrance of the law.

So Frank Spencer reluctantly retired as a gunman, and took up ranch work. He got a job on the Campbell spread, and at the age of thirty-five, started to settle down.

Except on payday. The saloons in Kamloops were not as good as the saloons in Calgary, but they had whisky that was as good, good enough in that first terrible winter to persuade a cowhand to make the ten-mile ride into town at the end of the month. At the Dominion or the Colonial, the conversation at the end of Saturday night often went like this:

"What are you looking at, you dumb Frog?"

"Not at you, saddle tramp."

"You want to watch your mouth, Frenchie."

"I am not looking for any trouble, Frank."

"You are fucking right you are not, you yellowbelly frog-eating son of a bitch."

"I'd hate to say what I seen you eating, big-mouth."

"Why dont you fuck off back to Montreal where you came from, Foster?"

"I dont come from Montreal, I come from St Foy."

"Then Foy off to Saint Fuck, Froggie."

"Piss off back to Pittsburgh, big-nose Yankee."

"Ah, you make me sick."

"Yeah?"

"Yeah."

"Yeah?"

"Yeah, Yankee."

At which point someone else would offer drinks to both disputants, or attention would shift to an argument in another part of the room. Kamloops was not Dodge.

Till one Friday in May.

"You riding into town, Frank?"

"Yeah, what do ya want, Pete?"

These were the same two men. How a French Canadian from St Foy got the name Pete Foster might seem a puzzle now, but in those days a lot of hired riders were paid for whatever name they announced the day they arrived. Pete Foster was as likely a name for a man with a French accent as Frank Spencer was for a man with a Tennessee accent.

"Here's five bucks. Bring me four bottles of rye whisky."

"You putting up a year's supply all at once, Frenchie?"

"If you're nice I'll give you a glass with plenty of water, Spence."

"Hell, I cant remember what water tastes like," said the Tennessee bad man, now the Thompson Valley not-so-bad man.

In town he ate some Chinese food, picked up the Campbell ranch mail, and bought a new hat, then picked up Pete's whisky and headed back to the Double W in the middle of the afternoon. At first he just took the time to look at the end of spring and the beginning of summer. The grass was still green on the south slopes where the sun could not beat all day. The cattle were starting to graze upward. In six weeks they would be up among the trees. They had a regulated life but a pretty good one. All they had to do was pay a few inches of burnt hide for a life of eating and drinking.

All this musing made Frank Spencer desirous of a reward himself, and that last word, "drinking," did it. Here he was, carrying four bottles of whisky ten miles for that Frenchman, and no suggestion of any recompense. He decided that he was morally entitled to some of Foster's hooch. Action followed decision the way a coyote follows a limp foolhen, and in a trice Spencer had a cork between his teeth. After that the ride back to the ranch was more pleasure than meditation.

By the time he rode up to the old log bunkhouse, he was not guiding his horse at all, except for the last moment when he persuaded it to approach the open door and stop a step short of entering. Pete Foster, having heard the noise of his approach, met him there.

"You remember my whisky, Frank?" he asked.

Spencer jumped or slid off his horse and plunged his hand into his saddle-bag, coming out with a bottle at a time, numbering them as he handed them over to the other wrangler. He got to three.

"Where's the other one, Frank?"

Spencer reached in again and came out with the last bottle. There was about an inch and a half of whisky in it.

"This here was my commission, and I thank you for it, Froggy."

Pete Foster was incensed. One bottle of whisky came to most of a day's hard work. He stood there in the doorway, three bottles of whisky in his arms, unable for a moment to speak or think, while Frank Spencer led his bay gelding to the stable and started to take the gear off it. Pete Foster was really mad. Eventually he could speak, though he was not thinking so well.

"Spencer!"

Spencer continued to remove things from his horse.

"God damn it, Yank, I want a dollar and a half!"

"Dollar and a quarter," said Spencer.

"I want my fucking money, *câlice*!"

He should have had the sense to be alarmed by Spencer's mathematical accuracy.

Spencer just grinned, and slapped his saddle down on the big rail in front of the stable. He reached for the blanket. Foster reached for

Spencer, forgetting about the three bottles, which fell to the ground. One of them broke. This made Pete Foster furious.

"Tabernac!"

He spun the American around by the shoulder and threw a fist at him, propelling him against his saddle. He should not have done this. He was now speaking the language his opponent had learned in a lot of ranch yards and saloons in Arizona and Kansas. In that language your hand reaches for your belt, and if you have a six-gun there it speaks the next few words for you. This being a ranch outside Kamloops rather than a street in Laramie, Spencer was not wearing a six-gun, but he had a Bowie knife at his belt, and he reached for it. Now he felt a lot better about getting into a fight with the hot-head from St Foy.

But angry as he was, Pete Foster was not entirely stupid. He took a look at the big knife and decided that he could make do with two bottles of whisky for now. Leaving them on the ground for safe-keeping, he turned and lit out for another part of the ranch yard. Frank Spencer chased him, but though he was just drunk enough to fight, he was too drunk to find a man.

A couple hours later Pete Foster figured that the disagreement was settled. He could not get over losing the whisky, but he figured that when Spencer got sober he would see some sense and pay him back. Pete headed for the bunkhouse, where two other men were lying down and smoking. There was one bottle of his whisky on the table. He decided to go to the stable and find the other one. But as soon as he reached the yard he knew he was in trouble, and he knew where the other bottle had gone.

There was Frank Spencer on the porch of the big house, with a Winchester in his hands. He was as drunk as hell, but he was an American man of the west, which meant that he could shoot a jumping rabbit even if it looked as if there were two or three of them. Pete Foster took to running again.

He made it halfway to the bunkhouse. Frank Spencer, now a picture of efficiency, snapped one .44-calibre bullet into the middle of

Pete Foster's body, which quit moving all at once and dropped to the hard-packed earth.

But other bodies were now moving fast. Legs came running out of the bunkhouse towards the fallen man. Frank Spencer's legs took him to the stable. He grabbed Campbell's best horse, threw the first saddle he saw onto its back, and rode through the yard, waving the Winchester and promising loudly that he would use it again. But the men offered no interest in him. They were busy getting a wagon ready, lifting the bloody Quebecker, taking him to the new hospital in Kamloops.

Frank Spencer, on Campbell's favourite bay, carrying Campbell's favourite rifle, rode south.

Pete Foster died at four in the morning. While he was doing it he just had time for one word.

"Caprice."

Caprice wasnt the only French Canadian in town. A no-account would-be hard case named Loop Groulx was sitting in the Canadian Cafe ("Chinese and Canadian Cooking") having steak and eggs and nips out of a small bottle of rye whisky when the woman came in. There were a couple of dusty wranglers sitting at another table, and two or three Chinese kids hanging around the candy counter, obviously expert and bored from having to stay in sight for too many hours a day while their parents sold fried stuff to the cowboys and town people.

She found a table as far from the men as she could, and sat with her back to a wall, where she could watch the door and the tops of passing people visible over the curtains that started halfway down the big window. At the hotel she had washed up but she hadnt changed. Now she took off her hat and placed it with her whip on the chair beside her.

Everyday Luigi saw her from the kitchen, where he was scouring a huge wok. Now that he could see her dark red hair and more of her face, he wished he were forty years old again.

"Wash that wok, Roo," said Soo Woo.

So he scoured, but he looked as often as he could into the other room, and he saw Loop Groulx watching her too. He saw Soo Woo approach the woman, and it was the first time he had ever seen the Celestial boss shuffle his feet.

"Let me have some English tea," she said. "And may I have some fried rice with chicken in it?"

"Onry poke fry rice," said Soo.

"That will do nicely," she said.

When the owner-waiter had brought the teapot and cup, she took out the book she had been reading the night before and opened it on the table and began reading.

It was a drab olive green book with this information on the title page:

Marlowe's Faustus

Goethe's Faust
(from the German)

by
John Anster, LL.D.

With an Introduction by Henry Morley
London

George Routledge and Sons
Broadway, Ludgate Hill
New York: 9 Lafayette Place
1883

There was also a rubber stamp that championed:

The "Better 'Ole" News Stand
(W. Hill)
Idlehour Theatre Building
Shaunavon, Sask.

But she was not reading the title page or the page with the stamp on it. She was, as she had been the night before, snagged on page 103:

> Then did I in creations of my own
> (Oh, is not man in every thing divine!)

Build worlds — or bidding them no longer be —
Exert, enjoy a sense of deity —
Doomed for such dreams presumptuous to atone;
All by one word of thunder overthrown!

She knew it meant something to her, but she wasnt sure what. She had the six lines memorized, but still she stared at them on the page and looked hard the way she sometimes did just before the other meaning edged past her eyes into her delight.

Build worlds? The first time she had read it aloud she had read and memorized "build words," and so was surprised to find "worlds" when she looked again last night. Build worlds? She supposed they did something like that in the Idlehours Theatre. Idle hours, her mother in St Foy had said, are reserved for the Fiend.

Last winter in Arizona she had met a middle-aged woman who told her a story over a pot of tea in the American Cafe in Prescott. She could not remember her name, except that it started with a C, but she remembered the story. Mrs C said that she had been so lonely on her first homestead after her husband disappeared that she had taken to writing poems and tying them to tumbleweeds and watching them roll southward out of sight. That was how she won her second husband, a man with a face like a coyote and a clear heart.

When the fried rice was placed in front of her, she continued to read, bringing her fork to a blind mouth, and wondering whether the thunder was the answer to everyone who builds a world, or only to the unholy. Her mother would have said that the notion of building a world was blasphemy. Her mother had been unhappy when Caprice announced that she was going to become a schoolteacher. A schoolteacher should be a nun, so that someone else will have protected her from the things in books.

Loop Groulx was one of those unpleasant men who feel affronted when they see someone else reading a book or scrupulously obeying the law. He was especially unsettled on this occasion because he was sensitive enough to realize that this was a beautiful woman. That she was reading a book and not even looking around the cafe upset him more. When she got up and left, he followed her out.

Drying his hands as he walked, Everyday Luigi followed.

☆ ☆ ☆

They were lying in the sweat house early in the morning. The first Indian had built it or its ancestor many years ago, so he felt that having contributed his share, he could wait for the young fellow to bring more hot rocks. The second Indian felt that it would be presumptuous of him to carry rocks into his elder's sweat house, so he would wait for the old man to bring them. There wasnt much steam left, but he felt too good right now to run out and sit in the cold creek.

"Some of the white men from across the medicine line have asked me whether they might be permitted to visit a steam house," said the second Indian.

"Did you tell them that it would be difficult because our sacred laws suggest that the red man's spiritual wealth depends on his keeping the mysteries of the divine steam?"

"I never heard of that," said the second Indian.

"Well," said the first Indian, "it is not strictly true, but I have always found that the white man places more value on our stuff if we can convince him that we are religious about it."

"That will be of value to me when I come to expressing myself and our tribal beliefs in art," said the second Indian.

"What did you tell the white men from across the medicine line?"

"I said I would consult the master of the steam."

"Did you mention a price?"

"I am an artist. I dislike discussing such things."

The first Indian was not altogether happy with this artist's search for himself, and especially the self-absorption connected with it, but he could not help feeling a little amused by it. For one thing, it provided him with a feeling of greater wisdom, and made the role of teacher more sweet somehow.

"These petitioners you mention, they are the ones who came here to play that interesting game?"

"Baseball."

"An interesting game. You do not have to tell everyone I said so, but from what I have seen I find this brace-ball more interesting than sukkullilaka."

"But sukkullilaka is our traditional sport. It hearkens back to the misty origins of the people. Our greatest players have always been honoured equally with our most intrepid warriors and hunters."

The old man went out and brought in some more hot rocks. It was probably that word "misty" that did it. He poured on the water and lay down again, the tiny hemisphere now suffused with steam.

"I played sukkullilaka when I was younger. I represented our village in the great tournaments that occurred before you were born. But now that my playing days are over and I can watch the game as an impartial spectator, it seems rather over-simple to me, trying to get a ball between two posts. I dont even care for the ltpiq involved. Even though it is our honoured and cherished tradition to wager on the game, as you would likely suggest."

"I shouldnt wonder. You probably do not see well enough to know where to place your bets."

"I can see well enough to pop you one even in this fog, young man. What do you think we should charge the Yankees to be initiated into the sacred cult of the steam house?"

"Well, I was not thinking of their beads and fire-water. I rather wondered whether they might let me play their game with them."

"Why?"

"A voice tells me it might have something to do with my quest for an art form."

The reply was obvious, but the first Indian did not voice it. That was how he got to be the first Indian. Instead he got up to face the cold creek at last.

"Ask them whether they could use a first-base coach," he said.

A wagon full of potatoes in gunny sacks was creaking and rattling past the Canadian Cafe as she stepped out onto the wooden sidewalk. It was planting season as soon as the first warm dry winds swept through the valley, and already the fields along the riverside were tilled and heaped, and runnels of irrigation water were snaking over the dry earth. In the more distant fields men with their jackets off for the first time this year were sowing the season's first alfalfa crop. Big white clouds piled over the tops of the Cascade mountains to the west and stopped there. For the rest of the year, till the cool days of late fall, there would be few disruptions of the great blue arc of the sky. It would rain once at the end of June and again at the end of August, for twenty minutes or so each time. Birds would go crazy in the instant puddles. A calf might get stuck in the mud on the bank of the Thompson River. But for now the days would get hot and very dry, and Caprice would put her blue knitted hat away for the summer.

Now, her book tucked under her arm, she listened to her boots knocking on the wooden sidewalk as she walked toward the hostler's to check on her horse. She could probably trust the man, but she liked to see for herself, to see her horse. She liked to talk to him a little when she stuck him somewhere.

There was no scarcity of eyes turned her way as she walked, even though she didnt bounce at all. There was no scarcity of minds and mouths making comment, either. As she passed before them, the men and women in the shops and in front of them found sentences or fragments of sentences shaping inside their heads or directly in front of them.

"Where the hell did *she* come from?"

"Now there's one fine lookin' woman."

"Oh, Lordy, look at that."

"That creature had better stay away from places she'd better stay away from."

"Wait till Gert the Whore sees *her.*"

"Why, she dont bounce at all. It aint natural."

"Wonder how old she is."

"I think I seen her in Fairview one time."

"Looks like Strange is following her."

That last referred to Loop Groulx, who was often called Strange Loop in these parts. He was walking about ten percent faster than she was, trying to appear as if he were just taking his usual toothpick stroll after chowing down at Soo Woo's. But it was his intention to catch up to this book-reading girl around the time she got to the hostler's. Behind him was Everyday Luigi, walking about one percent slower than Loop was.

Strange Loop didnt seem to have anything special to do, and in this sort of town, at this time of year, when you see men driving wagons out of town, loaded down with seed or barbed wire, other men buying gear at the hardware, and ranch wives at the grocery store acquiring enough supplies to feed a crew, the sight of a man or several men with nothing apparent to do is suggestive if not clearly disquieting. Strange had been around town all winter, spending enough money to eat three or four times a day, and drink as often, and no one had heard him enquire about spring hiring at any of the ranches or the railroad. And it was clear that he was no pilgrim. If this had been the United States, he would have been carrying a tied-down six-shooter. As it was, he probably had a gun on him somewhere.

When Caprice walked back of the hostler's storefront to the corral, he followed her. She didnt appear to notice him, but went to her handsome black horse to ask him whether he was satisfied with his quarters. This irritated Groulx even more. He had to talk to her.

"Hello, Freckles," he said.

"I'm afraid you've mistaken me for someone else," she replied. And worst of all, she did not look at him as she said it, but continued to run her bare hand over the horse's neck.

"I couldnt help notice you was reading a book back there at the Chink's," he said.

"Good for you."

"I'm kind of a reader myself."

He was trying to keep his voice in a light bantering mood, but he was just the kind of would-be hardcase who sounded like a schoolyard bully even when he was asking his mother for another biscuit.

"Oh, I could tell that, Mr — ?"

"Name's Groulx, Ma'am. First name's Lionel, but folks call me Loop."

A perceptive eye, none of which was around, would have noticed that she stopped her hand's movement on the horse's neck for half a second. At last she turned and looked at the man. He was about an inch taller than she was.

He was gratified by her interest but he didnt know why it had come about.

"Tell me, Mr Groulx, why did you follow me here?"

"Well, like I said, Ma'am, I'm interested in books, and I was pleasured to see another book-lover in town. You a schoolteacher?"

"No I'm not."

Groulx had an unjustified confidence in his ability to talk up a woman, even though he had not overly impressed Gert the Whore. He had expected this beauty to trade her name for his, but here she was at the advantage. If this were a gunfight back in Utah or Arizona, one of them would have been dead by now.

"What are you readin', anyway?"

"Goethe. Are you a devotee of romantic poetry, Mr Groulx?"

"Cant say I am. Only poem I can remember is *Captain My Captain*."

"Well, Mr Groulx, I have been riding all week, and I think I had better go and have a rest. You'll excuse me, wont you?"

She gave her horse a final pat and began to walk back toward the street, but as she thought to pass the hard-case, he grabbed her upper arm. He was a little unsure of his motive — was he asserting the natural prerogative of the hunter-and-gatherer male, or was he perhaps imploring her that she look again and consider that he was deserving of a little more attention, as a gift at least.

That was when Everyday Luigi made his move. Out of the dark noon shadow into the bright sun he came, arriving with two hands against Loop's chest. He pushed, and Loop's grip on the woman was released as he himself stumbled several boot heels backwards.

"What the fuck do you think you're doing, Wop?"

"Just leave the lady alone, Strange."

Luigi was really scared. He had lived in a lot of towns, east and west, and he had been bruised and cut from time to time. But he had never offered himself this way. He had never seen a woman like Caprice, and he had never done what he had just done to Loop Groulx. Oh, shit, he thought.

"What the fuck do you think you're doing?"

And Groulx bashed him. He hammered him and kicked him and clobbered him. He thumped him against the rails of the corral, and stomped him into the ground. He moved faster than one would have thought possible, hitting the middle-aged Italian immigrant with both fists, elbows, the top of his head, his right knee, and both boots. He hit him about fifteen times, and only stopped because he noticed the woman walking away.

He thought she was heading for the street, whether to escape or to get help from the Provincial Police. But she was only walking far enough to get distance.

When she had reached the right distance, he was suddenly aware of her intent. It was familiar but in the circumstances impossible to believe.

In one moment he saw her take her coiled whip from her side. In the next he saw her shake it loose. Before the next he felt a sharp crack across his chest, that drove him again back on his boot heels, then his hat was knocked from his head. He was still trying to stand steady when the whip grabbed his foot and pulled it away from the ground. He fell on his ass. The loud smacks of the whip were met by geysers of dust beside him, where he had got to his hands and knees, and now he scrabbled, trying to get to his feet again, but she was too fast. She was also amazingly strong. He got his hands off the ground for a half-second, but another blow on his back sent him belly-down on the ground, his face a few inches from some moist horse buns. Then she stopped.

She stopped, so he turned and sat on the ground to face her, but there were about a half-dozen people there now. He was too weak to do anything. There were too many people there for him to do what he wanted to do.

The woman turned and walked away, coiling her whip as she went. Everyday Luigi limped after her. The other people, three men and two kids, looked at Strange Loop for a while, then left without saying anything. That was something at least.

She hadnt even dropped her damned poetry book. If she had he would have picked it up and thrown it into the corral. Maybe he would have to do that with her. First thing he had to do was go and get a new shirt. He thought about how he would make her pay for it. He was going to make her beg for it.

☆ ☆ ☆

Frank Spencer had got a long way south by the time Caprice arrived in Kamloops on the train. But a day later she was in the hand-tooled saddle on her black, and headed in the same direction. Sometimes she found someone who remembered seeing the desperado a week earlier. Most of the time she travelled the dry brown valley south, past green lakes and blue lakes, along a quick dark green river. She had found out as much as the people in Kamloops and at the Campbell ranch knew about him, the litany of cowtowns and mining towns he had mentioned when he was bragging in a Kamloops bar.

In Fairview she let herself spend a couple nights in a hotel, and she let Cabayo spend a couple nights in the hotel's stable. She talked across the hotel bar with John Kearns, an amiable Irish Canadian with a slow way of talking and a disregard for Yankee gunslingers. He had an interesting tale to relate about an incident in the Bucket of Blood, the unofficial name of his establishment, a week earlier.

"Seems like he might have been the baddy you're looking for, Miss," he said. "He had a lot to drink, and when he got a skinful, he enquired as to whether any of the miners wanted to compete with guns or knives or fists. Nobody took him up on it, but laughed at him instead. Then he said there was a Froggie up north a ways — begging your pardon, Miss — "

"Quite all right, Mr Kearns, I know you are only reporting Spencer's language."

Kearns pulled a couple beers for some men covered with white dust, then resumed his story.

"Said there was a young French Canadian chappie up north a

ways who wasnt laughing at anyone any more. That would probably be your brother, I take it."

"That was Pierre. Spencer shot him over a bottle of whisky."

"Right here in Fairview I have seen a lot of bad things happen to people over a bottle of whisky, or even a glass of whisky," said Kearns. "We are only fifteen miles from the Yankee border."

"My brother never fired a gun at anything but rabbits and snakes, Mr Kearns."

"Well, I hope you find this Spencer fellow, Miss. I also hope you dont find him."

"I'll be going across the line at Nighthawk tomorrow, Mr Kearns. If I come up this way again, I'll let you know what happened to Frank Spencer."

"I am more concerned with what happens with you, Miss."

Caprice looked down at her bare hand, her fingertips on the glass of gin, at the smooth water the glass slid on when she moved it back and forth a little on the gleaming bar.

"Is this reality? — so like a dream
All seems! May I, upon some future day,
Resume my visit? — learn the grounds and root
Of these your doctrines?"

"Come when it may suit," replied John Kearns. "So you have read Marlowe's tragical drama of the doctor's inadvisable quest?"

"*Oui*, that I have, sir. But I was speaking from Goethe."

"You're a lovely lass, Miss, and I dont like to see you going on this quest you are on. You should be a poet instead."

"Mr Kearns, you are also, from what I have been able to tell, a lovely man. And probably a poet. In my own country I was a poet. I even produced a little book called *L'Ancien Barre du Jour*, which was not hated by the critics. But now I am in another country, and here I am not a poet. I am a sister."

"You are perhaps a fury," said John Kearns, and with a tender look at her, went to satisfy some loud miners at the other end of the bar.

A few minutes later she was standing at the edge of the clay cliff that held Fairview above the long brown valley with its green river running south. Bare brown hills with occasional short pines rose on the other side. Shadows were falling into the valley but the evening sun still bathed the range land above it. Thinking of her only other departure from her home country, the dream she could hardly remember, she sat on a boulder, making sure to check the ground for snakes, and gazed down at the still green banks of the river beneath her. The frogs there were beginning their rumble. The Midi had had a sky like this, and a warmth that rose from the earth when the sun was departing.

She looked up and down the valley, and now she transformed it in her mind. She planted long vineyards on the higher slopes, and created fruit orchards as far as she could see, north and south in the valley. She put a house in each orchard, red tile roofs and yellow stucco walls. She made one house with a huge trellis of red roses over the kitchen door. And after consulting with her own patience for a moment, she saved a corner of that orchard, and spread out a baseball field on it. She didnt know exactly how to fashion it, but she knew that it would be taken care of.

If you just had ordinary eastern eyes you would see a long shallow valley, brown in the honest sunlight, blue on the slopes of the hills, green among the trees on the hilltops. You would see the Monashee blue if you were far enough east, the Cascade blue if far enough west. You would see the enormous quiet bow of blue sky above, and if you were looking actively you might see a hawk up high. If you had Indian eyes you would see the hawk's head bent to look below him with eyes even better than yours. But if you had ordinary eastern eyes you might be satisfied or even transported by the lovely morning light bathing the bunch grass and producing bright rectangles on the bench lands. You would see the blurry grey-purple of sage, and along both sides of the green river you would see dark green tributaries of potato rows, swathes of alfalfa. You would spy the marks of men, the wooden troughs that carried water to the potato fields, perhaps some sun-silvered wooden troughs that had once carried stream water to placer mines. Of course you would see the sunflash off the rails laid here half a decade ago, and the shiny yellow telegraph poles, the wires that sing when you throw a stone that hits them. If you are a particularly smart boy from town, you might walk along the line, looking for the fresh copper lengths at the bottom of each pole. You can earn a dollar on a good day of coppering.

If you have ordinary eyes and a good heart you will stop working or riding for a minute or two and look ahead of you for twenty miles. In all likelihood you wont see anyone else.

But if you have another kind of eye, you might climb to an outcropping of rock in the valley slope and look closely at its surface.

There along with the thin lichen you will likely spot the signature of a small shelled creature from under the sea. With the kind of eye that can turn away from the range and focus on a rooted boulder you may look millions of years into the past. You will read the first writing of the Thompson Valley, a story left by a departing sea that never saw a sailor. Mr Fraser left his pages for us, but he was only an index-writer with Scottish eyes and a star-gazing friend lost in another valley. He was a figure in a long story, mistakenly persuaded that he was the maker of that narrative. He had company in the northwest, more than he imagined.

If you have normal reader's eyes you will see the Europeans here sitting down to pull the small cactus off their trouser legs. You will see the people in high boots acquiring the skill or habit of looking around the ground and rocks before they sit down. You will know a newcomer by the sunburn on his forehead. You will be able to distinguish the varieties of darkness in skin, the suntanned European, the half-breed with a Scottish name, the Lebanese cowpuncher. The people with perpetual red faces are the English who never tan but live an entire summer with sunburned noses and necks.

If you are a curious reader you will see a familiar crumbling of rock, and look closer, to find what you more than half expect, light blue agate, opal, jasper. Once you are pretty sure you found some garnet. If you had been here a lifetime or two earlier you might have found gold and silver, or at least copper. If you were a miner for wages now, you would be certain of finding a seam of coal every day you went down the shaft.

But if you were an Indian you always knew these things were here, part of the earth. Curiosity was to be expended on the white men.

"How could you get to be so old and not have a woman?" asked the second Indian.

"I have had women all over the world," said Everyday Luigi.

"How is it that you were not able to keep them, or at least one?" asked the persistent native artist.

Everyday Luigi tried to remember the correct way to allow an enigmatic Triestine expression to pass over his face. It was especially difficult with the bruises and abrasions.

"I have always travelled a good deal," he said. "Sometimes one travels because of the women about whom the question of keeping arises. In all cases it is complicated to travel the face of the globe with all that extra baggage."

"Explain it to me in more believable language," said the second Indian. "Imagine that you are talking with an aborigine who does not believe that story about a globe."

The first Indian was there, but he was not saying anything.

"Are you a Catholic Indian or a Prostitute Indian," asked Everyday Luigi.

"I am an animist, with Catholic overtones."

Everyday Luigi found this hard to respond to. The doctrine of his church regarding divorce and annulment and sexual sin would mean little to a man whose escape from guilt was a matter of choice between the confessional and the spirits in the forest. He decided to find a way to drop the topic.

"Anyway, I am too old to acquire a woman," he said. "I am nearly fifty."

"Then why did you allow your face to get into such a condition over a young woman who had been in town for less than a day?" asked the second Indian.

"It was a matter of honour," said the more or less white man. "Of *cavalleria*."

The first Indian, who had in the normal course of things, picked up some Spanish, knew the Italian was talking about horses. But was he thus referring to the young woman, admittedly coltish, or the site of his humiliation? It was well known around these parts that Soo Woo's swamper stayed away from horses the way Gert the Whore stayed away from church.

"We Indians are pretty well known in our regard for honour," said the first Indian, "but when we come to acting upon it the results are always manifestly different from the events of yesterday. Your face looks pretty funny in the context of honour."

"You're just talking like an Indian," said Luigi, who had work to do, but who hated walking past the smiles of the Celestials working in the laundry.

"Are you serious?" asked the second Indian. "I've never heard an Indian talking like that. In the context of honour. Come on!"

Everyday Luigi weighed the disadvantages of staying here and continuing this fruitless conversation, and going back to his job with its smiles. There was also the job, of course.

"Well, honour is different for you Indians and us Italians. For you it's all about fighting, and for us it's all about protecting women."

"Well, you sure dont know much about fighting, I'll give you that," said the second Indian.

"I have spent some time in places like Utah and Wyoming," said the first Indian. "The immigrants there seem to understand a connection between honour and fighting quite well. They seem to be very much interested in death. They carry honour instruments on their hips down there."

Everyday Luigi felt about guns the way he felt about horses.

"There arent many Italians down there," he said. "The Yankees need to import thousands of Italians. They would be a good influence. They would teach the Yankees that honour has everything to do with protecting women and nothing to do with guns and the things people do with guns."

The two red men had really come to town for the game, but whenever they could they tried to satisfy their curiosity about the white men. They had never before thought there was a difference between Italians and other kinds of white men.

"What do you think the young woman's idea of honour might be?" asked the first Indian. "Does it have to do with fighting or with protecting Italian men?"

Everyday Luigi decided on the laundry and the smiles. At least there the task of trying to carry on a conversation in English was more a problem in getting started than a problem of having started and being unable to see a reasonable ending.

The team was giddy, as will often happen at the beginning of a season. They were filled with confidence, and showed it by their imitation of children on the short train trip west. For some, the imports from Minneapolis, this would be their first road game as Canadian ball players, specifically as Kamloops Elks. For the others, simultaneously envious of the money the Yanks would be getting and hopeful that the addition of the pros would take them to the Provincial tournament in September, it would be their first chance to strut in another town, one of the nicest parts of the game.

Even without the Yanks they were a pretty good club. Last year's Provincial tournament had taken place on their home field, and they had lost to New Westminster in ten innings.

We can look back to what they looked forward to. These young men would indeed run away from their own league this year, and go to the championships, and come home champions of the Province.

The Indians, if they had been asked, could have told them so. They would have directed their memories to New Year's Day that year, only a few months ago. It had been a warm bright day, as if the hard white sun knew something was up and were trying to make the best of things as long as it could.

People in the Thompson Valley were acting almost as if they were responsible for the mildness of the winter. At least they felt as if they should show proper appreciation for it. On Christmas Day Santa Claus rode the length of Main Street on the cowcatcher of Engine 373, carrying his enormous sack and wearing a red union suit with no white fur. On New Year's Day, the town team and the CPR side took off their jackets and played a baseball game in front of a large crowd of picnickers. It was not an overly serious game, and there was a little mud around home plate, but the joy and effrontery of playing the summer pastime on January 1st, hangovers ebbing away as blood coursed through bodies and brains, filled the eighteen players with pride, that they could for an afternoon deny the conditions of their employment.

Then in the sixth inning there was a chill, and the light dimmed a little. The game was suspended for a half-hour as the moon slid across the face of the warmth. The ball players and their spectators cheered and toasted the eclipse of the sun, and cheered louder when it reappeared. The game continued, and the town team, whose Minnesotans had not yet arrived, eked out a narrow victory over their local rivals.

If the Indians had been asked, they could have told the townies they were going to have a good year. As long as the pitching held up, and if they could execute the hit and run.

Now, or rather a then that we call now, the train was coming to a stop, and the young men were switching crumbs off their vests, running combs through their hair, ready to step off the train and dazzle the local citizens. Baseball players have always loved to dress up fancy off the field. These young fellows were sporting candy-stripe suits, wing collars and cravats, watch chains across their vests, straw boaters on their heads, and elegant walking sticks in their hands. Their hair was shaved short and parted just off the middle. Then as now, baseball players liked to dress like pimps. If there had been motorcars then, they would have driven here in the kinds of vehicles that pimps favour. No one has ever explained this similarity of tastes.

In fact one of the Kamloops outfielders *was* a pimp. But the rest of them had regular Thompson Valley jobs, even the stars from across the line. Some of them worked on ranches, but most of them had relatively easy jobs in town. The second baseman was a teacher at the Kamloops Indian School. This was Roy Smith.

As the train squealed and steamed to a stop, Smith remained sitting while his team mates staggered to remain upright during the last jerks of the car. He was looking out the window, forward and back along the platform. He didnt see what he was looking for.

But she was there. From her perch on the top rail of the loading pen she watched the regular passengers and the dandies step down from their car. She knew he would be the last one off, and she smiled at her knowledge. It was not a matter of pride but it was a matter of amusement to her that she could figure him out so easily while remaining a puzzle to his methodical and serious mind. It drove him crazy, for instance, that she spoke English with a barely discernible accent. Well, not crazy. With a mind like that he would never know a minute of craziness. At certain moments, when he was a little too much convinced of his role as teacher and wise moral guide, she would put on an accent and a demure feminine whimper. That would always stop his paragraph and make him just a little cool. Then she would see about warming him.

She would see. When he finally stepped down, carrying his beaten leather bag, stovepipe pantlegs wading through the steam that was still drifting across the boards of the platform, she put her gloved hands on the rail on either side of her and then she was the best athlete within a mile, as she landed on her feet and walked quickly but without haste to his side.

"Hello, teacher," she said.

He was really happy to see her. Just about everybody was happy to see her. Utter strangers were happy to see her walking along a boardwalk or riding past on a high black horse or sipping tea at a dry camp somewhere on the Interior Plateau. But Roy Smith had to pretend that he was not happy to see her here.

"I know why you're here," he said.

She put out her gloved hand and pushed a cowlick back into place above his forehead. That would have made just about anybody happy.

"I came to watch a ball game," she said.

Whether with their mothers or with women who have their own ways, young men somehow have to sulk. Roy Smith was sulking now. As he and Caprice walked to the Chinese restaurant, he said nothing. Observing this, she walked beside but at a little distance. Her strides were equal in length to his. For fun she walked in step, and sulking, he tried to change his rhythm.

But when she had her tea and toast in front of her and he had his out-of-town beer, he began talking again.

"Is Frank Spencer back in the Valley?"

"I dont know. He's back in the country."

She had her gloves off. The teacup looked wonderful as it was held by her long bony fingers. They were not soft and white. The backs of her hands had freckles on them. But her hands were not cracked and toughened like the hands of a ranch wife, either. They were strong enough to control a powerful horse and to propel a whip. But they were wonderful to look at as they busied themselves at toast and strawberry preserves with a white tablecloth as background.

"What are you doing in this town, Caprice?"

"I told you, handsome. I'm going to a ball game. I am a supporter of the Kamloops Elks."

"Caprice, I have already heard what you did two days ago. Do you think you can cause a public scandal like that and avoid the consequences?"

"He followed me to the hostler's, Roy. He could have killed the poor little man who tried to stop him in his ugly little game."

"Damn it, it makes me crazy to know you could get hurt or killed doing what you're doing in some town I cant get to quick. Or some place I havent even heard of."

She knew he was right. It was not easy to find a thoroughly peaceful man in this kind of country, and there were thousands of women who had given up hope of ever finding such a man. She knew that Roy Smith wanted her to forget all this trail riding, to forget Quebec, then, to remember what she did best. He was the only person within two thousand miles to have read anything she had written. It would have been hard enough for him to ask her to combine the sensibility that had made her a poet with the dusty routine of a western schoolteacher's wife. To ask her to give up her hate was too complicated for these two minds faced with their now undeniable love. This should all have been a long drama in verse, all this death and hate and love and whatever that fourth force was. That fourth force made a person surrender to something a verse-dramatist would call fate, a destiny. Necessity. Family revenge belonged to Jacobean tragedies, all that blood and all those curses, and the off-stage horrors. No one could imagine taking such a scenario seriously into a personal modern life. It was theatre. Even the words were stupid, silly. They should be intoned by a tremulous voice or the shrieks of an old matron driven crazy by blood and sword-clash. She would never say the word fate or the word revenge out loud, especially to Roy Smith. But family revenge was something she had heard of on this continent, too, in recent times on just this sort of landscape.

"Teacher?"

It was a new tone, a quiet voice that said all fencing and parrying was over.

"Yes?"

"That man I had my run-in with? His name is Loop Groulx."

"That's what I heard. From what I was told, he has been loafing around town all winter."

"I heard his name mentioned in Arizona, Roy."

☆ ☆ ☆

In her saddle-bag Caprice carried a yellowed and brittle page from a two-year-old issue of the Kamloops *Sentinel*. There was an advertisement on it that read:

> STOLEN! FROM L. CAMPBELL'S RANCH!
>
> By Frank Spencer, a horse, saddle and bridle; and a .44-calibre Winchester repeating rifle. The horse was a bay, with part of its forehead white, and branded Lc on the left shoulder; the saddle was of California make, double cinch, and block stirrup; narrow; the bridle had hand-made reins and snaffle bit. Anyone delivering the same to the undersigned at Kamloops will be suitably rewarded.
>
> L. CAMPBELL, June 25, 1887.

On June 25, of course, she was riding south through Nevada, and she would not see the advertisement till her first mail in Prescott. But she knew what the horse and gear looked like, all right, and she knew what Spencer looked like. In her saddle-bags she was carrying a photograph of the Campbell Ranch crew at a picnic, fifteen men standing stiff behind a long outdoor plank table, eyes squinting at the sun. She carried another picture of him in her head. In this picture Frank Spencer was bleeding.

Anyone who thinks that it would make a nice holiday to ride a horse from Kamloops, B.C. to Prescott, Arizona should try it some time. Then try to ride back again, not in a straight line, but from town to town, ranch to ranch. Try riding to Prescott and back and try to look beautiful at the end of the ride. Try handling the problem of food and laundry and bookstores. Eat a lot or a little of jerked beef and stale tortillas. Put on a wet shirt in the morning and let the sun dry it on your back. Try explaining to rousters and ranch wives and local lawmen what a woman is doing alone on such a ride. Try to stay away from men like Loop Groulx in all the mining towns and rail heads along the way.

Once she had picked up the mail in Prescott she had a picture to show sheriffs and marshals and hotel keepers as she rode the dry country northward again. But most of them said it could be anyone squinting in the sun. Whenever she asked questions in a town that Spencer had bragged about on the Campbell ranch, men told her they hadnt seen him for years, or they had never heard of him. In the southwest corner of Utah she saw a picture of him before she got around to asking her tired questions. It was a drawing of his face with a beard on it, and his name was printed under the drawing. Under the name was the information that the administration of another county would like to know where he was.

"That bill's been up there for four years, Miss. We dont exactly expect to see that critter show up here. The mines are doing so bad even the whores have left for California, begging your pardon."

"Then would you mind if I take the picture with me?"

"Miss, you can have anything you want in this town, I'll guarantee you that."

As she rode through Oregon she often showed this picture to people, many of whom said they remembered seeing it a couple years ago. Some of them offered the opinion that Frank Spencer was probably dead or in jail somewhere, or maybe in Canada. She could check in Walla Walla.

In Walla Walla they told her they had never had the pleasure of Mr Spencer's company, but they had heard of him. He used to send letters to a convict called Groulx. Always had Canadian stamps on them but no return address. Never mentioned whereabouts in Canada he was hanging out.

"You from Canada, Miss?"

"I am from Quebec."

"Wherever that is, you must be a long way from home. You ever need anything, you just ask, y'hear?"

She didnt need anything but information. Or rest. If the trail had not been leading north now, she was not sure she would stay on it. If it werent for the now unwelcome force that was moving her without revealing its name, she would sell her horse and get on a train east. No, she would not sell her horse. No.

In Oregon she talked to several liars, and stayed overnight in a town forty miles from the ranch where Frank Spencer was resting up from an accident in the weeds. When she rode along the Snake River in Washington she looked right at Mr Campbell's horse, but at such a distance that she didnt see the brand.

She was tired now, and she was not using her eyes as much as the constant tamping of her spine was using her. When she passed through Nighthawk she told the first Canadian she talked to that she had nothing to declare.

It can be pretty dangerous to stay in a town after you have humiliated a person everyone perceives to be a potential bully. Strange Loop did not have a bad reputation as a gunfighter and brawler here, but he was far from refined. His language was no better than it should have been, and he spent most of his time lounging around in the bars or tracking mud into the Canadian Cafe. Strange was an outsider several months ago, and could not now (or rather the present then) be considered a citizen. That is, he didnt work. But if a newer outsider who was a man had come into town and thrashed him at the hostler's, that stranger would have to keep an eye out for retaliation in dark places. Nobody knew what the situation was likely to be if the stranger was a woman, or a girl, as most people called her.

"What kind of girl beats a man with a whip," was the semi-rhetorical question of a young woman wearing laced boots in the bar of the Nicola.

"I'm not so sure she's a girl," said Gert the Whore.

But Gert was of two minds, or three. She didnt much like Loop Groulx, or men like Loop, partly because they were brutish and dirty, and partly because they tried to get as much as they could for as little as they could pay, nothing if possible. On the other hand, she felt a little like the most famous desperado in town who loses a bit of glamour when Wild Bill rides in. On the third hand she liked the whiff of danger that had crept into town. She knew that danger and business went together.

"Well," said Addie the afternoon bartender, "it seems to me like there's two kinds of women. There's the kind you want to be your mother or the mother of your kids, and there's the other kind."

"Listen," said Gert, "there's only one kind of man, and you're it, an asshole."

"Nice language, Gert. We sure know what kind of woman you are."

"You'll never find out," she said.

"No, but I mean it. This one with the whip aint natural. You sure couldnt imagine marrying her, and she's too big to even imagine getting into the bedroll with."

Everyday Luigi, his face varying in colour from yellow to purple, was having an amaro at the bar. He didnt like either side of this conversation. It was this kind of conversation that had enlivened his nights with the Kamloops Italian band a few years ago, but now it was fixed on a person he knew, and loved.

"Capriccia should take her whip to you two," he said.

Everyday Luigi was tolerated, but there wasnt anyone in town who would admit to caring about him. A man who went to work for the Chinaman. Gert the Whore had once taunted him by offering a free sample, and was of two minds when the little man turned and left with speed.

"You find your true love, Dago?" Addie winked at the girls.

"Ah, leave him alone, Addie," said the one in the laced boots. "You might bruise his feelings."

Everyday Luigi didnt even get the lame joke, but he gulped the rest of his brown drink and left anyway. He wanted to be on the street as often as he could today, between deliveries and odd jobs. He wanted to keep an eye out for Loop Groulx.

At the Canadian Cafe there were three ranch wives having tea and scones with orange marmalade. Their husbands were in town because it was Saturday and the first day of the baseball season. They were in town because they could get a ride and look at the shops. Their names were probably Ruth, Clara and Jeanette.

"Now be fair, Ruth, that Frenchman Groulx had it coming to him."

"I agree. From a *man*. But what kind of woman comes riding into a peaceful town, comes riding *alone* into a peaceful town, and gets into a fight the first hour she's here?"

"What was she supposed to do? Just let that filthy devil have his *way* with her?"

"He wasnt trying to have his way with her, from what I have heard. She butted into a quarrel with the Italian."

"It was hardly a quarrel, Ruth. That filthy devil was killing the old man."

"Well, I wont have any truck with a perfect stranger who comes into my town and starts a brawl. A scandal. And a woman! Can you imagine doing such a thing, Jeanette? Of course not."

Jeanette was imagining doing such a thing. She imagined doing it to several different men. She imagined being nearly six feet tall.

"It is just not *natural*," proclaimed Ruth.

As one can imagine, there was at least as much talk about the whipping as there was about the ball game around town.

"What would we be doing if it was a man who did it," asked the first constable.

"The same thing we're doing now," said the second constable. "No one has entered a complaint, have they?"

"I wouldn't want to be Loop Groulx," said the first constable. "Do you figger he's lit out?"

"I wouldnt want to be that girl," said the second constable.

"I would," said the first constable. "Only I'd carry a revolver the next time I saw him."

"You *are* carrying a revolver."

At the baseball grounds the young athletes were beginning to throw baseballs at each other while other men in vests were laying lines of quicklime on the ground. There were already dozens of boys running around, kicking holes in the dry earth, throwing cactuses at each other, looking for snakes to bash.

The ball players on both sides were like everyone else, more likely to talk about the incident than the game.

"Tell you what I'd do, I'd take a whip to *her*," said one of the first basemen.

"You dont even know how to use a baseball bat," said the second first baseman, "what do you think you could do with a whip?"

"It just aint right for a woman to ride around alone like that, beating up on fellows. I'll wager she's an invert," opined the first first baseman.

"I dont care what she is. I'd like to get her in a hay loft," said the second first baseman.

J.C. Tunstall, the manager of the Kamloops side, had been listening. He spit a stream of tobacco juice between the feet of his first baseman. This was always a signal that he had something to tell one or more of his players. If he hit your foot it was a sign that you would be sitting on the plank this day. His own players now became quiet like boys waiting for admonition to be finished. The players from the other side listened in. They could enjoy what he had to say without having to appear contrite or compliant.

"I dont want you boys to talk like that about her. She might be anything, she might be everything you say. All I know is that she is one hell of a lookin' woman, and she could probably beat the tarnation out of any three of you. And one more thing. She's Roy Smith's woman."

"That lucky son of a bitch," said one ball player.

"That poor bastard," offered another.

"Say, where the hell *is* Roy?" put in a third.

Roy was in a second-storey room at the Nicola Hotel, out of uniform, out of his regular weekend clothes, too. He was lying on his back, and on his left shoulder lay the head and loose red hair of the most famous person in town. There was a single sheet covering the two long bodies as high as their waists. The rest of the bed covers were on the floor at the foot of the brass bed.

"I wish I could see you more often," said Roy Smith. "It aint much fun going home at night and imagining you sleeping under the stars in Arizona or some such place."

"Teacher, I'm surprised at you. If you say aint, what are your little Indian children going to say?"

"I wish you would forget all this unhappy travelling. I wish — "

"Shh, I know what you wish."

Indeed she did. He used to say it every night. Now he seldom did. There was a kind of hope held out, from one of them, maybe both of them, that when this trailing was over with somehow, when they heard some news about the pursued, maybe she would say to herself and to him that she would be what he wanted. He wanted her to be Mrs Smith. When she left Quebec such a notion had never passed through her mind.

But here she was, a poet, with a schoolteacher's left leg lying under her long right leg. She turned her head and took his left nipple in her mouth and gave it a slightly more than tender bite.

"When are you supposed to be at the ballpark?" she asked.

"Right now," he said.

"Are you supposed to do this before a match?"

"Game. A game."

"Ah oui, un game."

"No, I am not supposed to do this for twelve hours before a game."

"Now that you have broken the rule, what do you think about doing it one more time before you go to the game?"

He knew she was kidding. He thought she was kidding. She was probably kidding. He would get up in a few seconds and go. A minute or two more. Just kiss her body a few times, and then go and play ball. Just a few kisses on the freckles above her breasts.

The beautiful black horse did not feel very lucky, and his rider was just about asleep when they came through Nighthawk again. They had nothing to declare. The horse had to watch for snakes himself, and there was more than one cactus adhering to the skin on his tired legs. A tumbleweed sped out of the flatland and fetched against his back legs, and he did not flinch. Grasshoppers clacked across his face, but he kept it down. He still had a sore haunch where he had brushed against an ocotillo a few months ago. She had got most of the tiny spines out, but there was still an ugly festering there.

She looked a little better. There was dust in the folds of her clothes and lightening her dark red hair. Her nose was peeling less now as she had been pointing it north for a month or two. She was thin where she had been slender.

They did not want to make camp tonight. She was determined to rest in Fairview, and she wanted to give the black some oats and carrots. But would they make it? It was as if they had marshalled unlikely powers of endurance to reach the boundary, and now that they were back in the country they might collapse at any moment.

"Poquito más de heroismo, Cabayo", she murmured, leaning forward even more on the saddlehorn.

But they reached what she knew had to be Reed Creek, and she knew it was downhill now, that for a few seconds at a time they would even be in shade. When they came into sight of the first miner's shack, the horse lifted his head at last and offered an intimate snort. She loved him for his generosity in the middle of pain. She sat with her back straight and her dusty braids falling straight behind her shoulders.

"Tú eres mi alma, Negro", she said out loud, and his ears twitched. He saw the dry creek bed passing by his left, and he saw horse droppings in front of him on the wagon trail that had widened a little from the horse path higher up.

When they passed the big house where George Atwood directed the operations of Strathyre mill, a man with a swede saw stopped his work and raised his wide-brimmed hat. That was the way it was in Fairview. It was the first time she had seen that since they had left here in the late spring.

It was late in the afternoon now. The gold-pickers in the shafts were making their last loads. In an hour they would be joined by prospectors who congregated nightly at Moffat's saloon to discuss the situation and partake of the proprietor's famous good cheer. She rode down out of the coulee and onto the grassy bench where the lower town had grown. In a few minutes she almost fell from her saddle at the front door of the hotel she had left more than a year ago.

It was a two-storey log and plank structure, or rather two of them attached, one set back ten feet from the other. Over the upper-storey windows of the forward half were the words, Golden Gate Hotel. That had always been its name on the registry, but for most of its short life it had been called the Bucket of Blood. Since John Kearns had taken it over, however, it was coming to be called simply "The Fish House."

Mr Kearns was a devout Irish Catholic and Mrs Kearns was a tolerable cook, so on Friday nights the Catholic miners and some others with a taste for something other than beef would gather at the Fish House and eat a lot of finny creatures pulled from Osoyoos Lake and the Okanagan River. Sometimes a man and his wife might put away a dozen little yellow perches. On the best days they would devour rainbow trout with butter and lemon. Fresh water clams were not popular, but there were satisfactory feeds of wide-mouth bass and, when the government man was away making his rounds in the Kootenays, some nice red inland-bound salmon.

There were a lot of hotels in Fairview, some just one-storey saloons with a few back rooms, others that had been mentioned in Vancouver newspapers. But the Bucket of Blood had three things going for it: it was farther than some from the stamp mills, there was fresh fish on Friday night, and it had a dance hall, where clean prospectors and shaven miners would go to shake a leg on Saturday night.

Caprice was really happy to see John Kearns. This was partly because he was the hotel man and where there is a hotel man in a growing town there is a bath and a bed, and partly because of the good talks she had had with him on her way south.

"Didnt find him, eh?" said John Kearns.

"I'll tell you all about it tomorrow morning," she said. "Right now I just want to get clean and go to sleep for fourteen hours, and then get clean again, and eat some pancakes, and then sit in your lobby out of the sun and look out the window at other people going to work. Can I have a room?"

Kearns ran a big hand through his thick curly rug of hair, and cleared his throat.

"You bet," he said. "But it'll take fifteen minutes to get it ready for you. Can you hang on that long?"

"Of course," she said. "Or rather, I hope so. I am going to see about my horse. Unless you have a nice bed with clean sheets for him."

"We've had a few guests in the digging trade who looked a lot like him."

"I recall that you have a first-rate stable, Mr Kearns. I will be back in fifteen minutes."

When she came back around front there was a commotion in the street. Seven men and six children were watching as two other men were punching each other in the middle of the hard-mud street. Unlike most fights, this one did not feature swearing and shouting on the parts of the combatants. They simply pounded one another and shoved one another around in their inexpert way. When she came into sight, walking slowly on her long thin legs and carrying her whip, they stopped their flailing and smiled at her. If they had not already had their hats knocked off they would have lifted them.

It entered her mind that if this had been going on in one of the towns she had passed through in the past month or two someone would have discharged a revolver by now.

When she entered the small lobby with its carpets and animal heads, she saw that Mr Kearns was not looking out at the scrap, but rather counting out some coins into the palm of an Indian man.

"Thank you, Tenny," said the latter.

"You dont have to thank me," said Mr Kearns. "Just bring me some more of those critters with the speckles all over their backs."

"Can I have a bottle of fire-water?"

"Piss off."

The Indian man smiled with big perfect teeth and walked out, rattling the coins in his fist.

"Sorry about the language, Miss. Didnt see you coming in."

"Mr Kearns, what is going on out there in the street?"

"Fistfight. Dust-up."

"I can see that, and I am too weary for a lot of questions and few answers."

"Well, let me put it this way. Before you came there were going to be three loose beds here tonight. Now there's two. Those two gentlemen are discussing which one of 'em is going to get the last one, the other having been claimed by a pistolero from Mr Atwood's claims in Nevada."

"I dont want to cause trouble, Mr Kearns. You should have told me you were out of rooms."

"Not true, Miss. There is always room for you."

"But it is embarrassing and unpleasant to have men brawling in the street for the last bed, I mean when one is the cause of it."

The rug-headed man turned the register book and held out the elk-horn pen.

"When it gets close to the weekend we get filled up. It is normal for men to sock each other to get the last indoor sleep."

"That's rather unpleasant, isnt it?"

"It's a tradition," said Mr Kearns. "Your hot water will be ready now. I'll have it sent up right away. See you in the morning."

"I'm so tired. Yes, I'll talk to you in the morning."

"You want fresh peaches with those pancakes?"

The ballpark gave off the scent of fresh lumber. People were in the habit of attending games in their buckboards, parking them around the perimeter of the outfield except right field, whose boundary was the river. But there was a new grandstand, and that is where the unaccompanied ladies and drifters sat. Boys and girls wandered around the grounds, vaguely aware of the game but not the score, except for one ten-year-old who sat in the grandstand directly behind home plate with a pencil and his school scribbler.

In the second inning, Ed Chesley hit a ball that rattled off the spokes of a wagon in left, and Kamloops was ahead 2–0.

Caprice was reminded of a snowy day in the high country of New Mexico, a day when she and her horse had both been persuaded to abandon the sky and look for a valley farther north. All through the baseball game the wind from behind the high cottonwoods along the river bank carried a flurry of white puffballs across the playing field. The locals considered it an omen or at least a part of the home field advantage. The Kamloops Elks just laughed at the idea, they were that confident. One of the Minnesota lads continually cracked jokes about playing the great Canadian game in arctic conditions.

In the fourth inning Willy Schoonmaker slid into home plate with his spikes up, driving the catcher off his knees and onto his back. There were gutteral threats from the crowd, but the Elks were ahead 3–0.

"I cannot help wondering," said the first Indian, "why these people call themselves elks."

"Well, the elk is a beautiful and noble animal," said the second Indian. "As a hunter and an artist I respect all the animals, of course, but the elk fills me with awe when I see him standing with his head up."

"That elk there does not have his head up. He is all crouched over with a stick in his hand."

The second Indian had his mouth full of ice cream. His older companion had tried some and liked it immensely, but had not taken a second bite. One had to put up with certain sacrifices to retain the kind of dignity one was expected to show in the ceremonial meetings and the photographs.

"The elk is admirable in its hauteur," said the second Indian, licking his fingers. "On the prairie there are Indian people who name their children after elk. I have even heard of cases in which fathers have pretended to see an elk at the birth of their children so they can call them things such as Running Elk, or Elk Who Fears No Hunter."

"Elk, however, are stupid. I do not know how you young people do it, but we always found it easier to have the elk come to us than to go stalking him among the trees. All we had to do was put a salt lick by the side of the lake, or a snare made of vines for them to stumble into. Then we picked up our bows and picked out the one we wanted to eat. Even Coyote could get himself an elk for the winter."

"Do you call that sport?"

"Crouching down with a stick in your hands. Do you call that sport?"

"Times are changing, old teacher. That stick is called a Louisville Slugger."

"Do you think we should crouch down behind the willows and wait for the elk to stick his tongue on the salt lick and then bang him with a Louisville Slugger?"

"Times are changing. Maybe we would have more success doing what that man behind the brown-and-white horse is doing, crouching with a .30–30 Winchester."

"You saw him too, did you? I was beginning to have doubts about these old eyes, but it is wonderful what a proper traditional diet will do for them."

In the fifth inning Joe McCrum stepped into a gopher hole while chasing down a high fly, and two unearned runs crossed the plate, tightening the score to 3–2.

Everyday Luigi was at the Canadian Cafe, getting another tub of vanilla ice cream. When he came out onto the boardwalk with the weight hanging off both ends of the pole across his shoulders, he saw two men come out of the Bank of Commerce and mount their horses. Out of habit he checked the brands. They were different from each other, but they were both unknown in the area. He would have stayed and watched which way the riders were headed, but Soo Woo had a very strong attitude toward melting.

Still, he had some data filed away. Someone might need it.

When Everyday Luigi got back to the ballpark it was the sixth inning. The cotton was falling like Christmas, and the locals had a man on second with one out. There was a ripple of excitement around the ring of buckboards and through the grandstand, where Gert the Whore could be heard excoriating the manliness of the Kamloops pitcher.

"You shoulda spent a quiet morning in church, ya dumb bunny," she shouted, and her companions laughed heartily.

The boy with the scribbler and pencil looked at her and then at her friends with irritation and lust. Baseball was a complicated game, but it was going to be necessary in the coming years. He would find out. Baseball would be beautiful when some things were not.

"Ball two," said the umpire.

"You coulda fooled me," shouted Gert the Whore, and her companions guffawed.

The banker's wife hustled her kids off for another dose of ice cream.

The next pitch came off the bat twice as fast as it had come in. Smack, went the bat, and the ball hit the pitcher right on the head.

"Hooray," shouted Gert.

But the ball landed right in the hands of Roy Smith the second baseman.

"Phooey," said Gert.

Roy Smith moved like a cougar. With the ball in his sore hand, he ran over second base, much to the surprise of the runner who had not even thought of returning there yet. Roy Smith had two put-outs, and the pitcher, though he did not know it yet because he was still lying with his face on the ground, had an assist.

"Darn it all to heck," said Gert the Whore.

At the end of six innings it was still 3–2.

Roy Smith dropped the ball at the pitcher's box as he trotted off the field, no expression on his face. Ball players love this moment. They always run off the field with no expressions on their faces. A smile might make it look as if they were pleased by an extraordinary stroke of mortal luck. A smile might make the victims feel a little better. If you act as if it is all in a day's work, your luck will stay good, and you will appear invincible to your opponents and fans.

Caprice sat in the grandstand and did not applaud. This was, after all, an away game. But she kept her grey eyes on Roy Smith as he joined his team-mates on the bench. Some of them were smiling; that was all right. She looked intently at him to see whether he would glance in her direction. She was really proud of him when he didnt. It would have been nice, though. Hooray, she said inside.

She would cut the piece out of the *Journal* tomorrow if it mentioned that play.

It was not going to matter now who won the game. She knew that this moment for Roy Smith was a lot like that moment for her had been when she was still a poet and not a fury.

The instant of inspiration seemed now to be reflected from all sides at once, from a multitude of sunny and snowy circumstance of what had happened or of what might have happened. The instant flashed forth like a point of light, and now from puff ball to puff ball of vague circumstance confused form was veiling softly its afterglow. In the virgin womb of the imagination the word was made flesh.

The boy with the spectacles and the scribbler watched the white stuff blowing across the outfield, and wondered whether this was what manna looked like for the people of Moses exiled in the desert.

"Ice cream here," shouted Everyday Luigi.

On the fresh yellow wood of the plank on which Caprice was sitting a jagged rip appeared. Then there was a smack like the sound of a Louisville Slugger creating an extra-base hit. She moved like a cougar, even as the other spectators in the ball park were gathering their wits. She was off her seat and running before anyone else had decided that what they had heard was a rifle shot.

Roy Smith ran toward her while other men ran for their horses or for cover. A man on a brown-and-white mount was already over the ridge and out of sight, even of the Indian eyes that had been alone in seeing him. There was an awful commotion in and around the ballpark, women picking up their skirts and screaming or cursing, depending on who they were, men looking for their children, children trying to save their ice cream from accidental loss.

Roy Smith had his baseball arms around the tall woman with the gleaming red hair. He held her and again had no expression on his face. Another woman in her place might have had her face buried in his chest. She was looking with her grey eyes over his shoulder, perhaps scanning the hillside.

The boy with the scribbler still sat in his seat directly behind home plate, wondering whether this was a suspension or a forfeiture of the game.

From up on the hillside she could hear the rumble of heavy machinery at the Strathyre quartz mill as she sat near a window and read last week's *Okanagan Mining Review*, the first whole Canadian newspaper she had seen in over a year. On the tablecloth in front of her were the remains of an elegant breakfast. Mr Kearns had told his cook to work his skill to the edge, and Caprice had done justice to the cantaloup and the trout and the pan-fried potatoes and the toast with gooseberry preserves, and the goat's milk and the three cups of French coffee. Mr Kearns told her that her ebon friend at the stable was receiving the equine version of this service as well. It was the kind of welcome that removed all doubt about motives. She knew that her host was going to give her a lecture afterward, but for the moment she was grateful for the night between clean sheets and the sunshine that was falling across the valley and glancing along the silver knife that a few minutes earlier had spread thick butter on perfect toast.

She allowed her fancy to play with the idea of staying in Fairview, of forgetting her bitter quest. The newspaper in her hands explained that Fairview would one day soon become "the leading city of the Okanagan Valley." She watched little Jimmy Kearns at another table, his head bent over a book, and imagined the school they would need here, imagined a cottage beside Reed Creek, lady slippers and buttercups growing without urging in its yard. She smiled as she imagined work-dirty miners doffing their hats to a schoolmarm taller than most of their number.

But she was not a schoolteacher. Roy Smith was a schoolteacher. She was riding the grub line. She was what some people called a saddle tramp, but it was not a good idea to call her that to her face. She had spent more than a year meditating on death, and that is not a schoolteacher's occupation. Roy Smith would like her to be the wife of a schoolteacher, the mother of some of the children in his school one day. Mr Kearns, she knew, was going to encourage peacefulness, too.

The beautiful table land she was spending this day in, and the optimism in the faces of its people, could almost have persuaded her to leave accounts in the hands of the Provincial Police, or to forget her fate as nemesis. Except for the last word her brother had pronounced on the hard dirt of the Kc.

John Kearns had been watching her as she alternately scanned the thin newspaper and looked out the newly scrubbed window at the bright high morning. Now he signalled a small ex-cowboy to take her used dishes away, and approached her table himself. When she smiled at him he saw in her bright grey eyes that the exhaustion she had arrived with had now been succeeded by a kind of out-of-time languor. He sat down at her table and asked her how the trout had been.

"It was the best meal I have had in a year."

"It was probably the best one I have served in a year."

"I think that last night I was in such a state that I said something about having been away only a month or two," she said, with a little wonder in her voice.

"Something like that. I did not think it was the time to disabuse you," he replied, friendliness in his tone.

"I was just thinking that I wish I lived here."

Kearns smiled.

"His servants he with new acquist
Of true experience from this great event
With peace and consolation hath dismist,
And calm of mind, all passion spent."

She smiled his smile back at him.

"I have been wondering about peace and consolation a lot lately, Mr Kearns. I know that here in the west poetry is a consolation to a lot of people who feel as if they have been exiled from the earth their families have assumed to be their right home. Even in the meanest little railhead in Arizona I found people spending their scant coin on travelling recitation shows and desert-eating opera companies."

"I am Irish," said John Kearns, "It is my lot in life to consume whisky, which I manage in some quantity, so that it has been said more than the once that I am my own best customer. And to remember the words of the bards and minstrels."

"Some people would say that a scattering of mine shafts on a hillside of rocks and rattlers was a strange place to be reading poetry, Mr Kearns."

His big open face with its roof of thick curly hair turned to gaze at her and offer a look of amusement. It was the look that a poet devises just before uttering his favourite lines.

"Ah, but I cannot read or write a word, my dear lady. I was brought up in the family tradition of illiteracy."

"You are fooling with me, sir. Since leaving Quebec I have not met a person, man of God or instructor of youth, who knows as many poetical words as you do."

"That is because I am blessed not only with a copious thirst but also with a tyrannical memory. I have had many a poem read to my ears, and what my ears have been assailed with my heart has engraved. Even while I try to disremember the Protestant self-assuredness of Mr John Milton, the splendour of his versification settles in me like gold in a vein of quartz."

Like most poets who wander anonymous among people who know nothing of their other life, she was tempted on the one hand to tell him more about her publications, and determined on the other hand to guard her knowledge, believing that it is the reader's job to come to the poetry. One should have friends of the regular person as well as admirers of the poet. One should not sacrifice one to the other. John Kearns knew her as a person who could recite the words that he would never hear from a prospector, and he knew that she could do more than repeat a verse. She would not tell him any more about her book. Later she would send him a copy on the stage. It was pleasant to imagine his opening it, and giving it to Jimmy Kearns to read aloud.

"I am armed with more than complete steel, —
The justice of my quarrel."

"Ah," said John Kearns, "are we then to trade passages from our wise and musical instructors?"

"It seems to me, sir, that you began such an undertaking," she said.

"You took as your subject justice," he replied, "but another person might look at the strain in your eyes last night and give your theme another name."

She smiled at him, and lifted her unbraided hair back over her shoulder. The light of the window played through the several dark shades of red there.

"I have heard that lecture from another man more than a year ago," she said.

"Heat not a furnace for your foe/ That it do singe yourself."

There was something that arose from the middle of her warm and rested body that told her that this was a more than pleasant dream, this morning of the bright sun. The light on the tablecloth was certainly preferable to the dark cold ashes of another night's camp-fire. She had wakened more than a hundred times lying on the ground whose name she did not know, and she was capable of doing it a hundred times more. But waking with her bitterness at sunrise near a canyon creek had nothing to do with beauty. Sparring over English poetry with a man who was indisputably a friend should be more than a dream. It could be something a person might call a life.

"You are a kindly man, Mr Kearns. And you are certainly right. Sometimes when I stop riding or thinking I look at myself and I do not see the woman I thought of growing up to be. I have not been able to write a single line of poetry in over a year, not since I heard of my brother's death. I thought at first that it was because I could not be a poet again, had no right to be a poet again until that man is brought to justice."

"To vengeance."

"All right. I thought that the bullet that stopped my brother's heart had also struck mine. But when I am able to see myself clear I know that I have poisoned my own well. I know that."

She was staring out the window now, at the empty boardwalk in front of the general store across the way. John Kearns left her to her silence for the space of a minute.

"Ride to Kamloops, Miss. Ride to your schoolteacher. Take the stage to Kamloops. Or take the train to Quebec. Your horse will thank you for returning him to the more civilized grass that was his home. Forget Frank Spencer. The Provincial Police will not forget him, I promise you. If you are interested in justice, leave justice to them. Remember this country, and remember the talks you have had with me. Try to be more sensible in the things you choose to remember, will you, Miss?"

She turned from her gaze across the road and favoured him with a smile that almost transformed her freckled face.

"You are a true friend, Mr Kearns. I will remember my talks with you more fondly than anything else I have known in the west."

She thought it should be more than a pleasant dream to sit in the morning sunlight and drink coffee where she could smell the new wood in a building at the centre of a community's faith and optimism.

"So will you go to Kamloops and forget Spencer?"

"No."

John Kearns uttered a sigh and rapped the knuckles of his enormous hand against the side of his curly head.

"Then come to the dance tomorrow night."

"I will. And if you are not too drunk, I will save a dance for you, my true friend. If Mrs Kearns does not mind."

She had seen Mrs Kearns entering the room with a fresh tablecloth.

"I certainly do not mind, Miss. But this night you had better get another night's sleep such as you got last night, for he is a dancin' devil, that Irishman," said Mrs Kearns.

Her husband got to his feet, facing Caprice and placing his hand over his heart. Then with a futile attempt at an Irish accent he offered a final passage from the deathless anthology.

> "When you do dance, I wish you
> A wave o' the sea, that you might ever do
> Nothing but that."

A lot of beautiful things are dangerous, Everyday Luigi said to himself as he lugged the gunny sack with its clinking load over his shoulder, up the dry slope, his feet slipping in the sand, toward the crest overlooking town. That river, for instance, emerald green, cold and sweet, will carry you to the other river that has grown impatient during its long flow southwards, to a turmoil in a canyon where no man would live, once wet. This woman, for instance, taking her long steps up the slope in front of him, has not said more than ten words all morning, but each word was encased in emerald and sounded like emeralds being dropped on a pane of glass. The morning had been warm before breakfast, so the summer of the great Interior Plateau was begun. Snakes would be lying in the shade already. Capriccia was not wearing a jacket any more. Her red checked shirt was tucked into her tight trousers, and her trouser legs were tucked into her high soft boots. When she took those long climbing strides, a poor immigrant had to keep his own silence, but language spun around inside him. Some other feeling was being brewed into loyalty.

On the ridge there were some ponderosa pines, maybe five inches through the bole, but they were scattered. Bunch grass ruled the soft earth, with the occasional clump of greasewood, a colony of little cactus here and there. Wagon-wheel ruts had cut a crooked path along the edge of the crest, and they led to a cattle-guard made of lodgepole pine lengths over a pit. Lodgepoles also made up the first segments of the fence that led off with barbed wire across the tableland from the cattle-guard. Luigi put down his sack and straightened his back. He wondered whether they were going to talk this morning.

But he had a notion that he had better not be the one to start. So while she stood and looked down over the town, he opened his sack and took out the whisky and rum bottles, standing them on the top railing of the fence. Standing a round-bottomed bottle on a round pole is not the sort of thing one can do quickly, and Luigi was a little concerned with the silent woman's patience. So he was glad that the earth was soft, because though he had a lot of experience with other people's whisky bottles, he had little experience with tall angry women. Eventually he managed to get a dozen bottles standing about four feet apart along the railing.

She was still standing against the sky, gazing down at the town, probably, he knew, especially at the ball grounds and the railroad station. She might have looked for a while at the grey hoodoos that stood in a line below the crest on the other side of the valley.

It was still not the time to speak, so he gave a short whistle, making sure not to allow a rising tone that might suggest arrogance at the end.

She looked for a while longer at the town and up the valley. Then she turned on her heel, and as she walked she pulled her soft gloves tighter on her large hands. She looked careless, or perhaps preoccupied, as she took a stance about fifteen feet from the arrayed bottles. The sun was to her right, but it did not appear that she had thought about checking it.

Luigi was to her left. He felt a shiver that he could not satisfactorily explain as she took the whip from her side and uncoiled it on the ground in front of her. She flicked it in front of her, then flicked it behind her. When it cracked, he was not ready, and he fell back a step. He looked, but all the bottles were still there.

She cracked it again. Its end snapped an inch short of the bottle furthest to the right. She cracked it eleven more times, her body bending forward so that he could see the powerful muscles of her back pressing the fabric of her shirt. All the bottles stood.

Everyday Luigi recalled a time at the stage station in Ogden,

Utah, when he had been given a chance to try out a driver's whip. It was all he could do to lift it and try to flail it at the air in front of him. A revolver, for all its kick, is a toy for the hand compared to the effort it takes to play a bull whip.

There was a smile on Capriccia's face!

She was shaking the beautiful and dangerous leather out on the ground in front of her. He could see her breast rising and falling, hear her breath coming. She took off her flat-brimmed hat and tossed it to him. He caught it.

"Nice catch," she said.

He dropped it. Quickly he bent to pick it up from the clump of grass it had fallen on. As he did so he spied a pointed stone. It was an arrowhead. Usually you found arrowheads along the river. He wiped the dirt off it across his pant leg.

It was perfect. Beautiful. He put it in his pocket.

Caprice was ready. She stepped forward with her long right leg, and snapped the whip. The bottle farthest to the east fell off the rail toward her. If one were counting one could then have counted to five. The second bottle flew ten feet up into the air and landed the other side of the fence. Five. The third bottle flipped high and to the left, right at Luigi. His hands went out but it bounced off his thumb and fell to the earth along with the hat he had been holding.

"Nice try," she said.

He picked up her hat and dusted it off and put it in a ponderosa. If there were bottles to catch, he was going to catch them.

The fourth bottled landed neck downward in a cluster of cactus. The fifth was soon seen to be spinning on its side between two wheel ruts.

Luigi counted to fifteen. The first Indian held his breath. The second Indian counted to one.

Then six seven eight nine ten! Broken glass flew in the sun like loud alarmed birds. For the following moments there was a natural quiet on the flat, animated only by the quick breathing of the tall woman, smile gone, red hair in a cascading tangle.

Everyday Luigi lifted his hands as if to clap them, thought better of it, and turned to retrieve the hat from the tree. Caprice coiled the thing in her hands. A rabbit tore away across the bench as fast as he could.

Behind their rock the first Indian paid his young companion what he owed him. The second Indian was tremendously pleased, not because of the fifty cents but because the older man had been right about a hundred times in a row.

"Oh, that was beautiful," he said.

"I would not have chosen that word," said the first Indian. "Noisy, perhaps."

"Dont be a sore loser," said the second Indian.

"Oh, I expect to get my money back the next time we go fishing."

"That cowperson is an artist," said the second Indian.

"Another artist. Now everyone is an artist."

"No, you are a critic, venerated friend."

Farther away, up on the second bench, two ordinary white man's eyes were watching with the aid of some field-glasses supported on the saddle of a brown-and-white horse. They watched the extraordinary woman and the tired Italian disappear over the edge of the tableland.

Higher still, in the cloudless sky the eyes of a patrolling hawk had picked out the scampering rabbit.

Emily Peachtree Guano was finding the west as exciting as she had always dreamed, if quite a lot harder work. The famous Iroquois princess, known as "the Belle of Caughnawaga," was Canada's most famous poet, and in the decades after Confederation she rose to the challenge posed by her nation, the difficult task of knitting the Dominion together in the face of the Yankee threat of manifest destiny. Many British and especially Scottish-born men in the worlds of politics and industry credited the railroad with the successes of nationhood. But the women of the far-flung provinces and territories, the sensitive men who hungered for the arts as much as for beef and gold, the librarians and schoolteachers of the mining camps and logging towns, knew that the young country's life would depend on the breath of culture pumped into its lungs by the poems and sketches and ebullient humour of the woman in the white buckskin with the bear claw necklace. Emily often felt tired on her long buckboard rides across the coal hills and along the tumbleweed draws, but she felt a deep need, an almost mystical call from the pine forests. She would be the only lady in small towns of married and commercial women, and the only woman in smaller communities of men who had not seen any females other than their horses and mules for half a year. Clad in feathers and hides she would stand before them in the Methodist church hall and recite verses about God and the whispering voice of the dark woods.

She would tell them:

> Something so sacred lies upon the ground,
> Like to a blessing to a holy mound,
> A calm we sense but cannot yet propound.

How true, how true, the heads in the pews would think. The minister of the church would explain in his thank-you speech that the Great Spirit of the red race was but another name for our Lord.

"My God is lovely, dark and deep," she would tell them.

Well, a dark God, they would think, not the best sort of thing for the children to hear. But poetic.

"And now my partner, the actor and monologist, Mr Hartley McBride Schooner, will join me in a sketch entitled 'An Oar in the Fiery Lake.' "

At this point the men in the crowd would straighten their backs. Men who spent their days moiling for gold hankered for narrative and drama. They did not have an ear for lyric. That was for the women folk and the gents who change their shirts every couple days.

Emily and her ugly little partner had been a great success all through the West Kootenays and the boundary country, and not just because they were a novelty. Entertainers galore trooped through the mining towns there, following the rail north from Spokane. California opera singers and even Pennsylvania comedians drew big crowds of the sophisticates in Nelson and the Irish immigrants in the Slocan Valley. It had been years since anything had been thrown at a performer, though unrehearsed and patronizing entertainers might have to shout over the thumping of boots as the hard-working audience made for the box-office to get their dollars back.

The beauteous princess and the squat trouper had their act down cold, and no one ever walked out. Partly for patriotic reasons and partly out of curiosity about the rumour that she had a wooden leg, the crowds at Emily's recitals outdrew San Francisco Sally and Her Ocarina Chorus.

So when Miss Guano and her effects arrived in Fairview on a springboard from Camp McKinney, the future boom town was ready for her. The rent at the Bucket of Blood was agreeable, and the prospect of a warm bath there encouraged the princess to prepare an especially humorous and artistic evening for the locals. She was particularly pleased by the readiness of the male citizens to lift their hats when she came into view.

"May I have your autograph, your highness?" asked John Kearns.

"I am not called that," replied the poet. "Call me Miss Guano. If this nation is to be drawn together and its heart filled with hope, it must be with the spirit of democracy and fellow feeling that reigns on the forest floor. It may have been my fortunate lot in life to be born with the blood of a princess and the breath of a muse in my ear, but I travel this broad Dominion secure in the knowledge that its myriad people have the touch of their enlightened maker in their hearts."

Kearns was attempting to catch a glimpse of her ankle, but the skirt she was wearing came to the floor. If there was some way to get her to climb something he might be satisfied about the rumour.

"Do you have an autograph book?" the princess asked.

"No," he said, "I mean will you please endite your signature in the guest registry?"

The ugly little man who was with her had put down his Gladstone bag, and was now making a note with pencil in a leather-bound book. This exchange would form part of a humorous sketch in their next engagement at Okanagan Falls. By the time they got to Kamloops they would be able to offer an entire half-hour on the lighter side of a literary tour in the Kootenay and Okanagan valleys. Emily Peachtree Guano was renowned for her topicality as well as her rare gift from Polyhymnia.

That evening she spoke the words that the wives and husbands of Fairview were persuaded that they had been thirsting for.

> Yon western mounts that soothe my heart
> Will ever offer gold;
> Yet richer stories told by God
> Are sweeter, truer told.

John Kearns was there, and joined his decorous handclap to the grateful applause of the community gathered in his Iroquois-decorated hall. But a month later he could not remember the words that were uttered from the pine-bough-framed stage.

On the train back to Kamloops most of the Elks were playing rummy. Roy Smith usually liked rummy, playing with the intensity and light-handedness with which he played second base. He won more often than he lost, and generally arrived home with enough coin to spend on special treats for his pupils at school on Monday. But tomorrow those children were going to have to make do with their regular fare. Tonight Roy Smith was staring out the window at the rivershine under the full moon.

He was imagining a woman with a rifle bullet in her.

He knew that the Provincial Police would "continue their investigation." He had joined them looking for a spent cartridge case, but there were dozens of them lying on the ground about where they figured the rifle man had stood. He had been with Caprice while they questioned her. Did she have any enemies.

"How do we know the shot was intended for me?" she replied.

But the police "had a theory."

"Did Lionel Joseph Groulx say anything to you after you beat him up the day before yesterday?" asked the first constable.

"I did not stay around to hear what he had to say."

"Did you have any dealings with Groulx before the incident?" asked the second constable.

She found something to do with her shirt-tail while she was not answering the question. Roy Smith waited as expectantly as did the officers of the law.

"I had never seen him before the day in question," she said.

"You never knew he existed?"

"I had heard his name mentioned."

Back in her hotel room she found something else to do with her shirt-tail. Neither of them felt much like making love, beyond an expression of care. It was as if they sensed the vulnerability of the flesh, and did not want to bring it to an edge of unwariness. They would sin, but not sin deeply. Neither would they talk directly about the baseball game and its outcome.

But he loved no beauty as much as he loved the beauty that happened when one of them took off her shirt. When the warm weather arrived she wore nothing underneath it, and when one of them took off her shirt her long smooth back appeared, a valley down the middle, with light red down picked out by the afternoon sun that came through the blind pulled over the window. Long smooth muscles that almost brought tears to his eyes when she began to turn toward him, and then when she turned toward him, one high little breast followed by a second, sweet soft firm muscles, the freckles above them. There was such a distance from her breasts to the top of her trousers.

"You are so tall," he said.

"You have mentioned that."

"You are so long," he said.

"*Toi aussi,*" she said, with a smile.

Something, he did not know whether it was he or she or something else, fetched her nakedness into his arms. Still they did not want it all, they wanted to hold and to be held. He wanted to speak but not speak, not speak if it would deprive him of this holding, being held, of this beauty.

There they were, a lot going on in each head in that room. Three of the relationships were as immediate as can be, as close as rain water on a rose. Her body and his body, nearly the same size, cleaved to one another. His head reached with all its care for her lovely strong body. Her head felt the ball player with his quickness. Feeling his body she felt her own there, and he felt his, she doing the feeling of it for him. Only their heads, touching one another, could not know what was held in reserve in the other.

They knew only the speech they had rehearsed so often. Will you be Mrs Smith. Yes, some time. Will you give up this terrible adventure and come home with me. No. Why not. You know, you have read the things I have read. Those are just things to read. Then why did they get written. Why cant you just write it then. I am writing it, that is what I am doing. I dont understand you. But I thought you were a teacher. I teach the ABCs, you are living in a different alphabet.

Moments like that, no matter how wonderful and difficult to understand, pass by, and people return to ordinary language.

"When does the train leave?" she asked.

"It is on a siding now. It will leave when the police are satisfied that they can let it. I would like you to be on it with me. You know I have to be at the school tomorrow morning."

She pushed him and he fell across the bed on his back. Then she fell on him. He could feel her hard breasts through his fancy shirt. What could he do? He put his arms around her and hugged her to him, knowing that he had to leave. He lay with his legs together and she lay on top of him with her legs together. She felt like a good friend.

"Please," he said.

"You dont really have time. You have a train to catch," she said. But she moved one knee toward his waist.

"No, I mean please come with me."

"Why are you going?"

"I have to," he said. "I have a duty to my school, to my pupils."

"I have a duty as well," she said.

"That is not a duty, *ma chérie*. That is something else."

A locomotive whistle sounded through the town, hit the mountain, and sounded back through the town.

She got up and retrieved her shirt.

Now, or really a later then, the train was chuffing eastward after a short stop at Savona. The moon lit the surface of the lake and suggested the darkness of the hills on the other side. I have a duty to my school, he was saying inside his head with his forehead against the glass. He tried to make the phrase coincide with the clacking wheels of the train, but it would not fit the joined rails.

I have a duty to my pupils. I love Caprice. I have a duty to my pupils, and that is a duty to life.

He thought of how awful it was to be getting farther and farther away from the bushwhacker. But the bushwhacker was probably gone over the hill. If he has any sense. The Provincials will be looking for anyone suspicious, and they were suspicious of Loop Groulx.

A baseball park is supposed to be a refuge from all that sort of thing. It is supposed to be a place where time and death and disease and duty are forgotten. It is the field for play, a funny sort of place that is at once free from all the constrictions and dangers of life, and bound perfectly to rules that we obey though we know they dont matter. There are not supposed to be any bullets in the baseball park. Rifles and bullets are not a game.

The rummy players were getting a little louder as the train approached Kamloops.

Rifles and bullets and the insane travels of that dear woman are not a game. They are at once too true and insane.

But what about baseball? Isnt that insane? Isnt that what makes it so pleasurable? To run as hard as you can to get back where you could have been all the time by staying there?

Somebody behind him melded and a hubbub arose. Dont get so excited, an infielder said. It's only a game.

It would have been better if his thoughts could have coincided with the clacking of the steel.

But if what Caprice and Frank Spencer and Loop Groulx and even Pete Foster were playing, if that too is only a game?

For a second before he blinked the train was sitting still and the moon was racing on the lake. Then the train was moving again.

If that is a game, it is a game in which people get cut and shot and killed. It is a game in which you do not know whether the other players are obeying the rules. You dont know whether you are obeying the rules. Before you find out the rules you could be dead. The inventor and master of that game does not assume that he has to explain all the rules to any individual.

When I went west on this trip I was a ball player, he said to the window. Now on the way back I am a schoolteacher. If that rifle had not gone off I might be a card player. No, that is too tidy. If Caprice had not been there I might have been able to get an hour or two of sleep.

For some people the meaning of the word "game" is animal victims. An animal that wanders into the wrong place or is too tired to run any more, might find itself standing in the gun-sight of a man who is on his holidays. If the man happened to be working at his job at the time, the animal would be a quarry or simply dinner. But if the man with the gun is a Yankee on his vacation, with all the latest equipment and a good supply of whisky, then the soon to be dead or wounded animal is called game. It happens with birds, too. When they get shot they are called game birds.

Another word that people with guns like to use is "sport." When the word was a lot younger it had more letters at the front, and meant something one does when one is on holiday, away from the usual occupation of carrying something for somebody else. A Yankee or some other person who walks along looking for an animal to shoot says that he is engaged in a "sport."

Unlike the situation in other sports, in this game the visiting team usually has the advantage. The visitors usually go home with the trophy.

The Thompson Valley was the home of a highly successful group of British and Irish landholders. Among the most successful were two brothers named Clement and H.P. Cornwall, proprietors of a big spread along the river. Their home was known all across the Interior Plateau as The Manor. Clement Cornwall, by some measure the more forceful of the brothers, was a graduate of Cambridge University, and so became the County Court Judge of the Cariboo region, which was pretty handy to his vast economic concerns, as his land empire was popularly, or at least publicly, called "the gateway to the Cariboo." The year after the Provincial baseball tournament came to the Thompson Valley, Clement Cornwall became a senator.

The Cornwalls were English gentry. In fact all through the Interior of the province there were large ranches, later called cattle companies, owned by English gentry.

And English gentry, as much as anyone else, are interested in sport. Indians had their games. Cowboys had their games. Most people like to gamble in one way or another. Even God, some people would say, has his game. Roy Smith used to think about that when he was trying to explain to himself how he had managed to fall in love with a five-foot-eleven-inch red-headed freckle-faced French Canadian woman who was determined to stay around places where bullets can determine the score.

For Clement Cornwall the game was the English fox hunt. Some of his cowpunchers were interested in rodeo. His cook was a devotee of fan-tan. One of the young men in his land office was a right fielder. But Clement Cornwall looked upon the non-growing season, or the portion of it free from snow-cover, as fox season. Two decades ago he had imported thirty of the best hounds from the Midlands, along with all the proper costumes and musical instruments, and for two decades he and his guests from as far away as the coast and the Peace River country had been engaged in the chase. At the meet the guests would always acknowledge Clement Cornwall as master. H.P. Cornwall was usually the huntsman, and some of the more career-minded young gentlemen from the Douglas Ranch were generally the whippers-in.

The only trouble was that in the Thompson Valley and on the hillsides along the Valley, there were not many foxes. In England there were plenty of foxes, and terrier men and earth stoppers hired for the hunt generally knew where they were. In fact the fox hunt, though it depended on the availability of English foxes, was given its traditional form by Yorkshire gentry who acknowledged Squire William Draper as master of the hunt in 1726. Squire Draper explained that the sport was designed for the "express purpose of reducing the number of lamb killing foxes in Yorkshire."

In the Thompson Valley there were quite a few lambs along with the cattle, though not many of them fell to foxes. But agriculturalists did complain of coyotes.

"The coyote," said Clement Cornwall, "is an excellent fellow for this sport. He is clever, abundant, well adjusted to the terrain, and most important for the game-loving members of the hunt in such wide open country, endowed with far greater stamina than his little British cousin."

Some cowboys liked to shoot coyotes, or shoot at them, when they had the chance, especially from horseback. It seemed like a game, and at the same time could be explained as a necessity. Coyotes were thought of as lowly creatures. If you did not like a man you might call him a coyote.

Indians who had become cowboys could never quite figure out why their fellow riders liked shooting coyotes or expressed disgust at the animals. The Chinese who had once been gandy dancers but had had to find other work since the driving of the last spike, wondered why the Europeans bothered to shoot or chase an animal they were not going to eat.

The English gentry, a few of them in scarlet coats and black velvet caps, the rest in black coats and top hats, listened to the cheers of the huntsman, watched the hounds sniffing at the ground, and occasionally rode their horses hard.

Quite often the chase would be successful, and this is the way the game would be ended: the big brushy coyote tail would be cut off and handed by the master to a rider who had combined gentility and purpose. The head of the coyote would be cut off and presented to another superior player. And the pads removed from the coyote's legs would be distributed to the runner-up. Then the body of the game animal would be thrown to the hounds.

That evening there would be a festive dance at the Manor.

There the members of the hunt would pass remarks praising the endurance and cunning of their adversary. Someone would offer a measured phrase concerning the superiority of the game to mere "spectator sports." Another would offer a moderate defence of cricket.

In town Everyday Luigi, working for Soo Woo, who had contracted for the job, would all day have been weeding and seeding and generally tidying the baseball grounds. He would have been removing as much of the animal shit as possible, and filling the gopher holes.

That night he would see a gentleman from out of town framed for a second in the light coming from the door of the little frame house by the river where Gert the Whore lived.

Somewhere in the night and across the river and probably on top of the bluff, a coyote made his usual call. Everyday Luigi thought it might have sounded as if the unseen animal had called out something like Tally Ho. But not really. It was more like Yip yip yip yahoo.

Toujours le bon Dieu reste muet
En dessinant les lacs et les forêts.
Les matins frais et lumineux qu'il crée
Ne font que pleurer les êtres destinés
A partager les ombres désolées.

Pourtant un coeur qui bât rempli de haine
Est presque

How silent is the sagebrush on the flat!
The sky above the mountains growing blue
Belies a heart that rises filled with hate,
And nearly tempts the fury from her task
Of solitary justice in the west.

How silent is the God who drew the hills!
The sky above this rider on her search
Belies a soul consumed with wondrous hate,
And almost lulls the nemesis contrived
To bring some sunshine to a brother's grave.

How quiet is the morning on the trail!
The turmoil in a waking dream is spent
Before the dew has dried upon the pines;
Yet when the first loud crow bespeaks his pain
The sound converses with a rumoured death.

How quiet
the morning breaks
my concentration
on the target.

Ordinary English eyes
would see a flood of light
coursing down the valley
like a ghost of ice.

Famous hunter eyes
penetrate the shadows under rocks,
behind the sage
a fear not yet dried
by the rising fire.

Black and beautiful
the shadow in my heart
rides without luck to south,
to north, to a west
too wide.

A bullet too fast
and another not quick enough
have spoken a tongue
I have only begun to learn

Then did I in creations of my own
(Oh, is not woman in each thing divine?)
build worlds — or bidding them no longer be —
exert, enjoy a sense of deity —
doomed for such dreams presumptuous to atone;
all by one word of thunder overthrown!

Over-throne! The rumble of those words
is my sport, a seizing of His speech
for my dire purpose
and my duty.

A tumbleweed may speak, a crow
may utter wisdom, a fox
never appear to furious eyes,
thus telling what I dread to know.

Heat not a furnace for your foe,
that it not singe your self;
nor find fair view
to cast it out
for eyes turned inward to a shadow
that speaks from dying lips.

How silent is the sagebrush,
till wind from noon-day furnace
burns the fancy
to words conceived in
unfer

"I have been thinking about Coyote," said the second Indian.

Oh, I have been waiting to say something like this, thought the first Indian. It is a nice thing to have a youngster around, because a youngster will always feed you some good straight lines.

"Excuse me, what did you say?" he asked.

"I have been thinking about Coyote."

"You dont think about Coyote. You imagine Coyote."

Now the proper thing to do was to leave it there, with a kind of vatic elegance. It didnt take an artist to understand that. But the whippersnapper didnt understand it yet. The first Indian saw him open his well-toothed mouth, and knew that oracle would have to give way to lecturer.

"Think. Imagine. What's the difference?"

He would try one more time.

"Coyote is the difference," he said.

"Oh, you are just playing with words again," said the second Indian.

A perfect lead-in to a lecture. But the first Indian decided to save that one for later. He had a lot of things to save for later, but he did not know how much later he had left to him. When it came to riding or walking or especially standing with a solemn stillness that was expected of old Indians, he envied his protégé the carelessness of youth. But sly wisdom and the opportunity to effect puzzling rejoinders was a compensation. Yes it was.

"Let me tell you a story about Coyote," he said.

"Is there any way of stopping you?"

But the second Indian had been manoeuvring for this all along, and they both knew it. They sat down on the riverbank and turned their faces upward, as their people always did in a situation such as this. Neither knew why, but it seemed right.

"This is the story of Coyote and the Word-Eater. In the days before writing, Coyote used to sing for his supper. He would sit at his camp and sing the deer song. Oh deer, wise and mighty deer, here is only a lonesome friend waiting for you to appear, et cetera."

"Not the best words I have ever heard for a song."

"I dont know the exact words, of course. That was just an example. Not really an example, just a poor old man's substitute for the magic words of Coyote. If I knew the right words, there would be a buck with an enormous rack here right now."

"Point taken. Go on," said the second Indian.

But he couldnt help looking around, just in case. Not an animal in sight, if you didnt count the Double W cattle on the bench opposite.

"Well, one morning after a deep night's sleep, Coyote woke up and felt a strong hunger for mountain sheep. So he decided to sing the sheep words."

"Oh sheep, plump sheep, I have wakened from my lonesome sleep," suggested the second Indian.

"That will do. But when he tried to say the words out loud he was surprised to hear nothing but the stream that hurried by his camp. He tried and tried again, and though he could hear the words inside his head, he could not say them to the air. He tried the deer words and the porcupine words, and even the skunk words. But nothing happened. So he had to make do with lily roots."

"Lily roots are delicious," said the second Indian.

"When you wake up day after day with a powerful hunger for meat, you soon lose your taste for lily roots."

"Ice cream is even better than lily roots. I wish I knew the words to the ice-cream song."

"Do you want to hear the story at all?"

"Of course. Sorry. Continue."

"You know, I *could* just go back to the village and be a grandfather.

I dont have to ride all over the plateau with you, keeping you out of trouble and showing you how to tell the difference between an edible tree bark and a split-rail fence."

"I know. I have apologized. And I *am* interested in the adventures of your old friend Coyote."

"He is your friend too. He is probably watching you right now."

"I have never been able to figure him out," said the second Indian. "Is he a god or an animal or just a goof? Is he an Indian with magic powers? How come he uses a bow and arrow? If he can do so many supernatural things, why does he wind up all covered with skunk piss and things like that?"

The first Indian did want to get on with the story, but here was a chance to teach his young charge that sometimes a case of knowing something is to know with certainty that it is not quite knowable.

"He gave order to the world. So he keeps falling into messes."

"Maybe you'd better go on with the story," said the second Indian.

"Now Coyote knew that this not being able to sing the animals into his camp was a new problem, and whenever there is a new problem it is caused by a new being in the land."

"We Indians could have told him that," said the second Indian.

"I would rather have thought that was too obvious to require commenting upon," said the first Indian. "Do you think a story is just a story?"

"Sorry."

"So he left his camp and began tracking. He found deer tracks and hare droppings and Sasquatch prints in the river mud. These last he filed in his prodigious but captious memory, for later reference. He trailed through the willows and across the dry land for three days, never doubting his logic, but growing more hungry every day. Already characteristically thin, he was now quite gaunt, what a friend of mine from San Angel would call a *coyote flaco*."

"Where is Sam Ann Hell?"

"It is a fine neighbourhood of Mexico City."

"What does that have to do with the story?"

"Very little. I just like once in a while to demonstrate a certain breadth of referentiality."

"Sometimes you do not sound like an Indian to my ears."

"You have ordinary Indian ears. Listen. On the morning of the fourth day Coyote woke up from a dream of feasting, and saw some unusual footprints leading up from the riverbank to his camp. At the near end of the trail of prints he saw, when he opened his other eye, a creature he had never seen before. The Old Man never told me about you, he said. For this was an odd looking animal. It looked like a man or a bear. It had a man's face but it was covered with long white fur. It stood on its hind legs, about the height of a black bear, and its face was smiling like a white man with a land claim."

"Is that part of the story, or is that the part of a story that is not just a story?"

"Wait. Now Coyote said to the apparition, animals come into my camp only when I call for them. Not any more they dont, said the creature, you sure as hell did not call for me. That would be impossible, of course, under the circumstances, and in any case you do not know what I am called. It is my job to give the animals their names, said Coyote. The Old Man said so."

"This is really complicated for a Coyote story," said the second Indian.

"I'll say. The Old Man never told you about me, said the creature, so I will have to introduce myself. I am the word-eater. Are you the reason I have gone hungry for most of the past week, asked Coyote. Oh no, said the word-eater, that is attributable primarily to your silly pride. You could always track down some poor witless beast and eat it. You just cannot call them into your camp any more. Every time you try it I will eat your words. Why are you tormenting me this way, asked Coyote. Why do you want to eat my words while I go hungry? Well, come on, said the word-eater, I have to eat too."

"I like that," said the second Indian. "What I can follow of it."

"It's not that difficult. Well, said Coyote, what's to stop me from saying the word-eater words and bringing you into my camp to be turned into breakfast? Try it, said the creature. Of course Coyote could not say the words. He could hear them in his head but he could not project them into the air."

"A kind of reciter's block."

"Precisely. So the word-eater went away, laughing as he did so, and Coyote made breakfast out of lily roots and insects. For another week he fretted about the situation, once in a while trying the deer words or the goat words, but to no avail. He took to moping around his camp, eating choke-cherries and saskatoons to vary his diet. One day he found himself idly drawing pictures in the dirt with a stick. Then he decided to try drawing on a big rock near his camp-fire. Using berry juice and who knows what else, probably minerals of some sort, he drew a picture of a salmon. There was a splash at the edge of the river, and when Coyote looked to see what was happening, he saw a big salmon flopping around on the ground."

"Aha!"

"Aha, indeed. The first thing Coyote did was to eat the salmon. The second thing was to begin a drawing from memory of the word-eater. It took him hours and hours to get it right, because there were no conventions regarding the illustration of such an odd being. But eventually he got it right, and sure enough, there was the word-eater, walking into camp. Wordlessly, Coyote ate him."

"I just imagined something," interjected the second Indian.

"Uh huh."

"Why didnt Coyote eat him the first time he walked into his camp?"

"He didnt think of it."

Sometimes you didnt need a mysterious phrase to do what you needed to do. Or sometimes you couldnt think of one fast enough.

"That wasnt a bad Coyote story," said the second Indian.

"Thank you. Now you know the source of all those stone writings you have seen."

"You mean the pictures on big rocks along the river and sometimes by the road and once in a while on the hillsides?"

"All done by a hungry Coyote."

"But sometimes there are representations of people in those

pictures, I think. I am not as good a reader as I might be, I am not so much a reader as I am a creator of art, but I think I have seen representations of people in some of those glyphs."

The first Indian had a face like a stone, or like an Indian in a photograph.

"We have many Coyote stories," he said, "but we do not have the story on Coyote."

☆ ☆ ☆

The B.C. Express Company stage was on its way south, honey-bound, loaded with wealth. The six enormous horses had five of their twenty-five miles to make, pulling the wide tires over a road made of stones and holes. They were famous all over the continent. The stage was solid as the horses. People said it would take a rockslide to make a dent in it.

On the back of the stage the express packages were lashed. On the box sat Charlie Westoby, twelve ribbons and a whip stock in his hands. Charlie was famous too, among the passengers who subjected their bodies to the banging and thumping they would get on a ride to or from the Cariboo.

There were three passengers in the stage today, or rather that day. One of them, amazingly, was asleep, his limp body thrashing around on the back-facing seat. Sometimes one of the others would lift a boot to keep the body from particular harm. The two wakeful riders were strangers to one another because one was a part-time cowboy and the other was a journalist, as he called himself, from the Austro-Hungarian Empire.

"We're going through some patchy country," said the first rider.

"Apache country? I thought that was hundreds of miles to the south."

The foreigner looked alarmed but also excited. In his dispatches he often made things up, and in fact the parts he made up were quite frequently the best parts. But he also persuaded himself that imminent peril brought out the best in him.

"Naw," said the cowboy, "the Apaches are a Yankee problem.

Up here we got Indians who never give us any trouble. Up here us and the Indians understand each other."

"No fights with guns and arrows?"

"Guns?"

"The famous six-guns. The Colt."

"Naw," said the cowboy. "Only thing we ever use guns on is snakes and Germans."

The journalist leaned as far away as possible, but his thigh still lay alongside the other's.

"Only joshing ya," said the cowboy.

The journalist saw that his neighbour's teeth were showing through his moustache and that he was not packing a Colt. He grinned back. It was a good time, he guessed, to reveal his personal flask of whisky and offer it around to the non-sleeping passengers.

Mercifully, the stage slowed a little as it approached a hard turn that featured an overhanging rock and a precipitous drop to the unseen river below. As the eight thousand pounds of horseflesh impatiently picked their way around the quick bend, Westoby spied two men sitting their mounts and holding rifles in the crooks of their arms.

"Stop them horses and get your hands in the air, damn you," shouted one of the highwaymen.

If Al Young or Fred Peters had been driving that stage, it would have arrived at the B.C. Express headquarters robbed clean. But that day's driver was Charlie Westoby. Westoby was by no means any more brave than Young or Peters. Any man who would drive that route had to be brave and maybe a little infirm of mind. But he was extremely deaf. So when the highwayman hollered at him, Charlie assumed that he was offering a roadside greeting. He raised his whip hand in salute as he thundered on, only he did not hear the thundering.

"Good day to yez," he shouted back over his shoulder, as the horses picked up speed for a mildly frightful straight stretch.

His course was followed by four eyes staring with disbelief, anger and disappointment. But the rifles stayed where they were.

The two wakeful passengers had figured out what was on the minds of the two men sitting their horses at the bend in the mountain road.

"I am going to write a letter to the Express company," said the journalist, "and urge them to commend that driver. That is the kind of courage that makes the wild west what it is."

"That is a grand idea," said the cowboy. "And while you are at it, give a few words to the courage of our fellow passenger there. He did not flinch when he saw the firearms in the possession of the robbers."

The European had before now learned to expect condescension from the inhabitants of this dusty land. It did not deter his curiosity, his occupation as an asker of questions.

"Does the stage often fall into the hands of thieves?"

"First time I ever seen any," said the cowboy.

"Well, when we get to the company headquarters, I will be able to furnish a thorough description of those two men to the authorities. As a journalist I am trained in the art of observation and memory."

The cowboy had been holding the European's little flask all the while. Now he took a long contemplative pull from it before handing it back.

"Just tell them that one of the desperadoes was Loop Groulx and the other one seemed to be a stranger. Tell them the stranger was wearing the kind of hat they wear in Arizona, small brim, a little rolled."

"I had not noticed that," said the journalist.

The Nicola Hotel was the only lodging place to boast about in the Gateway to the Cariboo, and it enjoyed its monopoly. In the hot mining towns one would find dozens of small hotels with big bars, but when a boom is succeeded by ambitions to become a lasting metropolis, the numbers decline and the surviving hostelry becomes substantial. The Nicola was substantial. It got all the B.C.

Express business, and provided beds for any government agents or European journalists who were passing through the country of the Interior Plateau.

It also had the best poker game in town. There thirsty and speculative locals met travelling Yankees and Brits over the felt table. If we take a normal evening at the Nicola bar we will look at the table and see coins and paper from at least three countries. There is a Government of British Columbia twenty-dollar piece, 1862, with a crown on top and a wreath, if we could see it, underneath. There is a note for five dollars that informs the winner that he will be assured by the Bank of British North America, Victoria, V.I., 27th Sept. 1859. Beside it is a shiny double eagle from the U.S., and a pound note from Newfoundland. There are at the moment seven hundred dollars in the middle of the table.

The journalist from the Austro-Hungarian Empire was making notes in a little book, and receiving because of that some dour glances from around the room. He saw a hand drop seventy-five Canadian dollars on the pile of assorted money.

"Is the betting always this rich?" he asked the evening bartender.

"This is a peanut game," said the latter. "More than once I have seen a man lose his whole outfit, worth thousands, on the turn of a card. I seen small ranches get five times as big when a five-spot got turned over. I seen a rich Irishman throw his Spanish saddle in Gert the Whore's yard because he didnt no longer have the horse he rode into town on."

Most of the players were freighters. They all wore black stetson hats, high-heeled boots with jingling spurs, and bandannas, generally red, across their breasts. Some of them were drinking and losing. Some were drinking and winning. In his notebook the journalist gave them mighty scars across the face and added a few inches to their height.

The bartender looked at the German writing and thought it was English. He was interested in writing, and wished he could read it.

"What you writing down there?"

"A story of the wild west," said the journalist. "Facts about life in the big country, for people who are tired of their own stories."

"Lots of stories in this country," said the bartender. "Hardly any of them true."

"Ah," said the European. "The farther you get from the site, the more truth there is in the stories."

"Is that a fact?"

The journalist was looking at the mirror while those words were passed, and he could not believe his luck as he saw the two men with rifles enter through the side door. They had bandannas pulled up over their noses, so that only their fierce eyes showed under their pulled-down hats. He made mental notes to be transcribed and exaggerated later.

"All right, get all those hands in the air, damn you!"

He knew immediately who that was. It was the man who had yelled unsuccessfully at the stage the day before yesterday. The one who was not Loop somebody.

The desperadoes shared their work, but rather inexpertly, he thought, the shouter levelling his rifle around the room while the silent one scooped the money off the table, some of it onto the floor but most of it into the side pockets of his short saddle-jacket.

The bartender contemplated reaching for his shotgun but finally considered the fact that the desperadoes had not said anything about stealing directly from the hotel. He kept his hands above his shoulders.

"You," said the vocal thief.

"I?"

But it could not be anyone else. The fierce eyes under the small hat brim seemed to offer pain.

"Hell no, I'm talking to my sainted aunt. What are you writing with that pen?"

"History," said the European. He was puzzled that he should be able to say anything.

"Well, throw that pen on the floor over here. Easy. You aint putting me in history, damn you."

The journalist did as he was told, skidding the gold-nibbed pen across the floor to the gunman's feet. In a second it was smashed under a spurred heel.

Then the two robbers backed to the side door and out into the darkness. No one inside moved for a minute, and that was a good thing, because three rifle slugs smashed through the window of the door, and then horses' hooves were heard drumming away toward the river bridge.

A shadow that speaks from dying lips. That is what Archie Minjus called the artefact of his work as it smiled or scowled up at him from the tray in which it was delivered.

Archie Minjus was one of the few photographers in the Thompson Valley who had been there longer than the railroad. The railroad had brought work, brought a contract in fact. What the railroad wanted was picturesque scenes of glorious mountains and especially fertile valleys, shiny ribbons of track discernible as proximate to soil that could make a family's fortune. The railroad wanted easterners and immigrants who would be moved by images of profitable beauty. So Minjus travelled on the rails and stopped with his tripod to make pictures of the future.

Before the railroad and its interest in beauty his photographs did not show much in the way of glorious nature. This was because the men who were buying the pictures wanted to see themselves as winners already. A typical photograph would depict several men in rude clothes standing beside a sluice in front of a hill that had been stripped of trees and bushes and anything a poet might claim to be impressed by. If you look at photographs made before the railroad came through you will not see any scenes of natural majesty. It did not pay. There was no one who would offer gold for a memento of the land that was there before he arrived to make holes in it. Photography was expensive.

When he had worked in Victoria there had been some rich families who desired representations of their success, studies of their grand houses, or afternoons of croquet and tea parties. Here, though, before the railroad, he sold principally pictures of a defeated hillside.

But that was a living. Making death look alive by making it stand as still as death. Shadows on silver. Shadows that speak from dying lips.

Besides a living there was the curiosity that kept Archie Minjus poor, or if not exactly poor, at least far short of the fortune that he, like the gold seekers, thought he was seeking. At least when he first left Victoria. Victoria was a town filling up with photographers.

He was curious about people, what they looked like in this constant bright sunlight, what the Interior Plateau did to faces and bodies that had come here from so many diverse homes. He kept on making portraits of people who had not come to him, and every time he made a picture that was not commissioned he cut his income in half. Sometimes, accidentally, one of these pictures would prove fortunate, as did his famous study of the wild McLean brothers. Allan, Charlie, and Archie McLean and young Alex Hare stood with their hats off and leg-irons attached to belts, in front of a sun-beaten white wall, the McLeans handsome, their level eyes revealing no hatred, no fear, not even pride. Just a kind of level neatness and almost aristocracy. At least in the photograph. Their dying lips firm and sealed. It was said that when the three brothers were hanged together on the morning of January 31st, 1881, there were tears in Archie McLean's eyes. But he was fifteen years old. In the photograph his bandaged right hand is stuck inside his shirt. It suggests a story you would like to read some time.

Now, or rather the kind of now you are persuaded of in a black-and-white surface, Archie Minjus desired to photograph the tall woman apparently called Caprice. He did not know anything about her, but from the story he had been told upon returning to town, it sounded as if like the McLeans she had sand. That mixed with bad luck was his favourite appeal.

He must have had some artist in him, because he made a slow and indirect approach to her. He was from the west all right, but when this impulse to make his own pictures was upon him, he did not go direct to his quarry. Yet he could not just stay in his rooms and sing the Caprice words. Eventually he had to approach. He waited till she paid for her breakfast and left the Canadian Cafe. Then he abandoned his fourth cup of coffee and followed her out to the boardwalk.

"Nice morning," he said.

Most people here were reluctant to talk with her. But she had never seen this man in the worn city suit before. She was busy putting on her gloves, so she stopped to look at his face while she was doing so.

"My name is Minjus," he said.

Her gloves on, she now removed a book from under her arm and held it in one hand.

"I sort of live here, but I have just come back from some work I was doing around Savona," he said. "People have told me a little about you."

"Have they?"

This was more direct than he intended to be. Her grey eyes were looking at his hands. They were yellow. He lifted them before his face as if they were vegetables he was thinking of buying.

"I am a photograph maker," he said, turning his hands over and back.

"Are you?"

He took a couple steps along the boards, and she moved her long legs too, perhaps beside him. Thank goodness.

She might have been going to see her horse. She might have been going to pick up her mail. She might have been simply going for a walk after breakfast. Wherever she was going she went with long steps on hard heels, and she did not bounce.

"I wonder," he said.

"I would have thought you did not have time for wonder," she replied. "I would have thought that as a photograph maker you would be interested in recording what is."

So she was not a cowgirl. He thought he noticed some sort of little accent to her speech, but maybe it was refinement instead.

"There are some people who think of photographs as art," he said.

"Yes, I have met them. But not out here," she said.

They had passed the hostler's, so she was not after her horse. Soon they arrived at the river. She was looking at the ground near the bank. Where the earth was hard there were hundreds of old hoofprints, and where it was wet there were prints that were either new or newly moistened.

"May I?"

"I cannot afford a picture," she said. She had lifted her freckled face and was looking across the river, at the ribbon of dust that was the road to the Cariboo.

"I am not selling," he said. "I want to record you, as you say."

"That's a new one."

"I would like to take your portrait."

"Is that a fact?"

He was encouraged by the new mocking lightness in her voice.

"I can get my equipment and meet you here in ten minutes."

"If I am still here," she said, "that will be all right."

"I see that you are not carrying your famous weapon," he said.

"No."

"I was wondering. It would make a more appealing record if I could take a picture of you with your whip."

"No," she said.

☆ ☆ ☆

The two bushwhackers had picketed their horses in the meagre shade of a lone ponderosa pine, and were now crouched behind a boulder perched suggestively on the steep slope above the river. They were spying on the man below them. The man had pulled his one-horse wagon off the dusty road, and found a place where he could take off his boots, roll up his pantlegs, and dangle his feet in the slowly moving green water.

They had expected to see him take out a notebook and a pencil and get to work. But the man just sat there in his foreign suit, his delicate boots standing together beside him. He had draped his black cotton socks over the tops of the boots.

"That's him, all right," said the first bushwhacker.

"What the hell is he doing?"

"How the hell should I know? I never seen a Square Head journalist before."

"Well, what the hell are we waiting for?" said the other bushwhacker. "Let's get down there. Should we take our horses, or just walk down?"

The first bushwhacker made a point of casting his ordinary Yankee eyes up and down the valley and up the slope behind them, even across the river and into the scrub on the other side. There was a coyote standing still in the middle of an alluvial fan, but he did not see it. On a hot brown day such as this the only thing one was likely to see was movement. The only thing moving was the heavy green river.

They walked or rather slid down the sandy approach, their rifles in their hands. One of them was a .44–40, model of 1867.

There was so much sliding and clanking and cursing, that even the man with his feet in the water heard them arriving at last. Without lifting his feet he turned his head and raised his hairy eyebrows.

"Howdy," said one of the men, the quality of his speech affected by the ragged way he was breathing.

The other did not say anything, but carefully checked the road and the skyline for movement.

"Hello, gentlemen," said the man with his feet in the water. He touched the brim of his new black stetson with the first two fingers of his right hand. He did not seem to be as much interested in the weapons as one might have expected.

"What are ya doing?" asked the man who had spoken first.

"I am doing what I do every afternoon. A doctor who is very famous in my country instructed me to put my feet in cool water for half an hour every day. I have found that whatever cool water a person can find in this country is especially to be treasured."

"Thought ya might be fishing," said the bushwhacker, and guffawed.

The foreigner smiled. He had decided that his work here in the wild west would benefit from his attempting to be friendly in all encounters with the locals.

"As a matter of fact," he said, "I have been watching a considerably large fish for the last few minutes. Until you arrived he was moving his tail back and forth in a leisurely fashion and thus staying still in the watery sunlight. I was remarking that it has likely been several centuries since a fish of such size has been seen in the rivers of my country."

He had also learned that the locals appreciated acknowledgement of the grandeur of their frontier.

"This country of yours, that would be Australia, would it?" enquired the talkative rifleman.

"Austria. My name is Arpad Kesselring, or A. Kesselring when it appears in print."

"You any relation to the Kesselrings over by Vernon?"

"No, I have been in the New World for only about a year," said the journalist, idly moving his white feet in the water.

"You figuring on staying?"

"No, I am what we at home call a foreign correspondent. I was attracted to this country because of the opportunity to capture in words the drama that follows the death of the gold mines and the arrival of the railroad."

The talkative bushwhacker was hooked. Before the hold-up in the bar, he had never considered himself a possible character in a story. He had seen other men reading cheap soft books with drawings of miners and cowpunchers and outlaws in them, but somehow he had never really been able to connect those words and pictures with his daily life. Even when some stage got drygulched, or an Indian shot some drunk in Kamloops or somewhere, he never associated the event with a drama someone would want to read about in Australia.

"This country has got a lot of opportunities for a man which wants to go into business," he said. "My partner and me, we are going into business."

"Yes, I recognize you from the other evening," said the journalist. "You are Mr Lionel Groulx, but I did not catch the name of your partner...."

"This here is Frank Smith."

Nobody offered to shake hands.

Mr Kesselring took his feet out of the water and held them to dry in the hot sun. Loop Groulx sat down on the bank a few yards from him, his legs bent under him and his rifle laid across his thighs. Frank Smith stood where he could watch the road in both directions. The horse, disappointed by the meagreness of the grass thereabouts, gave his harness a shake and then seemed to doze off.

"Well, then," said the journalist, "I seem to be in luck. For a year I have been hoping against wish to have the opportunity to speak with some authentic western outlaws. Do you mind if I call you outlaws? I always clear such matters with the people I make interviews with."

Groulx looked up at his partner before replying. Smith was not even listening, or if he was he was giving no sign that he had heard. He was scanning the skyline for movement.

"I think me and Mr Smith would prefer to be called businessmen."

"Your business is holding up stagecoaches and poker games?"

Groulx spit a gob into the fine dust that covered the ground from the road halfway down to the river.

"Naw. We are going into the epsom salts business. We know a good creek just north of here that's just full of epsom salts. But a body needs lots of expensive equipment to get an epsom salts business going. Meanwhile we are going to look for a nice stretch of black dirt to grow some potatoes on. We figure there's a nice future in potatoes here, what with the railroad and all."

The journalist was pulling on his cotton socks and fastening his garters.

"From what I have seen, the good black soil seems to have been claimed along this valley," he said.

"Say, shouldnt you be keepin' notes?" enquired Groulx.

The journalist pulled on an elegant black boot.

"Over the past decade I have developed the art of listening," he said. "If I were making notes all the time you were talking I might miss something you were saying, something little but absolutely the key to the story, the egg that will hatch the bird in the reader's imagination."

"But what if you get something wrong?" asked Loop Groulx.

"I am a writer," said the journalist. "My principal responsibility is to the story and its reader, not to the repetitive details of the country I am writing about. If you were wearing a brown hat now, I would be serving the story well if I gave you a black hat, you understand?"

Groulx took off his hat and looked at it.

"But I *am* wearin' a black hat."

A magazine writer from the Austro-Hungarian Empire was not necessarily an intellectual, not necessarily a repository of the great traditions of the city of Vienna, or even the cafes of Budapest. But

A. Kesselring often found that the glamour of the wild west was placed in perspective by the relative simplicity of the minds encountered there. He decided that he was not going to be entertained by further discussion of his craft here.

"The last few days in town I have been hearing some stories about you and a tall woman with a whip," he said. "In my experience these stories are often exaggerated and distorted by eye-witnesses and late-comers alike. Would you like to tell me your version of the true story?"

"That's my business," said Loop.

By the 1890s the west had started to shrink. It had started noticeably to shrink by the time the first locomotives made the turnaround at Port Moody. Now or rather then it shrank with every word that was sent back from the dry country across the mountains and over the Atlantic Ocean. Some of the west spilled northward for a while and seemed to be expanding to its original size, but there too it would shrink, until the west became small enough to fit into eastern plans, to become a region in the eastern scheme of things.

Out in the west the west was also, by the 1890s, becoming the past. The more one looked around in the west the more it seemed obvious that it was the past hanging on for a while. It became more clear all the time that the future was getting ready to move in, and the future of the west was going to be the east.

That was an awful irony for the western person. The man in the west had always been pure, hard as the country he rode in, but pure. That was why he was out there instead of back where all the paper money was made. The woman of the west was tough enough to live under that sun and a long way from the stores, but she was innocent.

Now after all that work, after working so hard to make the west a beginning, they could not help seeing that the west was every day becoming recognizably the past. It was slipping from the land into the landscape of stories about the west. It was becoming a style in eastern theatres and those theatres were beginning to show up in the west, and the west was now on the stage and in books and in songs instead of out the front door or on the trail this afternoon.

How could men and women who were supposed to be pure and innocent, at least simple and strong enough to live with brown hills and green rivers, dry summers and fierce snowy winters, how could these people live with irony? With the future, the east, ready to move in, how could they help but feel that they had been used? They had been used, as a temporary necessity.

Were they supposed to go through the pageant of the dude ranch for vacationing easterners, put on wider hats and bigger spurs, and punch those dogies for an audience? Join the Indians who sold quickly-made moccasins at the train station?

People in Europe were accustomed to living with irony. It was expected of them. They wrote the books and the plays and the operas. They rounded up the philosophy and branded it and took it to the railhead. Even people in the east knew how to settle down comfortably in irony.

But when you arrange things so that there is a big country out there where the pure of heart and the strong of limb may try to prove that human beings can work hard and live as simple as the sun coming up every day, you are betraying them somehow if you change the rules and tell them they have to live with irony. The country out there was hard but not cruel, and the people were the same way. They knew how to live with hard. But forcing irony on them was cruel.

When a painter or a writer grew up in the west after the 1890s he was likely to show in his works how much he loved the past of his native country, but despised the present. He did not want to hear about the future. There is a possibility that he also loved his childhood a lot more than his adulthood. A lot of people feel that way. Two kinds of people like reading stories of the old west: young people and old cowboys.

Already in the 1890s there were stories of the old west. The mood that ran through them was nostalgic regret. But they were printed back east and arrived on the train from Montreal or New York. It was a theme that would pervade all future writing about the west, and then, looking across the medicine line, one would see that it was a theme that would pervade all Yankee writing for at least a century.

Even when Adam and Eve were chucked out, they were sent east.

That was their future. After that their descendants always looked westward. Some of them looked westward for hard freedom and some of them looked westward for a dream of empire.

But as soon as you get to the Pacific Ocean, with a train or something, all you have in front of you is the east. A rotting market spilling fruit peels into the harbour, probably. A landlord collecting paper money from people living on bamboo boats.

The east just keeps coming till it sees the tip of its own tail and begins to wonder what it would taste like. In the little shrinking strands of the west that are still left, stories are being written. They are usually called the last of something.

The last of the Mohicans.

The last of the curlews.

The last of the cowboys.

The last western hero.

In the absence of a complete silence we hear a voice saying come back, Shane. And hoofbeats. The hell with us. We are all Europeans now. Now we can write the books and plays and operas. We just have to look around in the past and find subjects. There we will find a cowboy rather than a business man. The west has shrunk so much that we can get it inside us.

It is awfully dry in there.

We walk around in our European clothes, carrying our eastern newspapers, and we have a little dry something inside us.

It feels something like a soul, only too dry.

Some of us wouldnt mind seeing the last of it.

"Did you ever wonder where we came from?" asked the first Indian.

They were eating the last of the bannock. It was getting to be that time when they would have to leave town and head back to the people. Either that or try the food at the Canadian Cafe. The second Indian did not mind chop suey, but the first Indian was older and he knew that when the Chinese came across the Pacific they did not bring any cooks with them. When the Chinese came they were all rock carriers and hole diggers. They left all the cooks at home in China. He knew that the sign in the window of the Canadian Cafe — Chinese and Canadian Food — was an exaggeration on at least two counts. He could not read it, but he knew what it said. He knew that the yellow man, too, could speak with a forked tongue. Maybe a chopsticked tongue.

He thought momentarily of sharing this fortuitous fall of words with the young fellow, but forsook it, knowing that he would have to explain it.

"We are from Deadman Creek," said the second Indian, or something like that. He had his mouth full, as often happened when the food was running low.

They could, of course, seize a few fish from the river, but the local service clubs were touchy about Indians using their sports-fishing facilities.

"I dont mean you and I. I am referring to the Indian people. Did you ever stop to consider where we might have come from?"

"If you mean in the metaphysical sense, I suppose the Great Spirit sent us here to suffer inferior hunting and landscape, so that we would be filled with a hankering for the Happy Hunting Ground. Do you think we were sent here as punishment for some failing of ours up there?"

The young were expected to explore heterodox thought, even to espouse heresies for a while. That way they would come back to the people's beliefs with fervour, having tested the alternatives. A certain apostasy was even encouraged, though never overtly.

"No," said the first Indian, patiently. "I was not speaking metaphysically. I intended my question in the purview of anthropology."

"Anthro — ?"

"It is a word used by the powerful race or faction to describe the ways of the subjected or impoverished people."

"Are we impoverished?"

"According to the white man we are."

"Are we subjected?"

"We are subjects."

"As long as we are not objects."

"Subjects of the Great White Mother. She calls us her red children."

"She had better not call me that to my face. I will tie her braids together," vowed the second Indian.

The first Indian had lost his appetite, which was a good thing, because the last of the bannock was just then disappearing down a fierce warrior's throat. He had lost his appetite because his memory was filling up. He thought about the story his grandfather told him fifty years ago. In the story his grandfather was a boy who was talking with the first white man ever seen in the valley. His grandfather's grandfather used to tell wild stories about men in shining metal from the south, men in shining metal on horses in shining metal, but few believed him because there were no horses. The idea of a man sitting on the back of an animal was all right for the visions and fables of the speaker whose job it was to have visions and tell fables. But his grandfather's grandfather was a hunter. His tale was ascribed to the ingestion of the wrong berries in too great an abundance. And when his grandfather's grandfather's grandson spoke with the first white man to be seen in the valley, he was not speaking with a man in shining metal, and he was not speaking with a man on the back of an animal. Do you men with hair on your faces ever sit on the backs of animals, the boy asked. Yes we do, said the stranger, and some day maybe before your death, you people will too. I want to believe you, said the boy.

"I was talking with a white man," said the first Indian, "who had an interesting idea about where we came from."

It was at this point that the young man lost his attraction to heresy. When the old men get funny new ideas the young feel obliged to maintain the lore of the tribe.

"How would the white man know where we come from? It is the white man who comes from somewhere. We have always been here. We have a sacred relationship with the valley because we are the valley. We are the voice of the valley. We are the first people, who bring breath and meaning to the life of our mother the earth."

"Will you shut up for a minute," asked the first Indian.

"Listen to me for once, old friend. If the white man starts telling you that we came from somewhere else, it just means that he is working up a case to take away our land."

"Oh, he will do that," said the first Indian. "He does not need a story to do that. He is going to make us live in the past, and his notion is that we do not need much room to live in the past. In fact his notion is that we are the past."

The second Indian made the gesture that signifies impatience if it is slow and anger if it is fast. He made it medium fast.

"When I was assigned you as my teacher they never told me that I was going to learn from a man who passes on the stories of the white man."

"I am trying to tell you what one white man suggested. The rest of the white men do not believe him. That attracted me. Will you listen, or do you just want to get on the back of your animal and ride home?"

"This is my home. This whole valley is my home."

"Well then, do you want to hear a story in the comfort of your own home? You do not have to believe it. You can join the ordinary white man in not believing the story."

That was neat. He had him there. The brow of the young fellow was uncharacteristically knitted. In a moment he sat down with his spine straight up, and adopted the listening position.

"This white man goes around the valley and other valleys, making drawings of the pictures on the rocks, and collecting old bones. He picks up stones with sea shells in them and carries them in a rucksack. He makes drawings of Indians. He makes big drawings of our villages. He buys jewellery and clothing from us whenever he sees something he has not seen before and can persuade a person to sell it to him."

"He is engaged in that anthro — ?"

"Exactly. He tried to buy my grandfather's grandfather's bow from me. Someone told him that I was the only person at Deadman Creek who had his grandfather's grandfather's anything. Of course I did not sell it to him, but I let him make a drawing of it."

"Your grandfather's grandfather would never have permitted that. That bow would never have brought down another elk if he had done that."

"No one ever knew what my grandfather's grandfather would do, or say, for that matter."

"I think I would rather hear a story about your grandfather's grandfather," said the second Indian.

"I think you just like saying my grandfather's grandfather."

"All right. It is my duty to listen. So tell me about your white man and his sack full of stones. Do you think his grandson's grandson will some day let an Indian make a drawing of his sack of stones?"

"I have learned in my many years never to forbid my imagination anything."

"But you instructed me early to remember that imagination is based on facts. That one should never confuse imagination with mere fancy."

"Good. The fancy would leap to the notion that metal men could ride on the backs of metal animals. The imagination would know that men inside metal could ride horses with metal clothes."

"You did not tell me that this was going to be a story about men on animals."

"Well, in a way it is. But we will leave that for later."

"Phew!"

"Now. The anthropologist told me it was his opinion that many years ago we Indians lived in a country far to the sunset called Mongoleum. He thinks that we came here over the ice from that place, following the elk and something else whose name I cannot remember. He told me that there are Indians thousands and thousands of miles to the south of us. Farther south than we can imagine."

"Fancy."

"He thinks we all came from Mongoleum and settled this land long ago before the memory of the people found its way into stories and dances."

The second Indian had lost the look of impatience. It was replaced by an expressionless stolidity such as that seen in a photograph. Then that was replaced in turn by a look such as that seen on the face of a coyote when it sees a fool hen up close.

"Not meaning to get back into the realm of the metaphysical," he said, "but do you think that this Mongo place might be another word for the Happy Hunting Ground?"

An enormous grey cloudbank had been rising from the mountains to the west, and now its shadow had crossed the two seated men and almost reached their grazing ponies. The ponies were far brighter in hue than the men. In a few moments there would be heavy drops of rain, the first of which would raise dust before the serious downpour arrived to make new mud.

"From what he told me about the place, I would not imagine that the Great Spirit would do that to us. It sounds more like a big reserve than a reward," said the first Indian.

"Even the fancy would never confuse a reserve with a reward," said the second Indian.

It was pouring rain. The ground and the horses smelled nice, but it was really getting wet.

"I will have to tell you about the camels later," said the first Indian.

"Camels?"

Caprice stepped down from the train at the Kamloops station, amidst the usual staring and the slightly audible remarks from men and boys working or loitering there. During the slow and beautiful trip eastward through the valley, she had had time to think in a way different from the way one thinks on horseback. As the train cruised by alfalfa fields dotted with white wooden beehives, she thought about honey. As it chuffed up a rock-strewn brown hill, she thought about Frank Spencer. Then she thought about a gun. She was going to Kamloops for three reasons.

In Kamloops the CPR tracks ran right along the middle of the street, and there were little chunks of coal lying on the packed dirt. The boardwalk was raised high, so that anyone walking along it felt pretty tall. Caprice seldom met anyone who was taller than she, and for this reason hardly any man ever saw her grey eyes looking back into his. For the first block she kept her eyes down, though, looking at the scattered coal. It was a habit retained from her childhood, when the children in St Foy would walk along the tracks with gunny sacks, looking for fuel to bring home to their cold kitchens. That coal hardly ever came in a piece bigger than a child's fist.

Later, when she was wealthy and her family was not, she would drop coins from the train window whenever it was passing through a neighbourhood where ragged children's clothes hung on lines behind unpainted shacks.

For the second block she kept her head up, her hat hanging on her back, and her bright red hair shining in the late afternoon glitter.

Lord, she was beautiful! You should have seen her.

At the post office the young man behind the rich yellow wood counter just gawked at her. He was average height, about five feet seven in his city boots. General delivery, in the month he had been working there, had been just about like general delivery in Hazelton, except for the volume. Until now. Nobody like her had ever asked for a letter or parcel in Hazelton.

She asked him for her mail and he asked her for identification. She was of the opinion that she was ample identification herself.

"Do you have another name? A first name or a last name," he suggested. He was standing as straight up as he could manage.

"What does it say on the letters?" she asked without impatience or cajolery.

"Well, that's funny. It just says Caprice. I didnt know what in tarnation to make of that. Five letters, all addressed just to Caprice. I figured it must be the name of a mining company or something."

"What name did I give you when I asked for my mail?"

"Well, yes Ma'am, you said it."

"Then that resolves the mystery, doesnt it?" she said.

When she put out her gloved hand, his naked one came forward with the five long envelopes. Usually he was a lot more insistent about identification.

Her second stop would have to wait till morning, because the Bank of Montreal was closed, and her third stop would have to wait till after her second stop. She did not want to go to the Indian school before supper, so she decided to go for the kind of walk that people enjoy after being on the train for several hours. She walked the length of the only real street in Kamloops, which was a treat for the cowboys and town wives along the way, and walked back again along the edge of the water.

As her boots left clear marks along the moist earth, so her thoughts traced their paths. For a moment it passed through her head that she would normally be considering a verse while taking such a walk. *Toujours le bon Dieu reste muet....*

But she was not contemplating a divine silence now. She was imagining a loud noise close at hand. On her left hip she carried a heavy coil of leather. In her left hand she carried a small carpet bag. But the other gloved hand was hanging by her right hip. Its finger tips grazed the side of her denimed thigh, till she noticed and let them trail back and up. Anyone watching was watching those fingers and that thigh, and not the imaginary Colt that was still safely back in the shop she had passed a few long paces from the CPR station. No wonder — that thigh was not ruined by a little lateral bulge of flesh that sometimes makes women's trousers look like breaches. But then it was not often that one was permitted to see a woman in trousers, especially a young unattached woman. Especially a woman nearly six feet tall.

Those permitted to see were seeing. Ordinary eyes were always following Caprice wherever she walked.

The walk had been just enough to make her hungry. But the train fare had taken nearly the last of her money. She could spend what she had left to ride to the Indian school, or she could spend it on supper and then walk to the Indian school. By the time she had walked back to the station she knew that Roy Smith would be surprised by a hungry woman rather than a tired one. So she went to the hack stand instead of the cafe. It was the kind of decision a young poet used to make in Paris.

Roy Smith was indeed surprised. He had not even begun consideration of his own supper. Instead he was sitting at the linoleum-covered table in his little teacher's cabin, parsing some English sentences with a twelve-year-old Shuswap boy. When she appeared in the open doorway, he stood up fast enough to knock his home-made kitchen chair to the floor. He was all for sending the boy to the residence right then, but she insisted that he finish the remedial lesson. It gave her an opportunity to sit back on a couch in the shadows and watch Roy Smith being a teacher.

That was the sort of job people would just naturally expect her to be doing. She watched the patience and quiet and knew she could never handle it. As it was, she did not like being seventy-five miles away from her black Spanish horse.

It was not too long till the boy, who had to be encouraged to speak his sentences even in a tiny monotone, picked up his books and left the cabin. Then Roy Smith turned in his chair and looked at Caprice almost lost in the shadow.

"So. You have decided to abandon your misbegotten quest and come to marry me," he said, with put-on alacrity.

"You have to feed me before starting any arguments," she said.

"All I can offer you is warmed-up beef stew and some bread I got from the Italian marching-band picnic. I'll put the pot on, and you go out in the patch and pick us some leaf lettuce."

One thing a five-foot-eleven-inch woman can do is eat. Well after Roy Smith had tossed his napkin over his bowl and leaned his chair on its back legs, she was still wiping rough chunks of bread around the stew pot.

"When we get married I'm going to have to ask the government for a raise, just so I can feed you," he said.

"You dont have to marry me. You can have whatever you want from me without making it legal."

"I want to marry you."

"I have tried that once already."

She was not looking at him. She was thinking of the envelopes in her carpet bag. She wiped her mouth with her napkin, dropped it on the table beside her bowl, and got up from her chair.

Roy Smith was surprised by how much he loved her, how much more than he had thought he did.

She walked around the table and stood so close to him that her belly was almost touching his ear. He turned his head and pressed his face against her midriff. She leaned against him so hard that the chair capsized, and in a clatter they fell to the floor, the chair sliding across it and out the open doorway.

"They'll see," he said.

She got up and closed the door.

"The floor's kind of dirty," he said.

She did not reply. She opened his shirt, and one red braid fell over each side of his chest as she fell with her open mouth on his nipples. The low sun came through the window and cast its melted butter light on them. She opened his schoolteacher trousers.

They were sitting in the dark on his little porch, a buffalo rug wrapped around them. The school and the residence were in total darkness. The only light they could see was above them, a black sky filled with hard low stars. Out of unquenchable delight he had his hand on one of her small breasts.

"He's here," she said.

"Who's here?"

"Spencer."

"In Kamloops? That would be really stupid. The posse quit looking for him nearly a year ago, but there are pictures of him at the railroad station and the police station and the post office. Everybody in Kamloops knows what he looks like."

"Not Kamloops. But he's here. In the country."

"Tell the Provincials. Did you tell Constable Burr?"

"Of course not."

"Caprice?"

"He's using your name. He calls himself Frank Smith."

"A lot of people use my name. I would like you to."

"Maybe. After."

That was a sign of progress. She had never come out and said maybe before this. Yes, after she was shot at, she had, once.

"You dont even have a proper name," he said.

The sign above the wooden awning read F.W. Foster General Merchandise. It was a big wooden building, strong looking, with seven steps leading up to the front porch under the awning. Storage & Forwarding, read another set of white letters. Freight wagons for the Cariboo hung around till they were all loaded before hitting the rocky road north as a noisy caravan. After a train of six or seven wagons had raised dust on their way out, it seemed quiet in the big store.

"*Too* quiet," said G. Delsing, a young clerk with new red sleeve garters.

It was not quiet a moment later. Boots were heard stomping the boards outside, and then the door slammed against the wall, as two men with bandannas on their faces appeared inside, rifles at the ready. Foster and his two clerks raised their hands.

"Give us the gold, damn you, or we will shoot your guts full of lead," shouted one of the masked men.

"There aint any gold, Loop," said the older clerk. "It all went out on the train this morning."

The other hold-up man was at the window, checking the street and the inside of the store. He gestured with his rifle, and the two clerks, hands high, moved over to become a common target with F.W. Foster.

"Get the cash," he said.

The villain who had been addressed as Loop went to the ornate cash register and banged the keys with his rifle butt until the drawer fell open with a ring. He scooped up the various paper money and shoved it into a flour sack. As he dropped the coins into the sack, flour dust made a little cloud that settled on his clothes.

"Keep looking," said the unnamed rifleman with the .44–40.

Loop pulled out and down on the drawer, and it fell to the floor. He put his free hand into the hole and came out with three little leather bags.

"No gold, eh?"

"That there is private," said F.W. Foster.

"Well, it is now," said Loop, and dropped the bags into the flour sack, coughing as flour got up his nose.

The other masked man started walking backward to the door, his Winchester aimed at the target. Loop started to follow him, then came back and stuck the barrel of his rifle under the chin of the young clerk.

"Give me them garters," he said.

G. Delsing tried to get the garters off while still holding his arms high. With exasperation in the eyes that could be seen above the bandanna, Loop reached up with his free hand and snapped the prizes up and off.

"Jumping Jehovah," he said between his teeth behind the dirty cloth, "talk about stupid!"

A few seconds later the three store men could hear horses' hooves tattooing the hard earth outside.

Up the street Everyday Luigi could hear them too. He was standing on the boardwalk outside the office of the *Journal*, a big tub of dirty laundry in his hands. The two riders approached fast, their horses wild-eyed. One of the horses was brown-and-white. The other was white-and-brown.

He stepped into the street to see better.

The first bullet tore a hole in the laundry tub.

The second bullet hit Everyday Luigi in the jaw and sent him sprawling against the edge of the boardwalk.

You did not often see shooting like that from the back of a quick-moving horse, at least not on this side of the medicine line.

There were those who considered outlaws to be a class of people who would simply not engage in manual labour. But outlawing could be one of the hardest jobs in the old west. Rustlers, for instance, often rounding up a herd at night, and running the cattle over terrain that no daytime wrangler would choose, ran risks and endured conditions that no regular cowboys had to face. Professional gun-fighters often had to make long rides by horseback that chafed and generally wore a man down, not to mention the long hours of dull practice. Drygulchers, bushwhackers, and hold-up men suffered assaults on their nerves that would send many an ordinary citizen around the bend.

Consider these two robbers, Strange Loop Groulx and Frank "Smith." Deprived of the opportunity to spend their leisure time in a normal home, a homesteader's shack or a boarding house, for instance, they had to improvise. They had to build a home, and they had to build one while no one was watching, in a place where no one was likely to visit.

Fortunately for them, it was only three or four years since the driving of the last spike on the CPR, so there were still a lot of unused and abandoned railway ties lying on the ground near the tracks. And ever since the retreat of the sea that had been left behind by the ice there had been high clay cliffs with outcroppings of rock on which one could sometimes find the prints of ancient shellfish that had simply grown their homes around their bodies. Now *there* is an aversion to manual labour.

With some of those railway ties, and some silvered boards torn from fifty-year-old prospectors' flumes, Groulx and his foreman and their horses laboured to create a cabin set in a hole in the clay. They then used clay and brush to disguise the use of wood, at least from the ordinary eyes of passers-by, and in that inventive residence they passed their eating and sleeping hours. Groulx had thought that they would stash their earnings there, too, but his foreman pled a greater expertise in such matters, and insisted that they inter the proceedings elsewhere, not far distant, but not easily accessible of a third party.

There the morning after their transaction at F.W. Foster General Merchandising, they cooked bacon and flapjacks and coffee over a smokeless fire, and conducted the conversation that always seems to follow some exposition.

"You figure Constable Burr and his boys are having a good healthy ride this morning, Frank?"

Frank "Smith," who was loathe to do any talking while the duo was conducting business, allowed himself a few words while his stomach was doing its duty. While he spoke, though, his bearded face was not animated. His eyes looked alive, but they did not seem to share the space occupied by anyone else in the room, or even by the man himself.

"The British Columbia Provincials are a hopeless gang of men," he said. "Canadian bulls never bothered me for a minute. They will never find a bad man until they get some help from the Pinkertons down south."

Loop Groulx was not a nationalist or a patriot. He was quite happy to accept that position. Furthermore, he was proud to be thought eligible for the role of partner to this storied Yank.

"That was a pretty good deal we negotiated last night," he said, jocular as he dared. "When you figure we can start up our salt business?"

The eyes above the beard were flat with derision.

"You really believe the honest citizens of this valley are going to appreciate us setting up our firm and joining their businessmen's association?"

"Well, maybe a little north of here."

"Bah!"

"Maybe east. You ever seen the country around Ferguson and Gerrard? Couple of coming towns. Nice country."

"Nah."

"Now that's a country that's going to go somewheres. Fifty years from now this province is going to be a big hinterland for Ferguson and Gerrard."

"Where'd you learn that word, hinterland?"

"Aint it hinterland?"

Sometimes Loop did not feel so much like a partner as like a student or an apprentice. It was "Smith's" turn to say something, but he was just smoking a little cigar and holding a hot tin coffee cup in his bare hand.

"How long you figure we should stay in this country, then?" he enquired.

Those eyes were a *long* way off now.

"Long as *she* is in it."

"That bitch with the whip? She's mine, Frank. A bunch of people heard me say I was going to get her, and so I got to get her. I just aint exactly figured out what I am going to do to her. But it's going to be awful. Maybe when I am done with her she wont be such a long drink of water."

Frank "Smith" spit into the embers of the fire. He flung his cup onto the ground. He stood up and went to the low hole that was their door. He bent down and looked outside at the brightness. He turned around. He turned around again and went outside and pissed on the ground. He came back inside and picked up his rifle. He got out his cloth and cleaned the rifle. He looked like a man who did not know what to do with himself on his day off work. He finally looked at Loop Groulx, and his eyes were right there in the room.

"She is nothing to do with you," he said to the ugly man sitting on his saddle. "She dont give a damn about what you said, and neither do I. Only reason she is in this country at all is because I am here. I killed her brother, and she wants to kill me. I figured on never coming back here, but she come all the way here from back east, and she come all the way to Arizona Territory looking for a meeting. I aint the kind of buckeroo to disappoint a lady."

Groulx had never heard so many words in a row from the man. Still, he had an itching, or an urge of honour.

"But I got to do something," he said.

"Dont disappoint me, Groulx," said his foreman.

☆ ☆ ☆

The second Indian did not have the ordinary eyes of a passer-by, and the first Indian could still see better than most people because he knew what to look for. It was he who had found most of the good places in their hunt for young inexperienced grouse. Young inexperienced grouse made particularly good eating, though some people frowned on the harvesting of them, because they were all white meat, right down to their legs. All you had to do was walk up to them and bash them with a stick or a stone. You could even kick them quickly in the head. Dump out the guts, put them on a stick, and suspend them over a fire. In a few minutes that luscious white meat will just slide off the bones as you pull them out between your lips.

Full of young inexperienced grouse now, they were hunkered behind a big clump of grey sage, watching the low doorway of the bushwhackers' hideaway.

"Why are we doing this?" asked the second Indian. "What do we care what those two miscreants are doing?"

The first Indian had been preparing this lesson for some time. It was convincing, he felt, in its simplicity.

"The people of my grandfather's grandfather's time, and the people of my grandfather's time — "

"Et cetera."

"Very well, etcet-era."

"No you dont. That is not an Indian pun."

"Do not assume all the invader's ways, but make use of the particulars that will bring strength to the people."

"Point conceded. But I do not see the advantage in the fabrication of a rather weak and obvious pun. It is not worth a plugged nickle."

Many of their conversations seemed thus to threaten a kind of dispersal, to wander into byways that did not lead to the advance of education. But the first Indian wanted it to be understood that he was in control of them, that he had a plan not easily apprehended by the ordinary wit. It may have been true, but there were those who doubted it; the second Indian, for example.

"The people of my grandfather's grandfather's time paid the price for not watching everything the newcomers were doing. In our time the wise man will know everything that goes on in this valley. If we do not watch them carefully, some day they will make us drink poison and lock us up inside big stone houses. That is what my father's father told me when I was younger than you are now."

"I think that is some of your fancy, revered teacher," said the second Indian. "Instead of that particular fancy, why do you not finally get around to your promise about the camels?"

The first Indian had been planning to do that all along. He had recently been thinking of himself as a story that should not be told too quickly. If he were a white man he would probably resemble a book, a very thick book, in which the things that happen do not happen precipitately, but rather in a roundabout way. He sometimes wished that he could read and write books. As it was he could read sign better than any member of the band, and he felt that he could probably write it better too. He thought about the experiments he had made in his early years, the pictures he had drawn on rocks that would probably never be found in his lifetime.

"If you were to travel east and south from Kamloops," he said, "you could look for a ranch owned by a man named Henry. He had three camels walking around there in their old age. Now he has one left."

"Wait."

"Wait?"

"You have not told me what a camel is," said the second Indian. "Is it another kind of white man with yellow skin?"

"Oh, I did not tell you what a camel is? In the rain the other night?

Well. A camel is something like a big horse, but it has a large hump in the middle of its back, and a long long neck that bends and wobbles. It also smells very bad. It smells so bad that if there were two of them around you would go back inside your family's pit house in March."

"You are sure that people with metal all over them do not ride them?"

"Ho ho."

"Then why would people have them around?"

"That is the kind of question you should ask not of your teacher but of the white men who brought them to this country. I believe that some white man thought they could carry more supplies to their gold fields than horses and men could. A white man told me that camels have to drink water only once a year."

"The poor things," said the second Indian. "Being thirsty and drinking water is one of the great pleasures of life."

"Well, trying to ride a camel is not one of the great pleasures of life. When one is on the hump on the back of a camel, one is being thrown around in every direction. The only thing one can do is hang on as tight as possible to the traces, and hope for a good strong wind. For the stink."

"It sounds like a terrible animal. Can you eat it?"

"I believe that it is probably very short of white meat. However, having spent a year with you, I would not discount the notion that there are people who would eat just about anything that walks, and great amounts of it."

While they spoke they watched a plume of black smoke as it rose thick into the air and trailed off to disappear forever. It came from a black locomotive that was pulling five boxcars and one passenger coach and a caboose westward beside the green river.

"Well," said the second Indian, "we will have to give the white men one out of two. They got themselves a pretty good animal when they got the horse. But this camel sounds terrible. Where did they get it?"

"According to Henry they brought them from Mongoleum."

"Well, that settles one question, anyway. This Mongoleum is not another name for the Happy Hunting Ground."

In the silence that followed, the older man ostentatiously scanned the valley and the hills for movement, making sure that his protégé could not see the indecision on his face. He did not know how much his face might be revealing of his thoughts, but he was pretty sure that he did not look like an Indian in a photograph.

How much should he tell him about his own experience with camels? Should he tell him anything at all? A teacher usually likes to present the image of a person who has gained great wisdom without ever making a mistake. It is the student's role to make mistakes. Still, the teacher is always saying that we learn from our mistakes. It is when a student makes a mistake that the teacher finds a hand-hold for some useful teaching. Now you see, there's where you are making your mistake; you have to hold it this way.

The really wise teacher knows, though, that his student will learn as well from his teacher's confessed and narrated mistake as from his own. Still, when the student finds out that his teacher has made mistakes, does he not begin the process of unbecoming a student? Or is that becoming a non-student? Becoming something else, then. When he ceases to be a student, does one not cease to be a teacher? And if not a teacher, then what? Something else? Something like a friend? A friend to this pup?

He decided to tell him a little.

"I once owned two camels," he said.

The second Indian glanced at him with curiosity. With pity, perhaps? With authentic interest. This was the old man who would not taste chop suey.

"Tell me, wise man."

The first Indian scrutinized his associate's smile. It was more friendly than anything else.

"I went to Grande Prairie to sell some horses our people did not want, and that is where I saw the camels. Well, I was curious. Here was a fact I had never before known."

"Do not tell me. You let a white man horse-trade you."

"In a way, it was worth it."

"You let a white man camel-trade you."

"It was Henry. He had three camels, and I traded a few horses for two of them. I thought it was my duty, as an investigator of knowledge."

"How many horses did you trade for these two animals with humps on their backs?"

"They were not our best horses. These were horses the people did not want."

"How many?"

The first Indian scanned the valley, east and west. The smoke from the locomotive had all disappeared, a miracle.

"A few."

"Five?"

"Yes, around that."

"More than five?"

"Well, a little."

"Twenty?"

"No, no, I would never trade twenty horses for two camels."

"All right," said the second Indian, "let me assume that you traded nineteen of the people's horses for two camels — "

"Thirteen. Old ones, mainly."

"Thirteen, then. Some older ones. What I am interested in, though, is what happened to the camels."

The first Indian shifted a little, to get a better view of the bushwhackers' doorway. The faint ripple in the air was still to be seen just outside it. They made a pretty good smokeless fire, those two.

"Those camels were probably unhappy to be so far from home. They did not want to be used like horses or mules."

"But they let you ride them?"

"Oh, I rode them. But I gave that up pretty soon. Once you have been around camels for a while, you are not the most popular person in the village. Camels smell a lot worse even than white men. I took to a kind of independent existence, a little distance from the village. Our animals did not like to be near the camels.

Any time they got the scent of them, they would start to destroy the immediate environment."

"So," said the second Indian, "what did you do with them?"

"Well, the stink was making me impatient with my function as a gatherer of knowledge, and the consequent disjunction between myself and my community. But I came to my decision to give up that particular study when one of the shaggy bastards spit on me."

"Spit?"

"An enormous gob right on my breast. I would have thought that an animal that drinks once a year would be interested in preserving any moisture. I was incensed. I had reached the end of my tether."

"So what did you do? Did you sell them?"

"I had already tried that. No, I did not even think of trying to sell them any more now, or rather then."

"You — ?"

"I shot the bastards. Left them for the crows and ants."

He peered over his forearm to read his ex-student's face. There was, surprisingly, a look of respect there, such as he remembered seeing when their association had been younger.

"So you reassumed your place as a full member of the band."

"Well," said the first Indian, "by this time I had learned to like my somewhat independent path. You will see me at Deadman on occasion, but on the whole I would rather be sitting here, watching the action. Now you have just missed seeing one of those pilgrims urinating on a rock. Splashed all over his boots."

The young man darted his eyes there and back. Then he smiled.

"Teach me all you know, Uncle."

"You call me that and I will kick your ass in those white-man's trousers all the way down the bluff," said the first Indian.

Sometimes you got the impression that anywhere there were mines or ranches or logging camps there were bound to be men scribbling verses in their little notebooks or on any paper at hand. You could ride deep into the north country and high above the timber line, go where rails and even horses could not tread, pack your summer's food and tobacco on your back, and head into the unknown boonies. Set up your lonely camp and boil your coffee and fetch out your pipe. Pull your braces over your shoulders, unbutton the top of your trousers, lean back and utter a deep satisfied sigh. But before your eyes are half closed you will see an old newspaper snarled in a bush. Do not retrieve said newspaper and flatten out the wrinkles, or you will fall victim to some late verses of a sourdough rimester. Unless you are one of the lucky ones who cannot read the Queen's English or the new world subornings of it.

Alas, Caprice, unsettled after her ambiguous visit to Kamloops and environs, made that mistake. She was sitting on the comfortable train chuffing westward alongside the green river, watching the green turn to white as it hurried by some round rocks midstream, and resisting the impulse to make a metaphor comparing that scene to her inner landscape. But these good instincts did not serve her as a reader.

For she spied on the empty seat across the aisle a discarded newspaper called the *Cariboo Sentinel*, and as any railroad idler would do, she picked it up and began to read it. It was a month old, but it was news from somewhere else, an amusement worth taking up for a few of the usual miles.

However, the last page of this smudgy rag was devoted to some verses in small characters bearing the fancified print that announced "Sawney's Letters, or Cariboo Rhymes." They were the outspillings of a transplanted Scot named James Anderson, predictably known as "The Bard of Barkerville."

Caprice was no fool, and she was no newcomer to the region. She knew all about this sort of thing. Certainly, if she had been sitting at a cafe in Montreal, she would now deposit the paper on a nearby chair seat, preferably in the rain. Even if she were in the lobby of the Nicola Hotel, she would not permit her eyes the injury of a single verse paragraph.

But she was sitting on a train with the window open to permit rapid air and some coal dust into the car, and her body was asking her why she was speeding away from the source of its pleasure. She read the poems.

> The rough but honest miner, who toils by night and day,
> Seeking for the yellow gold, hid among the clay —
> His head may grow grey, and his face fu' o' care,
> Hunting after gold, with its 'castles in the air.'

On the hillside two Indians were hunkered behind a big bush, watching the train go by. Even if she had been watching for them she probably would not have spied them. As it was, she had her head down and her eyes aimed at the paper. Whether she was reading now or seeing the naked white body of Roy Smith in the moonlight, we do not know. Of course not.

> There are some women on this creek,
> So modest, and so mild and meek!
> The deep red blush aye paints their cheek;
> They never swear but when they speak.
> Each one's a mistress, too you'll find,
> To make good folk think that she's joined
> In honest wedlock unto one.
> She's YOURS — or ANY OTHER MAN'S.

The bard was tremendously interested in honesty, and seemed throughout to find it only among the hardscrabble miners. Poets interested in honesty, and they spring up anywhere that men do not work in neckties, always seem to think that poetic skill is basically dishonest.

Caprice threw the paper out the window of the train. It flattened against the boards of the outside wall for a moment, then fluttered up and away, to disappear like coal smoke.

The hospital on the hillside smelled of laundered sheets and disinfectant, of gauze and unguents. Afternoon sun made the ward whiter than ever, so that a fly, fat and buzzing in furious anxiety, seemed a misdirected whizz of black, an interesting flaw, but too much alive to ignore. There were plenty of open windows, fresh air being the best medicine the valley could supply, but the fly travelled its erratic way from wall to wall, annoying everyone except the most bored patients.

Everyday Luigi wanted to suggest to Caprice that she pop it out of the air with her whip, but he had no spoken language now. He had nearly no life, and only a small portion of his lower jaw remaining to him. All the tongues he had learned in his travels over the skin of the earth would now have to stay in other people's mouths. He was in untold pain from the top of his head to the middle of his chest. In the middle of his chest he was happy that Caprice was back in town, but happy in the middle of such pain means something most people do not know about, and they are fortunate instead.

"He was really lucky," said Doctor Trump, "that he was holding that tub full of tablecloths. That slug would have done him for sure."

Lucky Luigi just lay there without assenting. Caprice smiled, not in reply to Doc's statement, but for the benefit of the little stout man from Trieste.

In the reception room flooded with sunlight from the high windows and the open door, Soo Woo was instructing the former ranch wife who had a good widow's job behind a desk.

"You give Roo whatevah he need, you risten to me? I pay foh it."

"Yes, Mr Woo."

"Mistah Soo."

"Thank you, Mr Woo. You are very kind."

The Chinaman had not been in to see his employee. He was a businessman, and hence busy. He was now halfway out the door.

"Mr Woo?"

Mr Soo turned, his eyebrows shaggy and elevated. The top of a face can speak as often, though not as many languages, as the bottom.

"Will you have somebody else picking up the hospital laundry tomorrow morning?" asked the widow behind the desk.

"I send the kid, you no nevah mine," said Soo Woo.

That celestial just about owns this town, thought the woman as she stared after his hurrying frame. But we all like him.

Doc Trump was looking at his patient. Doc was wearing his usual house-call and leisure-time outfit, a pinstripe suit of a certain age, with a vest and short tails and a string tie, the last poorly knotted. When one was standing close to him, and especially when he was talking, one lost the scent of disinfectant and unguent and picked up the odour of store-bought whisky.

"I've just come from delivering a baby for one of Gert's girls," he said, and one assumed that he was talking to Everyday Luigi in particular, though he was not looking at him except part by part. He was looking at his watch and holding Luigi's wrist. He was looking at a thermometer. He was looking at Luigi's bandage.

"Lilly Traff. Weasely looking baby. Big swatch of blond hair on him, hardly ever see that."

Click click click went a horse's shoes on the rocks sticking out of the ground outside the open window. Pain streamed from the patient's eyes.

"Kid is scrawny and got a face like a weasel. But he's got something about him, makes you think he's going to do all right for himself in a non-working way. When I saw that cap of hair, straight and thick and yellow, I thought this kid is going to do okay. When

I saw his yellow head gleaming in the lamplight, it made me think of an old Shuswap story I heard."

Caprice had not heard any Shuswap stories, but she did not press the point or lead the man on. She was there to visit the closest thing she had to a friend in these parts. She reached for Everyday Luigi's hand and he gave it to her eagerly. She squeezed it lightly, imagining his pain.

Everyday Luigi still thought he could talk. If you have been able to talk all your life, you think you still can.

"Ehhhhhhhh," he said. The pain was enormous.

"Dont try to talk now," said the doctor, as he so often did in this country of mining accidents and drunken brawls.

As they walked from the ward and into the sunshine, Caprice spoke at last, a quiet question from a strong heart.

"What happened to the bullet that was in the laundry," she asked.

The doctor limped along beside her, his breath expressing his tiredness and age. He shifted his black bag with the brown areas where it was worn.

"It's at my place," he said. "I'm going to give it to Constable Burr but I thought someone might want a peek at it first. Not that I approve, you understand. But what a person wants a person wants, you know what I mean?"

"Thank you, Doc."

Doc Trump's place smelled like a lot of things, none of them resembling the outdoors. Caprice looked around for a place to sit when he mentioned such a posture, but decided against it. It would mean moving something, and she could not see a satisfactory place to move anything.

"I'll just be a second," he said. "Make yourself at home."

It was as likely a place to make a home as any she had seen for over a year. Home was not an idea that had ever settled on her, anyway. It was the place toward which she had once carried a small bag of accidental coal. It had once been an apartment in a cobblestone *arrondissement* in Paris. For a moment, as she crossed the line at Nighthawk it had seemed to be a country that looked just like the country she was leaving, and the latter was as far from home as she had ever been. People were always offering her a home, it seemed, but she had never really seen one she could sit down in for long. She could not recollect Mr Kearns's ever offering the word, but he had certainly acted as if she could have one on his hillside.

Everyday Luigi had lived everywhere, and spoken with an accent wherever he had been, but there was a sense that his home was wherever his boot soles rested.

"Here it is," said Doc Trump.

"What," she said, halfway out of her thoughts.

It was the bullet, of course, scarcely marred by its passage through the tin side of the laundry tub.

"That's a .44–40, isnt it?" she said.

"It's a .44, anyway," he said. "In my unfortunate life I have seen more than enough of those."

"Thanks, Doc."

"Thanks?"

"For letting me see it before you gave it to the Provincials."

"Oh sure. I am doing you a favour."

Caprice took her gloves out of her hip pocket, a lovely movement, and started to pull them over her fingers. Doc Trump put the bullet into his vest pocket and picked up a book from a messy pile of books on one of the embroidered chairs.

"I hear that you are interested in poetry," he said.

It was a small book bound in greyish-white wrappers with a white label affixed to the front.

She hesitated. Was this another bard of the west? But she opened it to the title page, as polite book people will. It read: *Squire Hardman* / by / George Colman / John Camden Hotten, publishers / London, 1871 / reprinted from the original edition of 1829 / by Cadell and Murray.

"Go ahead," said the doctor. "You can keep it if you like, or bring it back to me whenever you want."

With an unready and really unbecoming smile, she closed the little book and took her leave. As soon as she had done so, the doctor took his first drink of the hour.

In the Canadian Cafe she let the book lie unopened while she drank her tea and ate some of the chicken and greens. She did not notice anyone else in the cafe, and when she noticed that she had not noticed, she was angry with herself. She had instinctively chosen a table near the wall and a chair from which she could easily see both doors. But she had not been looking. This time she was fortunate. Lucky Caprice.

She was thinking about Frank Spencer and Everyday Luigi.

What was Frank Spencer doing back in this country? There was an old picture of him from a Montana arrest lying in the files at every police station on the Interior Plateau. If he wanted to rob stores and stages, he could do it with at least as much safety on the other side of the line. He was after something other than gold. That was for sure. What else was for sure?

She poured her second cup of ordinary English tea, and opened the little book, as it happened, to page 5:

> The study of the whip was, to his mind,
> The "properest study" of all womankind,
> And woman's proper sphere — a boy's behind.

Her brows were knitted as she flipped to page 22:

> And here she spends her mornings, well content
> With tasks of teaching and of punishment,
> Adept at each, a true-born Pedagogue,
> Well pleas'd t' instruct, and still more pleas'd to flog.

She almost threw it on the floor, but she had never done that sort of thing to a book in her life. Instead, she left a note with it, instructing Soo Woo to give it back to Doctor Trump.

"Sapristi!" she said as she was writing the words, with a pencil that nearly went through the paper torn from her notebook.

☆ ☆ ☆

Two great golden eagles soared over the benches and canyon rims, now black against the sky, now or really then lost against the brown bunch grass of the hillside, rose suddenly on a thermal updraft, wings unmoving. They would lean left and cut into a semi-circle, down, then find a smooth glide thirty feet above the ground, knives across the grey pillars of the hoodoos. Their extraordinary eyes missed no movement on the arid floor, no groundhog dropping on all four. Their big feathers might someday hang in a Thompson pit house, but for now those two birds live in the sky, and no other creature need even think of ruling anything save his mere stride of ground.

The boy with the spectacles lay on his back in the grass, watching the golden eagles. It was Sunday afternoon, so his work was done at the store, and the ball team was playing in Revelstoke. He was allowed to take the train to games in Savona and sometimes even Kamloops, but if the game was in Revelstoke or Grande Prairie, he had to wait and meet the train in the morning, to find out what to write in his scribbler.

Someday he was going to take the train to Chicago. For now he focused his eyes as best he could on the eagles, and followed the traceries of his thoughts as if they were wings that could decide things anytime.

Another boy his age would have spent Sunday afternoon with a horse. Boys he knew dressed up like cowboys, with holsters and peacemakers, like Yankee cowboys, and stalked each other through the town and out into the trees. They wanted to be heroes. They longed for myth. They didnt want to be children. They wanted to be immortals.

Children do not belong in myths. They are used in fairy stories, but myths are the domain of immortals. Children are reminders of change, or potential, of what is called in some places "becoming." Children make sense in a town that is looking forward to greatness in the twentieth century. But cowboys and lone riders and dangerous misunderstood gunfighters do not.

So those other boys were out there among the trees, riding away from girls and mothers, riding away from the Provincial Police, eager for the end of changing.

"Seems like I have to change you every half an hour," his mother's friend said to his baby cousin this morning.

So Pecos Adams and the Charbonneau brothers were out with other hard cases, lightin' a shuck. But the boy with the spectacles could not ride a horse. The other boys gave him hell for his spectacles anyway, so he did not feel a severe necessity to learn the whoop-up trail. If there were no eagles up there now he would be on his hunkers at the riverbank, looking at something else.

Then he was looking at something else. It was an upside-down face with light freckles. He scrabbled to a sitting position, abashed, thousands of miles west of Chicago.

"Did I scare you?" asked the woman as she became less tall by sitting near him. But not too near.

"Why, I guess you did, Ma'am." He took off his spectacles.

"I am sorry," she said, putting her braids behind her wide shoulders. "But as you see now, I am not scary."

He was glad that she had not said "frightening," as adults often did when they were talking at children. He was attracted to the light edge of accent on her voice. He put his spectacles back on.

"I was just looking at the eagles. There's two golden eagles up there. Been flying around all afternoon."

"Three," she said.

He looked, but saw only two. She raised her arm and pointed at a tall red pine on the skyline of the near bench. He looked from the top of the tree downward, but saw nothing. Then the eagle on the third branch from the top spread its wings and turned its body slightly and he saw it.

"Three," he said.

"I have a slab of chocolate," she said. "Want half?"

"Sure," he said.

They munched the chocolate in silence, and after a minute nearly all their discomfort was gone. Bright hot sunlight has a way of burning away shyness, even the shyness of these kinds of people. So that now he found himself able to ask about it. She had come over and sat down, after all.

"I noticed that you always carry that whip on you," he said.

"I have noticed that you always have your scribbler, even when it is the summer holidays," she replied.

"Aw, that's nothing, I just . . . it's nothing."

"It is not nothing," she said. "I carried one around when I was your age. Still do."

She was smiling with her big mouth and her grey eyes, but not the way adults smile at children. So he stayed. Well, he was not sure exactly why he stayed. There was nothing else to do. But she was not asking him what he liked best in school, or what he was going to be when he grew up.

"That's all right," he said. "You're a girl."

"Sometimes I wish I still was."

But she did not add anything about how your years at school are the happiest years of your life. So she probably meant it.

Thus they started to talk, and they talked. Two people sitting on the grass at the edge of town, where yellow-and-black butterflies careered from bush to bush. Once in a while a farm buggy would leave town after a day of church and visiting, to raise dust the other side of the bridge. A young prospector rode across their field, leading a diamond-hitched pack horse behind his own mount. A coffee pot clanked against a frying pan where they had been poorly lashed inside a slicker. The rider looked at them briefly, then lowered his head and continued walking his hang-head animals toward the quiet Sunday town. If it had been Saturday afternoon, he would have presented a different picture.

The boy with the spectacles waited till the prospector was out of hearing and nearly out of sight, before turning the talk to the subject Caprice had heard so often in her meetings with youngsters down south.

"Where did you learn to handle a whip like that?"

"Spain."

"Gol! . . . Sorry, Ma'am."

Spain. If he asked her to tell him about Spain she might tell him a few stories, not the real ones, maybe the Spanish ones. She might tell him about how she got her black horse, or some of the story. But no, he wanted the other thing.

"Would you show me how to use it?"

"No."

The poor kid. A whip would go nicely with thick eyeglasses. But no. If he asked why not she would give him the talk she had given to kids in Arizona. As soon as people hear all about how good you are, there will be some hotshot who thinks he's better and you have nothing else to do but go up against him, and so on.

"Will you let me see how you do it? I never saw."

"Once."

So they stood up. She uncoiled the dark brown leather.

"Do you see anything around here you dont like?" she asked.

He squinted around.

"That hunk of fungus on the pine tree."

She took a long step forward and he saw for the first time how beautiful a woman's thigh is. But there was a hiss, and when he looked up the tree bark was bare.

He did not say anything for a while, but just stood there, listening to the little field sounds coming back. At last he spoke.

"Will ya just — ?"

"Nope."

Archie Minjus the photograph-maker was at war with himself. His purpose in life was to see the west on silver, to make enough pictures to persuade any ordinary eye of the great size of the world, not by producing grand scenes of the mighty skyline, but by picking up the details and holding them in the light, and in the shadow, too, where breathing things lie at midday. He wanted to make a million pictures and imagine a viewer with immense time on his hands, to whom he could say this is just the little I could manage to — To record? — If you like.

But his lot in life was to invent the west as it disappeared into the past. Every time he opened his lens upon a sun-silvered prospector's sluice with tumbleweeds piled against it, the subject disappeared, leaving its fossil imprint in a Montreal furniture store.

This way he had killed over five hundred Shuswap Indians. He had killed the McLean boys. He had taken the cover off his lens and sent the surviving Overlanders to their grave. Each was a shadow that spoke from dying lips. Working in the dark as he did, he worked alone, unless a darker Mephistopheles stood beside the fixer, keeping the score.

No, he was alone, he thought. As alone as he was when bent under his black cowl behind his tripod. He was as shy in the world as is a farm boy at a preacher's coffee party. He could not — never could at any time — be what society requires. He was abashed in company — would every moment be at a loss.

Though while he stood in the dark again, observing the black shapes appearing on the flat world in the tray, he heard his other voice telling him: my good friend, have no fear on this score — be but self-possessed — that is the only art of life.

Nonsense, he thought. He would sell that and a lot more to possess a lens and a film fast enough to stop the water over Deadman Falls. Every picture he had tried to make of that sudden white spill looked as if a ghost had trailed its shroud through the small opening between the rocks.

Sometimes he thought he should have stayed in Victoria and flattered the Colonial beldames. Some day he would like to show them all his study of the woman he was looking at right now.

Caprice was embarrassed to be overheard talking to her horse. Cowboys, she knew, did it all the time. A few minutes ago she had been apologized to by an elderly wrangler.

"Excuse me, Ma'am," he had said, "the way I cuss. Seems like I have lost perty near all of my nacheral decent words, from living too long with this mean-hearted mustang here."

His curly-haired animal flattened its ears in mock hatred, and the old man shook his fist at it.

But Caprice could see that the wrangler had been rubbing liniment into the horse's legs. She would bet that he made sure that it got oats, too, rather than leaving things to the hostler's boys while he himself went to fill his stomach.

Still, she was glad that she had been speaking to her black in Spanish when she noticed the photograph-maker standing inside the stable door.

His eyes had adjusted to the change from bright sunshine to dark livery stable quickly. He saw the shift in her grey eyes and then he watched her step away from the horse and stand straight. That is, taller than he. He saw all this as a series of pictures.

He held out an envelope without saying anything.

"What," she asked. But she took the envelope and pulled the photograph from it. He watched her face while she had her first look at the picture. It was his habit.

She had been photographed often enough, in Paris and in Montreal. Those pictures were what she took to be the image of Caprice.

But she looked a long time at this one without casting a glance up at Archie Minjus. It was the first time she had looked with someone else's eyes at this creation in the west. It looked like an invention. It did not look like a cowgirl. It looked like someone out of a story that was told long before men thought of the idea of making a record of their life on earth.

"It's for you," he said.

"Thank you, you — "

Where she began blushing you would not have been able to know, but the blush rose from the top of her shirt and filled her face and for a trice the freckles became part of the blush. Minjus watched this happening, without a photographer's eye.

"No, Ma'am. Thank *you*," he said.

"I am sorry if I was a little rude when we spoke before," she said. "The people in this town — "

It was the first time, since she was a girl, that she could remember being so lost for speech. Yet the middle-sized man with the yellow fingers did not look any more formidable than all the Europeans or desert coyotes she had run across.

But there must be something about him that disconcerted her. It was the best photograph anyone had ever made of her, but that could not, not surely, be enough to deprive her of speech, deprive her of pride. It was as if a ghost had stepped past without really being seen.

Like a ghost of ice. In this hot country.

He did not ask her whether she liked it. He knew it was good, as good as the world. He did smile a little, though.

"Can I — ?"

"It's yours," he said.

"There is someone I could give it to."

"Doesnt matter," he said. "Seeing it, that matters."

"Well. Thank you."

He held out another envelope. With a pleased awkwardness she took it, and holding both envelopes and the portrait in her gloved left hand, pulled the second photograph out to the adequate light.

In this picture there was an enormous bare rock with sunlight nearly washing it of all features. Standing in front of the rock were two men. They were carrying repeater rifles in the crooks of their arms. One of the men was Loop Groulx. The other was Frank Spencer.

No one dared look up at the southern half of the sky because it was one of those days when the sun is a broad white fury that fills the entire quadrant. Clumps of sagebrush in the middle distance seemed to be shimmering with transparent flame. Unseen animals, the ones that were not designed to huddle underground, were lying in whatever sparse shade they could find, their bellies rising and falling in the quickness of their breath. If you were somewhere in the valley you could see for miles and miles, bleached grass and rolling hills and dazzling white hoodoos on the cliffsides. If your head was baked because you were foolish enough to come out without a hat, you might hallucinate a big cool dark room in which you could look at the Thompson Oven Valley and hear an orchestra loud with horns and see big square red letters suspended in the air over the empty range.

On a day like this Soo Woo was glad that he had invested in ice cream. The nickels cascaded into his till as almost everyone in town came by. Riders covered with sweat, on horses streaked with white foam, stopped for a scoop of ice cream before heading toward an afternoon of beer. Children paced the street and wandered the sports field, heads down, hoping for a magic nickel.

Addie the afternoon bartender at the Nicola left his clients for a while on the honour system and hoofed it over to the Canadian for a paper cone full of ice cream. Like everyone else he started biting at it as fast as he could, because the moment he stepped into the sun the white stuff was dripping over his knuckles.

As he did he heard a conversation that was transpiring between awkward hand-licking and grateful sighs among some women perspiring fragrantly on the bench in front of the cafe. These were Gert the Whore and some of her attractive friends.

"I grant you that," one of them was saying, "but what kind of name is Capreese, anyway. Puts me in mind of Kapeesh, something that little Eye-talian was always saying. And you noticed how he was always following her around with his big gooey eyes. I figure they're both foreigners, anyway. Now look at him. If he ever does come out of that hospital, he aint going to ever say Kapeesh or Capreesh or anything again."

"I knew an Eye-talian in Victoria," said Gert. "He was called Luigi too, seems like they are all called Luigi or Jeevani. Anyway, this Luigi was just like all Eye-talians, thought he was God's gift to women, thought he ought to get it free. I remember just like it was yesterday, the time he asked my friend Myrtle if she would like to go to work for him. Said it was not right a girl should be in her line of work without a man to take care of her interests. That's when Myrtle showed him her cute little hand-size pistol with two barrels to it. Well, when the Dago saw that — "

"I had one of those little guns once," said a third woman. "A Yankee sailor gave it to me when he came up short — "

"Hee hee."

"I mean when it turned out he didnt have enough of those Yankee dollars. Well, let me tell you, I was pretty scarified when he come up with this thing in his hand — "

"Hee hee."

"Oh come on! I thought he was going to shoot me, and me bare naked and all. But he says will this square matters, and I said I never used a gun before. Well, to tell the truth we were both a little pie-eyed, so he says come on, I will show you how to use it right now, and he puts it in my hand with his arm around me and all, and the darn little thing goes off. It didnt make as much noise as a farting horse, excuse me, but you know how thin some of those walls are on Johnson Street in Victoria. Well, about one second after the thing went off, accidental, like I said, we heard a shout coming from the next room. Ow, shit, I been shot, excuse me, and a few seconds later — ”

“Do I ever know how thin those walls are on Johnson Street,” said Gert the Whore. “Puts me in mind of the time a friend and me went right through one.”

“What kind of friend?” asked Addie, throwing his wet paper cone onto the boardwalk.

Gert grinned at him with her lips closed. She did not show her teeth any more, not since she had turned thirty.

“A friend I had just met that night, if you want to know,” she said. “Well, anyway this friend was a Japanese fellow, pretty big for one of them fellows. Seems like he was some kind of wrestler back home, and he wanted to show me how Japanese wrestling worked. I said let me show you how Canadian you-know-what works, I told him. But he let on as how wrestlers in his country werent allowed to do any you-know-what, and he wanted to ease into it now that he wasnt a wrestler any more. So he gets me to take all my clothes off and he takes all his clothes off, except for this rag he has around his you-know-what, and let me tell you, he was a big fellow, legs as big around as most people are around, and a big hard belly. Now he is throwing rice or salt or something around the room, I cant quite remember, and now he's stamping his feet up and down in a squat, and then he rushes me — ”

While Gert had been talking, Constable Burr had come out of Soo Woo's with little spots of ice cream on his tunic.

“Puts me in mind of the time I had to arrest this big fat wrestler when I was a rookie,” he said.

“You're still a rookie,” said a female voice.

Constable Burr scowled while a young woman in a thin white dress applied a hankie to the ice-cream spots on his breast.

“Well, this chap was a Turk, apparently,” he continued. “He had been holding wrestling exhibitions all the way up the coast from San Francisco, and now he had his tent pitched on the fairgrounds in New Westminster. He had a licence and all, but I was assigned to keep a watch on the crowd when the longshoremen and millworkers started lining up to wrestle this guy. But as it turned out it wasnt the crowd that gave me the trouble. It all started when this long-haired Frenchman got his turn in the ring. The Turk threw his arms, you should have seen the tattooes on him, threw his arms around the Frenchman and commenced to give him a bear-hug. Well, the Frenchman gave the Turk a big kiss right on the mouth. That made the Turk really mad — "

"It was probly all an act," said Addie the afternoon bartender.

"Act or not, that Turk picked up the Frenchman and threw him down on the mat and started pulling his pants off — "

"I knew a Turk once," said one of Gert's lady-friends. "He was the nicest foreigner you ever wanted to meet."

"How about letting me finish my story," suggested Constable Burr.

"Always used to have little presents for the ladies and kiddies," she said. "Used to give me the sweetest Turkish delight."

"Hee hee."

"Hee hee. Funny thing about him, he couldnt talk, not *any* language. Used to make sure you were looking at him by standing right in front of you, and making these signs with his fingers."

"We see galoots doing that every day hereabouts," said Gert the Whore.

"No, I mean, he tried to say everything that way. Used to touch you on the arm or someplace and start whole *Sen*tences with all this finger business. Funny thing was, I got so that I could understand what he was saying. Well, anyway, it's a good thing I did, because it sure came in handy the time I got stuck under the dead moose. It was the craziest — "

"Biggest moose I ever saw," put in another female voice, "was up in Fort George. Me and some other actresses was putting on this show for the annual miners' day. Let me tell you, them miners got some funny ideas about a good time."

"Miners! Dont tell me about miners. I was almost married to a miner once. This was over in Three Forks."

"Three what?"

"Forks! Forks! Honestly, you have the sense of humour of a cow, Ruby. Well, this miner, his name was Halfbreed Dick. Never mind, I know what you are going to say. Anyhow Dick was as nice a man as you would want to see when he wasnt drinking. When we was alone I used to make him dress up like a wild-west Indian and then I would pretend I was a helpless schoolteacher from the East, just been kidnapped from a wagon train."

"Wagon train? When did you ever see a wagon train," asked Constable Burr.

"They got them in them books from the States. The Indians were always shooting flaming arrows at them. Anyhow, like I was saying before I got interrupted by the law, Halfbreed Dick was as nice as you could imagine, except when he got to drinking. Then he would get the notion in his head that he was a woman. Now Dick wasnt a little man. In fact he was over six feet tall and probly about two hundred and twenty-five pounds, had a bit of a gut on him. So when he would go swiping clothes off of clotheslines, I mean *wo*men's clothes, things would get a little hairy. Dick would get on these women's clothes on say a Saturday night, and go sashayin' down to the Miner's Rest, that was the noisiest and biggest saloon in Three Forks. Well, I didnt know whether to laugh or cry. One night he went crashing into the Miner's Rest, and there was these three Yankee women up on the stage, kicking up their legs so you could see all the way to China, and Dick — "

"Looky here," said Myrtle.

Everyone turned to look. It was Caprice in the bright sun. In her riding boots and French gloves and white shirt with the buttons on the man's side, she was approaching on the boardwalk. Her heels resounded and she did not bounce. The four women and two men gawked like small town idlers. Caprice smiled wordlessly at them all and paid her nickel. She smiled wordlessly again and walked away with her paper cone of ice cream. She would not spill a drop on her French gloves. Each of the female watchers had her own thoughts on the apparition. The two males were not thinking at all.

Gert consoled herself by picturing how bad that six-foot thing would look in a party dress.

Now Addie the afternoon bartender remembered his duty and hied his way to the Nicola. Constable Burr took a quick look at the front of his tunic and went his rounds.

The women did not resume their attempts at finishing a story. When Caprice showed up she put a stop to narration.

☆ ☆ ☆

With a lot of his bottom jaw shot off, and bandages swathing the rest, except for a little hole, Everyday Luigi was not eating very interesting food. Soo Woo went to the hospital four times a day with a broth made of something. He would not let the hospital people deter him or even suggest much in the way of care for their most interesting patient. Soo Woo had numerous contracts with the hospital that went considerably further than the laundry, and he possessed a power in the community that was difficult for its members to pin down. The only other person whose ministering he would trust, apparently, was the woman called Caprice.

She was there at Everyday Luigi's bedside now, ministering ice cream. As it melted she found a way somehow to tender it through that little hole to a valiantly swallowing Triestine. She did not spill a drop.

When she had finished that treat she offered a little warning and then showed the photograph to her patient. His eyes opened wide but not a sound came through the hole or the bones of his head.

"Yes," she said. "These are the two men who did it? Dont nod or shake your head. Just raise your hand for yes, and move it sideways for no."

He raised his hand quickly. There was pain in his eyes. Caprice placed her bare hand for a moment on his.

"The one who shot you was the taller one? The one with no moustache?"

He raised his hand.

"Frank Spencer."

Everyday Luigi wished that he could write all the languages he had learned to speak. That is what he would set his attention to when the pain was gone. When the horror of his face was there to replace it. If he decided to go on living. If he could write this language they used here, he would write down the question: who is Frank Spencer? He moved his eyebrows instead.

"Frank Spencer killed a man called Pete Foster over a bottle of whisky. There was a story some people told and at least one wicked newspaper man wrote that he killed him over an Indian woman who did not want to hear from either of them. But if there is one thing I know how to do it is to find the real story among the rubbish that people deliver to you as facts. The young man called Pete Foster was my brother Pierre. That is why I am here in this country."

Everyday Luigi moved his hand sideways. She took it as a random gesture rather than a sign.

"Am I talking too much? Is it too tiring for you?"

He moved his hand sideways, four times.

As a matter of fact it was tiring, but no one had heard this person speak so many words on one occasion. His enforced silence was responsible. He would not have spoken if he could.

"Pierre was a good cowboy. He could do anything with a horse and a rope that any other man could do, and he did it for twenty-five dollars and board a month, what these westerners call twenty-five dollars and found. The only thing he found he could not do was to speak English without his accent."

Luigi could not respond with a yes or a no, but he tried to offer something with his eyes and forehead.

"Yes, like you," she said. "Spencer talks with an accent from Tennessee, and he shoots people who do not."

Caprice stood up, and Luigi thought that she was leaving. But she was only walking a few necessary steps. She went to the window and opened it a few more inches. Then she lowered it again to where it had been. The injured punchers in two of the other beds followed her with amazed eyes. She knew they were there but did not seem to. She sat on the foot of the bed instead of the wooden chair now.

"So I have to kill him," she said.

The room was so still that a fly could be heard buzzing and banging its head at another window.

Then Everyday Luigi moved his hand sideways, once.

After she had left the two injured punchers spoke quietly to each other. They were both from the Lazy Eight ranch, an outfit that had a long record of broken bones and missing blood.

"She dont look like she could kill a sheep," said the first puncher.

"She didnt mention no sheep," said the second puncher.

"She dont look like she knows nothing about killing."

"You ever heard of the Amazons?"

"I dont know nothing about foreigners," said the first puncher, contemplating the dark blue foot that protruded from the bottom end of his plaster cast.

"The Amazons is them big women live somewhere in Europe. They only use men folks for getting foals on them, and then they kill them off."

"What happens if they get boy babies?"

"Same thing," said the second puncher. "Worse part of it is, if you're a man and one of them Amazons takes a fancy to looking at you, there's not a thing you can do about it. One look and you just got to be with her. Sort of like them young Indian girls but worse, because you end up with an arrow in you for sure instead of just maybe."

The first puncher waved his good hand at his partner.

"Ah, you're just bullywhackin' the way you was when you tried to tell me about the side-hill gouger. Besides, I didnt see no arrows on her, just that regular workin' whip she had on her hip."

"You're a poor sap if you dont ever learn nothing about the things they got in Europe," said the second puncher. "Some of them Amazons got snakes instead of hair on their heads. One look at them and a man turns into a hoodoo."

"Oh sure," said the first puncher. "I suppose you're going to tell me them braids she had hanging down her back was a couple of rattlers."

The second puncher evinced some semi-fictional exasperation. He turned over painfully in his bed and raised his voice to the quiet man with the bandages around his head.

"Hey, Dago," he said. "You ever seen any Amazons in your grub-lining around the world?"

Everyday Luigi moved his hand sideways, a little.

There was only one saloon bar left in the town of Exodus, and it had seen better days. In the late 1860s and early 1870s, Exodus had served the light-hearted assaying and serious drinking needs of all the gold-walk boys along Deadman Creek. Now it was largely made up of false-front stores with the paint long gone and fallen-down fences. Strange-looking dogs lay curled on the baked ruts in the main street. Rattlesnakes found their ancestors' holes a few boot-heel steps from any doorway. In this kind of gold country it took only a decade or two to make a ghost town, and Exodus was almost there.

The saloon did not have a name any more, because there was no competition. In fact there were no other businesses left in town. About half the former stores had people living in them, and about half of these were Chinese men who had been the last to dip pans in the creek, and about half of these had managed to bring women from the home country. There had never been any houses in Exodus. The placers had known all along that the most sensible shelter was the kind you can fold up and tie to the back of an animal.

So this afternoon, or rather that one, Frank Spencer and Loop Groulx were the only customers in the unnamed saloon. There were no idlers or grand-dads to pick a fight with, so they picked a fight with the owner and bartender.

"How's about frying us a couple beef steaks," said Frank Spencer to that worthy.

The owner and bartender was picking between his few remaining teeth with a splinter he had yanked off the edge of the shelf where a mirror had once been. He was one of those older men who seem to shrink rather than getting lines in their skin. He took the splinter out of his mouth and addressed the two strangers sitting at the only table with a bottle of New Westminster whisky between them.

"We dont do no cooking here no more," he said.

"Oh ho," said Loop Groulx in a whining voice, "we dont do no cooking here no more. Look, old-timer, we got lots of money, and we are as hungry as coyotes in January. Get us some grub."

The shrinking man behind the bar was not intimidated. He knew the Canadian frontier pretty well, and he was familiar with the uncouth. He was not familiar with the really dangerous. There had been sufficient numbers of rude men in his establishment, but there had never been any killers, as far as he knew.

"Sorry, gents. We aint even got a cook any more."

"Do it yourself," said Groulx.

"I aint even got any meat in the place."

Loop Groulx was stymied for a minute. He did not want the chance for nastiness to get away from him, but he needed an angle to operate from. He persisted along the narrowest of lines.

"Yeah? What the hell do you eat, then?"

"Well," said the owner and bartender, "I aint eaten since yesterday night, and then I ate a snake."

He put the splinter in his mouth. Groulx did not like this at all. He didnt know whether he was being got the better of. He often felt as if people were saying something he did not get, and he wondered whether they were enjoying something he could not follow.

"What do you mean by that?" he said, as if he might know.

"Leave the man be," said Spencer, without moving his eyes from their attention to the rectangular hole in the wall where a door had once been.

But Groulx was worked up now, and he was convinced that he was terrifically hungry.

"God damn it, Frank, the son of a bitch is asking for it."

Spencer did not like his name to be mentioned in such a situation. His eyes swept the room out of habit, and returned to the doorway.

"Drink your drink, and we will go."

As he said this he started to put on his gloves. The man behind the bar noticed that there was a big blue mark on the back of the left hand now being covered.

"To hell with that," said Groulx.

As he got up his chair got tangled in his spoon-handle spur. He kicked at it angrily, and the chair sailed across the room, striking a pillar and falling to the floor undamaged. This made Loop really angry. He rushed to the bar and tried to reach across it, but his hand fell short of the old-timer's shirt, which he had hoped to grab in his fist.

Frank Spencer stood up and walked to the door, his steps soundless on the puncheon floor.

"Let's go," he said.

Loop Groulx spun around and ran awkwardly to the door and out, almost falling from his riding heels. He ran to his horse, which skittered because of the unusual excitement. This made Loop even angrier. He punched the horse with both fists, cursing its parentage and demeanor, all the while grabbing for the rifle in the scabbard in front of the saddle. Finally he got the weapon loose, dropped it on the ground, retrieved it, and headed back for the nameless saloon.

"No," said Frank Spencer.

Groulx stopped in his tracks, but he lifted the carbine to waist level and aimed it at the black doorway of the bar.

"I said no, damn it."

Spencer was holding a hog leg in his hand, the long shiny barrel pointed in his companion's direction. Loop hadnt even known that the Yankee had a hand-gun.

"Let's go, I said."

Groulx looked as if the top of his head would come off and all his insides would go through it like a geyser. He wanted to shoot and shoot. He wanted the gun to get hot in his hands. He wanted to keep shooting till the scrabbly old unpainted building came creaking and crashing down. Then he wanted to keep shooting till there was not a piece bigger than the splinter in the old fart's mouth.

But there was a part of him that wanted to go on living. He put the carbine back in the scabbard and punched his horse again, once where it was white and once where it was brown. The horse's near eye showed a lot of white, but it stayed relatively still while the bushwhacker it was unfortunately saddled with got on. It knew it was going to get rowels in its sides, and it did.

But Frank Spencer was just walking his horse out of town, and in a few moments Loop Groulx had to pull his mount up and wait while the other rider caught up with him. It made him angry that whatever they were doing he was made to know that if left to himself he would not do it the right way. But this was a different kind of anger. It was confusing and bothersome because it was somehow connected with the question of who was going to get to fix that woman.

After they had been riding alongside Deadman Creek for half an hour, the bushwhacker who always seemed to know that he was doing things the right way broke the ban on speech.

"I think I already told you, I dont want you calling me by my name when there are other folks around."

"Aw, Frank, if you would of let me ventilate that old coot you wouldnt of had to worry about that."

This time the speechless riding lasted about fifteen minutes.

"It aint our job to go around letting a streak of light through strangers," said Spencer.

"Aw, Frank, you got to shoot that Dago," complained Groulx.

"Leastways there's one less fella talking more than he should."

Even the imperfect wits of Strange Loop Groulx understood that laconic observation to be significant. He closed his mouth, took his right foot out of the stirrup, and kicked his horse alongside the neck.

Everyday Luigi's head was full of pain and language. The pain was drifting across his brain like a torn garment in the wind, and the language was sometimes Triestine Italian, sometimes French, and sometimes English. Sometimes it was a sequence of loud words in a language he did not know. In front of him two men were talking about these days in the west.

They were Doc Trump and Archie Minjus, the photograph-maker. Minjus had been waiting till the bright morning sun could make its way to the white wall opposite Luigi's bed. He had his tripod set up and his big square camera aimed to capture and dispense with the wounded man in the bright new bandages. Doc Trump was grousing about the added difficulty of tending his patient with a circus performing in his work space.

"Think of it this way, Doc," said Minjus. "You are trying to preserve the west in your way and I am trying to preserve the west in mine. We are not in each other's way. We are brothers in a mission."

Everyday Luigi would have pronounced his agreement if he could have. He felt a kind of rapport with this man whose fate had him living here and there, speaking a language that other men did not know.

Doc Trump rather liked him too, but he had his own kind of image to maintain. He was known as taciturn and impatient. It came from three decades of trying to mend the results of stupidity.

Now he was all finished with the Italian for this morning, but he fiddled with his tools and satchel because he really did want to hang around and pass a few words with this picture man. There were not, after all, very many interesting human beings in this part of the valley. There were the rich ranchers from England and Ireland who were interesting to each other, who were making each other into judges and successful politicians. But there were not many men or women around who were interested in creating their own lives. Most of the old sourdoughs and young cowpunchers were interchangeable. They could have been identified at age ten and tagged or branded like range cattle. But this picture man seemed to give over some of his time to thinking, considering what the book men called meaning.

On the other hand, maybe all this was worth one cow pie.

"You know, you have to get my permission to aim that contraption at my patient," he said.

Minjus, recognizing a faint bond between himself and the other man, offered one of his rare smiles.

"The dry land," he said, "is also a garden."

"You know," said the physician, "that when you pick a plant it starts dying."

"Or it lives, preserved between the pages of a book that is seldom opened, for ever."

"I dont know anything about forever," said Doc Trump. "I just try to keep them rooted as long as I can."

Everyday Luigi liked those sentiments. There had been a few moments when he had wanted to pass on to whatever country was waiting for him, but now, as the pain was showing a few tatters, he was interested in this one again.

"I would like to have one picture of you tending your patient," said Minjus.

The photograph-maker had his own bedside manner. Doc would grump and mutter, but he would agree to have the emanation of light off his body make its mark on the immortalizer's emulsion.

"You know, I think that device of yours robs people of their souls. If I had a firmer grasp on mine I would tell you to pack up your gear and get out of my hospital."

"Thank you. Now there is not a great amount of light in here, but that old soul-stealer the sun has just about given us all we are going to get. So you will have to keep absolutely still while I am under this hood robbing you of your hope for heaven."

"All right, just hurry yourself up," groused the doctor. "I have some other calls to make this morning. Some people just cannot wait around for the sun."

Actually his next patient was a thoroughbred horse over at the Manor. In truth he was not in that much of a hurry to get there.

When Minjus had opened and closed his lens on the upside-down doctor and casualty, he read Doc Trump's professed impatience correctly and brought the topic of conversation around to the heart of the story whose edge they had both been trimming this morning.

"That Caprice woman, now there's somebody that does not evince a strong desire to preserve a certain quantity of the west," he said.

"I do not know exactly what she has got her heart set on," said the doctor, "but from what I have been able to gather she is intent on some expunging rather than some preserving."

Everyday Luigi knew more about the subject than both of them put together, or at least he thought he did. He could have told them a thing or two, but he could not write and he could not speak. He could think, though, and now he thought for the first time that the reason Caprice had told him what she told him might have been that he could not tell any other citizens. He would have smiled if he had had anything to smile with.

But of course they knew something. These two understood languages that everybody speaks but do not themselves understand. One of them could read messages on the skin or around the eyes, a kind of writing perpetrated by parts of the body most people never see or even think of. The other was able to decipher the script of the sun, a language that caused all others to be possible.

"In all your contemplation about souls, Doc, have you ever given any thought to that woman's soul? How long do you reckon she is going to be in possession of it?"

"In my opinion there is some question about whether she has a good hold on it right now," replied Trump.

"Speaking more practically, do you imagine there is a good chance she can keep her corporeal body alive much longer?"

Doc Trump closed his ancient bag, adept as he was at such punctuational gestures.

"Were you thinking of her corporeal survival when you showed her that picture of those two wrongdoers?"

"I cannot rightly say. I only felt as if I owed her something. I sort of sensed that someone should help her even if what he was helping her with was more her business than good sense. Do you know what I'm trying to say?"

Doc Trump grinned ruefully.

"Oh, I know what you mean," he said. "I come up against that predicament every time I have to patch up a cow-chaser that's more bent on working than living."

He might have said something similar about the relationship between whisky and his own familiar stomach.

"So. Do you think I should not have shown her the picture?"

"Oh, I think she knew those two were in cahoots. I think she knew Spencer was in the country. How did you get the picture, anyway?"

The photographer snapped his tripod's legs together. He was pretty good at gestures himself.

"One thing I found out a long time ago, Doc — the average outlaw shares one thing with the average lawman. They both think of themselves as acting out a story that's half drama and half history. They love getting their pictures taken. They are both already looking for the sympathy of the audience, even if the audience is going to be watching the story unfold, as they say, a long while after the players are all dead."

"Players, eh?"

Doc Trump never forgot his own role as the grouchy observer and commentator on the relentlessly passing scene.

He wanted a copy of the photograph, but he was not going to ask for it.

☆ ☆ ☆

Now she knew that it could get done either way. She could go riding again, on a rested black, and this time there was a better chance that she would find what she was looking for. But she would find it where it was, where it was waiting. Minjus had told her that all the time he was setting up the photograph, Loop Groulx was practising his mean look, but Spencer's eyes were always looking up and down the valley and scanning the ridge tops.

Or she could wait here in town. Whatever it was that had brought a hunted killer back into the country would finally bring him wherever she was. That was not very good either, because she did not live here — she was just an uneasy presence in the town whose main purpose was to supply the surrounding ranches and the stage lines. She was a long way from Quebec. He was a long way from Tennessee or California. But he had shot somebody before now, and he had been shot at.

Sometimes she thought of praying to God, as she had been taught to do at home and at the sisters' school. But *toujours le bon Dieu reste muet*, she murmured as she climbed the hotel stairs. In any case, even if He did listen without replying, he would not approve of what was in her heart.

When her key sounded in the lock she heard a thump inside the room. Without thinking she threw the door open, and it crashed against something, a man's figure. She rushed, swinging her arms and using her body. Her fist thudded against the side of the man's face, and the force of her rush slammed him to the floor. She was on top of him, and wanted very much to stay alive. She drove her gloved fists at his head, hitting the floor twice, but hitting his head more often.

"Jesus, Josef and Maria, stop!"

She was already committed to hitting him one more time. Her fist got him in the middle of the forehead, and at the same time she saw his face for the first time.

It was someone she had seen before, but she could not remember where.

"Please! Do not hit me any more."

She became aware that she was sitting on the chest of a middle-aged man in a vested suit. He had a thick moustache with waxed ends and a little blood in the middle.

"I cannot breathe," he said, in a convincing wheeze.

Caprice got off him and stood between him and the open window, so that she could see him better than he could see her. The man rose awkwardly, and threw himself onto the bed, his feet on the floor and his head hanging over his knees. He was breathing now in great gulps of air.

"Who are you?" she asked.

He waved his hand, signalling that he was trying to get enough air inside him to make words of.

"What were you doing in my room?" she asked.

Finally the man sat up straighter and turned his face toward her. It was somewhat worse for wear.

"Your nose is bleeding," she said.

He reached into his vest pocket and extracted a white handkerchief with lace edging. When he had taken the first exploratory swab at his upper lip he examined the cloth, then got up and continued his work at the bureau mirror.

"You are a violent woman," he said, his accent most noticeable in his attempt at the last two words.

"I can be," she said, "when it is forced on me. Who are you, and what were you doing here, I asked you."

"My name is Arpad Kesselring," came the answer. "Or A. Kesselring when it appears in print."

"You are the Hungarian newspaper reporter?"

"I am an Austro-Hungarian, and I am what is called in the civilized world, where women do not beat men, an international correspondent."

She indulged his huffiness because it did not sound at all daunting coming from the mouth of a man with lumps beginning to swell on his face and his suit covered in shiny dirt.

"I have lived in Europe, Mr Kiss."

"That is Kesselring."

"You changed it for professional reasons?"

"I do not see that that is any of your business. If my unfortunate father happened to have an overly common name for that region of the world, that was his business. If I happen to have one of the most respected names in journalism, that is mine."

Caprice smiled, indulgent still.

"And this, Mr Kesselringworm, is my room."

Such verbal behaviour was not usual with Caprice, but she was experiencing various levels of stress. She felt a little rueful about the physical beating she had administered to the silly journalist, and a little embarrassed about her low *badinage.* Still, when one is half-expecting a bullet in the back, it is a bit much to surprise a man in your room.

Kesselring straightened his suit as much as he could, and passed his hand over his oiled hair.

"It may be simply your room as far as you are concerned, Miss Caprice," he said then, "but for the literate people of the Empire it will be legend. It will be history. Most important, perhaps, it will be romance."

She thought of the Sunday morning she had spent in this room with Roy Smith, and allowed an unreadable smile to pass over her lips. But her eyes were wary.

"I hold no particular respect for your Empire, Sir. As far as I could see it is no more than a lot of pork-eaters strutting around in cut-away jackets and too many feathers. I lived, you see, in France."

Kesselring knew what she meant. The Empire may have been the most powerful and far-flung political entity on the continent, but in Paris it was grouped with a lot of other people to feel superior to.

A *déjà vu* slipped quickly into the room and back out the window. It went too quickly for a judgement as to whose it was.

"In any case," said the journalist, taking a pencil from his vest pocket and a notebook from his jacket, "it is my *arriviste* ambition to make you immortal."

"A lot of people have devised that plan, it seems," she said coolly.

"Yes, well perhaps I will be successful where others are not. May I engage you in an interview?"

He was annoyed that the instrument he flourished had to be a pencil.

"Was that your intention when you sneaked into my hotel room by a window on the second floor?"

It was his turn to smile. He performed a smile whose intention was to say that now the sparring is over and we have an understanding that the two of us are engaged in an activity that no ordinary citizen of these parts could hope to understand.

"Let us say that I was hopeful of conducting some research," he purred.

"I regret that it turned out so badly for you," she said.

Despite his gestures, she remained standing between him and the window. She looked out onto the street every few seconds, but appeared to remain emotionless.

"Not at all," he said. "Now if I may — will you explain, in your own words, of course, how you came to assuming a role, a destiny, if you like, chosen by God and social convention for the male of our race?"

Caprice was going to say one thing, but she didnt. Instead, she said another thing, looking with her grey eyes at the shiny hair of the portly man sitting on the edge of her rented bed.

"I suppose it happened after I saw what a poor job the ones chosen by God were doing," she said.

It was called the Industrial Residential School, but most people, including the pupils, called it the Indian school. There the fifty children on loan from the reserves were given a basic education. On top of that, the girls were instructed in housekeeping and sewing, while the boys were taught to farm. In these first years of operation that meant clearing the land. The white people who built the school felt that when the first generation returned home after their schooling the young men would put the Indian lands to the plow, and their wives would feed them balanced meals from their own gardens. It was a way of getting the west to the Indians before the east arrived.

Roy Smith knew a little about farming. His father had sold objects to farmers in Nova Scotia. But he had been encouraged by his father and brothers to go to Dalhousie University, and by newspaper editorials to head out west with the hope of developing a Canadian nation. Now he was a westerner, and charged with bringing a basic education to boys who seemed happy with the stove heat of winter and restless when the warm winds of late spring brought the scent of sage and pines in through the open windows. Then the happiest boy in class was the one he asked to wield the long pole that opened the top windows.

In the middle of the hot summer most of the children were gone to their creekside homes. Only a few remained for special instruction, the ones who had missed half the winter because of family death or forgetfulness. These he attended not in the haunted classrooms, but under a gnarled pine tree or at the table in his own shack. He watched with guarded despair as the shiny black head of hair bent over the arithmetic scribbler and the blunt pencil came to a stop hard against the paper.

And he too daydreamed about being away from there.

He thought about his last moments with Caprice. It does not seem right, he had told her, that I am bound here, that I have to stay in this one place while you are riding all over the country, whenever you feel like up and moving.

She had tucked her calico shirt into the top of her Levi's, and started to pull her gloves onto her long hands. The image brought her into the present, and when the boy looked up, expecting admonition or chiding, he saw that his teacher's eyes were not there for now.

"How long do you think you can keep up this continual moving around?" he asked.

His voice was part way to miserable, on its way to petulant.

"Until I stop," she said.

She said these things tersely now. They had elaborated the argument often enough in the past year and more. Now she let her few words remind him of all those that had passed.

"Or you are stopped," he said.

"I am not sure that those two possibilities are much different."

"Caprice, you are a poet, not a gunman. Not a gunwoman. That even sounds silly. You dont even have a gun."

That had been true until the previous day.

"I have a job," she said.

"That is not a job. Damn it, this is not Kansas, but it can be a violent land. You were not made for this sort of thing. You went to a sisters' school overlooking the St Lawrence River. You drank coffee in tiny cups in Paris."

"And in a tin cup ten miles outside of Tombstone."

"All right. But there are men here in this semi-civilized province whose job it is to carry guns and pursue thieves and murderers. I know, sometimes it takes them a long time. But it is their job. It is not yours. I can offer you a job, and — "

"Say it, Roy Smith. It will not stop me, but I would like to hear you say this anyway."

He was bashful, but he was afraid for her. He could speak, though he thought he sounded foolish.

"I can offer you love."

"I love you, Roy Smith. I have been in love only once before. You are the first time I have said it in English."

"Then what am I not offering?" he asked. "Why are you going on with this insanity?"

"I have got to do what I... a woman has... a sister — "

She did not like to say very much, and when she tried to speak and could not do it well, she liked it even less. She pointed to the black sky, reminding him that he had promised to take her into town before it got light.

Now he was back in the present, or rather what for him was the present. The Indian boy was standing up, holding the pencil out for his teacher to see.

"What is it?" asked Roy Smith.

"This," said the boy, holding the pencil incorrectly in his fist. "This thing. It does not understand my words."

Sometime after daylight had been pressing on the dry ground for a while, two of the Indian boys who were hacking at the couch grass with long hoes began to talk about their teacher.

"I once believed that he knew everything," said the first boy.

"He does. He knows everything we Indians do not know. He knows all there is to know about, what does he call it, about the world. He knows everything about the world," said the second boy.

The first boy slammed the surface of the earth with a long hoe that had traced a semi-circle in its flight.

"He does not know how things are between a man and a woman," he said, after grunting with the impact.

"Well, that is not the world," said the second boy. "That is a woman."

The second boy was not clouting the ground now. He was trying to lean on a hoe that was too long for him. The first boy slammed the corner of his hoe blade under the edge of a clump of brown grass. He was getting the hang of agriculture.

"For a time I could not believe that was a woman," he said. "She is so big. She is bigger than any woman I have ever seen before now."

"She is tall."

"She is taller than nearly any man I have ever seen."

"Many of the white men are that tall," said the second boy.

"She is taller than any horse I have ever seen."

"But prettier."

"No. No woman is as pretty as a horse."

The second boy banged his hoe against the first boy's hoe.

"Roy Smith is not the only person who does not know how things are between men and women," he said.

Then a competition of hoes ensued. Swinging side-arm, the boys clanged blade against blade. Their black hair swept about their faces as they swung, and their teeth shone white as they opened their lips wide in the first smiles of the week.

Roy Smith was watching them from the feed barn, where he had gone to make his daily check on tidiness. Those boys, he thought. We will never make farmers of them. We will never keep them alive that way.

He remembered that Horace Greeley said the Indians would have to disappear while the white people filled up the west. And James Fenimore Cooper said earlier that the Red Man's duty was to die and leave the new lands to the energy of a superior race.

But Roy Smith had to do what a teacher had to do. Maybe here on this side of the medicine line we can teach them instead of killing them.

Teach them what?

And how could Roy Smith teach anyone anything? His mind could not tell anything to his yearning. And his yearning did not know how to speak to any other part of him.

When he stepped out of the black door of the feed barn the boys spied him and returned to their punishment of the dry earth. Some schoolmasters would have been pleased by that, but Roy Smith was not.

Constable Burr was uncomfortable. No one had run up to him and said Constable Burr, you've got to do something, but he could sense that sentiment in people's glances, in the tone of a voice, even in the little shift in a man's pace as he approached.

He did not like being humbugged by two blackbirds that seemed to be able to talk to every stranger who passed through. He did not like his British Columbia Provincial Police uniform, especially the little cap with the short bill. He did not like the fact that the North West Mounted Police had a famous unofficial motto they did not deserve, in his opinion.

But mainly he did not like the complication of this case. The complication was a six-foot woman with a fancy European bull whip and a manner that pretended to be aloof but which had citizens falling all over themselves to find an excuse to talk with her.

He was uncomfortable because he did not know exactly what she had to do with the case. He could connect her with Loop Groulx, and he could connect Groulx with Frank Spencer, but he could not see what Spencer had to do with the woman. Yet he felt in his police bones that there was a connection between that polecat and the woman from back east.

If he could figure out why Spencer was crazy enough to come back to this country where the Provincials and the Mounties were both after him, he might have a line on what the woman was up to.

Up to above five feet eleven inches, said a nasty little voice in the back of his head. Constable Burr was about five feet eight and a half, just over the minimum for the Provincials, and, he was sure, the main reason he was spending all these years on the great Interior Plateau instead of down at the coast.

No one had come right up to him and said what are you going to do about this threat to our community, but the question had been asked, and not in a friendly way. There was a nasty editorial on page three of yesterday's *Journal*, whose main thrust was the accusation that the Provincials were not capable of handling a Yankee gun-slinger and his loutish companion, at least not the Provincials in this part of the world. It might be a good thing for the community if the Mounties would take over the whole situation, it suggested, or maybe we should hire some Pinkerton men from across the line. The editorial was unsigned, but Constable Burr knew that it was written by an unsociable old skunk from England who called himself editor and publisher. The name he went by was Cyril Trump. He was a cousin to the doctor, but he did not have the redeeming quality that man had. In fact he hardly ever let an issue go by without condemning the effect of hard liquor on the "last frontier." There was not a person in town or on any of the surrounding ranches that would say good-morning to the editor of the *Journal*.

Now Constable Burr was not only uncomfortable, but tired and dusty and in one hell of a burn. He had just spent the day since before sun-up riding up and down Scotty Creek looking for a hiding hole. Someone had mentioned seeing two suspicious looking riders in the area, and after riding with two junior constables for sixteen hours, all he had found was a dead camp-fire with some old cans and a cracker box. He knew his quarry very little, but he knew them well enough to know that they would not leave that kind of sign. That kind of sign was left by newcomers from back east.

He was hungry, too, but before he could think of the peculiar steaks at Soo Woo's, he had to hear something said right to his face. So he left his drooping horse at the hostler's and tramped over to the *Journal* office in the dying light. He knew that Trump would be there. He was hardly ever anywhere else.

He did not know that the foreigner would be there too. The

foreigner had been pestering him for days to grant an "interview." Burr knew that he should talk with the man who had managed to talk with the murderers and with the woman, but he had just told him to come back when he was not so busy.

"Ah, the protector of our civilization!" said Trump in his annoying British accent.

Burr saw that the foreigner had his pencil out but he did not care tonight.

"Trump. Do you know that Washington became a state of the Yankee union this year?"

"I do read the papers," said the editor superciliously.

"That means hundreds of bad actors came north, looking for greener pastures. Same with Montana and the Dakotas. Have you heard of the Johnson County range war in Wyoming? Do you think all those rustlers and gun-skunks and jailbirds are going to turn into Methodist preachers once they get on our side of the line? God damn it, man, do you think this Spencer is the only malefactor from down there we have to worry about?"

The foreigner was making notes. Trump was inspecting a sheet of type, his pasty English face betraying no great interest in the questions directed loudly in his direction. Without taking his eyes off the paper held high in his outstretched hands he gave his wry answer.

"He is the only one I am aware of who has shot a citizen in this town."

"All right. All right. Do you have any information that would make my job easier? Do you know something that would make the apprehension of Spencer and Groulx as simple as you have been suggesting it is?"

"I only know what I read in the paper, Mr Burr. But perhaps my colleague from Budapest could enlighten you further."

Constable Burr slammed the door on the way out. Trump would have closed it behind him anyway. This time of night in the first half of August, most doors along the street were open to let the baked air of the afternoon escape. But Trump was opposed to dust more than to heat.

"Now perhaps we can return to our business," said Herr Kesselring.

Trump was still making himself busy about the shop. He was looking at things he did not really have to look at. If he had not been a newspaper man he might have made a successful poker player.

"I dont recall that we had any business, Mister," he said.

"It is very simple," said the European journalist. "You make use not only of my expertise, I think you say expertise?"

"Some do. I dont."

"You make use of my expertise, and also the knowledge that I alone seem to have about these ruffians, what do you call them, desperadoes?"

"I call them assholes, but not in print," said Trump, checking to see whether his pencils were sharpened. They, of course, were.

An ingratiating smile crossed the bottom half of the foreigner's face.

"Well," he said, "You receive my expertise and my knowledge, and a by-line of some considerable international repute. Also, you will undoubtedly acquire the admiration of your fellow editors, and a share of the income that will result when newspapers and magazines in the larger centres make petition for the right to reprint the stories."

"Share?"

"It is the way things are done in Europe. I am sure that things are done the same way in the wild west," said Kesselring.

Cyril Trump did not have anything else to check over. The morning's paper was already thumping through the press, and would be on the stage north and south just after sun-up. He sat down heavily in his chair behind his desk and took a package of tailor-made cigarettes out from under a pile of paper. He was reflecting upon how wise he had been to leave the old country.

"Mister," he said, "what you are talking about is money. But you resemble a lot of people who come here from the east or farther east. You want big money, quick. Now, I am willing to give you a little money even quicker."

Like a poker player, he was looking at his opponent, but not so that you would notice it.

"I am listening," said the other player, but without enthusiasm.

He looked around for a clean place to sit, but there was no such thing. His suit looked better than it did after his contretemps with Caprice, but it did not look as good as he would want it to.

"I will pay you for your information, same as I would pay any rouster that came in here with news I can use," said Trump, his face in a cloud of blue smoke. "I dont give a cow flap what the out-of-town papers are interested in. I want to tell the people in the western Thompson Valley and parts of the Fraser and the ranches from the Nicola to the Bonaparte what they think about things that are going on here. They pay me three cents to find out, and they think they are getting a good deal."

His frontier idiom sounded oddly persuasive in a British accent.

Kesselring tapped his hat against his knee and put it on his oiled head. He opened the street door and spoke from the boardwalk.

"I will give you something gratis," he said. "Mr Spencer and Monsieur Groulx are residing in a peculiar hovel above the railway tracks somewhere between here and the lake. If you had the eyes of an extra-ordinary journalist, you would be able to see it from a buggy that had come to rest beside a rectangle."

Trump did not want to ask. He was a professional asker, but in this circumstance he would have liked to keep his aloof silence.

"A rectangle?"

"Yes. You know, when someone lifts a heavy railway tie from the ground it has been resting on for three years, it leaves a peculiar wet yellow mark inhabited by the low forms of life we seldom think of but which are never far from us."

"I agree," said Trump.

"Good-night, editor," said Kesselring, the smile now in his words but nowhere to be seen on his face.

He did not close the door. When Trump got up to close it, he saw the woman's face. Then he did not see it.

In the wild west, where men were men and life was hard, women were supposed to be one of two things — commodities or prizes. Bad women, such as those found in the dance halls and brothels, were the commodities, and went along with whisky and gambling, those things a tough man who had been ruining his health in the wild desired to spend his few dollars on when he finally got to town for a while. The beautiful or not necessarily all that beautiful daughters of ranch owners were the principal prizes, because they were relatively virtuous, somewhat educated, and likely to inherit land or stocks.

We are not here counting the wives of homesteaders, of course. They were neither commodities nor prizes. They were, like anything that was likely to produce, used as devices to prepare the dream of a future. Hard men riding into town were not much interested in the future, at least nothing beyond tonight and maybe tomorrow night.

One of these men was the reason for Caprice's worst experience that summer. She never learned his name, and all these years later, when we think of the old Thompson Valley days, we could never dream of finding it out. It is possible that on that occasion he did not remember it very well himself.

Actually, it was an unusual occasion. In the last decades of the nineteenth century in the west, women who were not there for the professional entertainment of men were pretty certain to be treated politely by them. Even drunks who bashed each other in saloons and on the street, burly men who employed language that would strip the varnish off a railroad car, did their best to be gallant to the women they outnumbered so thoroughly. What they said about them in their own male company might have been a different story.

Caprice, lightly informed with the secrets told her by the journalist and the photograph-maker, was planning to ride eastward before dawn the morning after next. She had spent the last half-hour at the stable, checking out her gear, lifting the thirty-pound saddle down for a slow inspection, wrapping black tape around all the metal parts of the bridle that would reflect sunlight. She talked to Cabayo in Spanish for a while, and saw to it that he was ready to walk and run if need be.

Now she was on her way back to the hotel.

She heard the late-night clamour pouring out with the odour of beer through the open doors of the Bonaparte saloon. She saw a light burning in the window of the *Journal* office. Her heels rapped the boards as she went by the barber shop without glancing at the old dusty joke about an Indian scalp in the window. She was crossing the side-lane just before the Nicola. A sudden weight with the stink of belly-whisky hit her all at once from behind, and she found herself lying face down in the rocky dust, a heavy thing lying on her.

"This is a Texas Bowie knife I got on your neck. You make one sound and I'll have your blood all over the ground."

The voice was in her ear. She could feel harsh whiskers against the skin of her neck, but not the knife. The stink of whisky made her want to shut off her breathing. She did not make a sound.

"Okay, you fucking bitch, you're going to get what you've been looking for."

They were in the complete shadow made by the solid wall of the hotel. She was not carrying her whip or the other thing, not that they would have helped her in the present situation. The man's enormous weight crushed her chest against the ground. She could hear his loud breathing. He was now sitting on her back. His hand grabbed the collar of her calico shirt and ripped it from her back.

"You going to turn over, or you want it like this?"

Those were the last words she heard him say.

There was a thud, and then his body fell over her again. She struggled to get out from under him, and then she heard the unmistakeable sound of a smashing bottle.

The man was getting to his feet now, making an animal sound in his throat. But even in the gloom he recognized the familiar remainder of a broken whisky bottle held four inches from his eyes.

"You are fixing to leave this place right now, arent you?" said a female voice with no ambiguity.

The man moved only his eyes, looking around the ground near the long body of the silent Caprice.

"You are not even going to stay long enough to grab your knife, are you?" said the female voice.

There was a fairly lengthy moment when no one moved at all. Then, with one more animal noise, the man moved on. He turned to look once, but that was all. The two women were quiet until they could no longer hear his boots.

The woman holding the top half of a broken bottle was Gert the Whore. She was wearing a low-cut dress of some dark colour and what people called French shoes. Her hair had earlier in the night been piled up in a fantastic arrangement, but now there were long curls spilling down here and there. A crocheted shawl hung from her shoulders.

Gert threw the remainder of the bottle down the lane, and picked up the assailant's knife.

Caprice had managed to turn so that she was half-sitting on the warm dark ground. Gert could see a scrape of blood on her forehead and tears in her staring eyes when she bent down to help her up. The front of the shirt had fallen away to reveal the breasts that Gert had had fifteen years ago. She put her shawl around Caprice's shoulders.

"Dont tell anyone," said Caprice.

She was panting with the shock that follows release. Her eyes were not in control of their seeing. She looked utterly vulnerable, and Gert did not know whether to like that or not. But she knew that she would not exploit it.

"We'd best get you to my house," she said. "We dont want to take the chance of trying to get you to your room without nobody seeing us."

"Thank you," said Caprice, and accepted the arm around her waist. She could walk, but right now she did not want to walk alone.

"In the morning I will fetch you some clothes from your room," said Gert when she had got the other woman onto a chair in the tiny parlour of her little house by the river.

Then she brought a cloth and a soapy basin and washed her from her forehead to her waist. There were going to be bruises, and tomorrow there was going to be stiffness. But for the moment all Caprice could feel was her passivity.

All she could feel was her childhood.

"It couldnt of been anyone from around here," said Gert. "I dont think I ever seen that one before."

She was rummaging around, looking for a night-dress, but stopped when she realized that she would never find anything big enough.

"Thank you for what you did," said Caprice. They were the first words she had been able to speak since her first plea.

"I just happened to be there. And I just happened to have a bottle on me. Well, I often do," said Gert.

"I did not know I had a friend in this town," said Caprice, leaning back against the chair at last.

"You had one," said Gert.

"Thank God. I mean thank you."

"I was talking about my kid. You was talking with him in the park. He talks about you all the time, or at least when he isnt talking about baseball or Africa."

Now Caprice's eyes were back in the present where they belonged.

"The boy with glasses?"

"My kid."

Caprice glanced around at what she could see of the little house.

"Oh, he dont live with me," said Gert. "It's bad enough for him around this town. He doesnt have a pile of friends, things being the way they are. I pay for his board with some nice Methodist people."

"He is a smart boy," said Caprice.

"That's the wonder of it," said Gert. "Because he sure has got a dumb mother."

Then like a mother she saw the head of red hair beginning to droop, and walked her charge easily to her fluffy bed.

She threw the Bowie knife into a box of abandoned weapons that lay in a corner of the room.

☆ ☆ ☆

"You have not asked me a question in two days," said the first Indian.

"Well, I have not thought of any questions," said the second Indian, evasively.

"You think you know everything?"

"Well, no."

"Because if you know everything, I am out of a job. It is my traditional task to instruct a promising youth in the ways of our people and the world."

"Oh, and you have done a wonderful job. In my opinion."

"You have opinions now, do you? Then my job is truly finished. I wish I had been born to Johnny Philip. Then I would have inherited the Eagle Dance. Ernie Philip and I were born the same day, but he got all the luck. He inherited the Eagle Dance and I got the position of mentor."

The first Indian was really worried not so much about the misfortune of his birth as about the years remaining to him. He did not think that he could face another tyro, start the whole process again.

"I am sure that there is still an abun-dance of things you can teach me," said the second Indian.

"I thought you were opposed to non-Indian puns," said the old man.

"You are the teacher," said the second Indian.

It was not that he thought he knew everything. It was rather that he could feel the sadness in his older friend's heart. He did think of him as a friend now, not just a teacher and taskmaster. He had felt recently that his questions were not attracting the happiness of explanation, but arousing a world-weariness in the white-haired man. He always thought of the white-haired man's loneliness, and he wondered whether he were perhaps a little in love with it. That was an ambiguous feeling.

"If you have no more questions to ask of me, you had better go home and report that happy news to your father and uncle," said the first Indian.

"I have a question for you," said the second Indian.

The old man stared at the river canyon before them, pretending, perhaps, that he could see whatever flotsam was surfacing there.

"Is it a real question, or is it what people on the railroad call make-work?"

"What is a real question?"

"Is that your question?"

"No, not the question I had in mind."

"Because if it is your question, it is a real question, though not the sort of thing I am charged with explaining to you. The customs of our people do not include it in my duties, and the ways of the world do not consider it important, at least not the world in these parts."

Here we go, thought the second Indian, this is exactly the reason why I have not been asking many questions lately.

"No," he said, "that was not my question."

"Not?"

"It is an interesting question, do not misunderstand me, but it is not the question I had in mind."

"Mind?"

"Oh, forget it."

He threw a stone over the lip of the canyon and watched it enter the white water. The first Indian watched it go over the lip of the canyon.

"I am sorry. I thought that I was using a device we old ones call the Neskainlith Method. But in actuality I was just giving way to my grouchiness."

"Actuality?"

"Good shot. I deserved that, and you are learning fast," said the first Indian. "All right, young fellow, what was your original question?"

"I have no more questions about origin," said the second Indian. "I think that they will be answered when we die and go to Mongoleum. I just have a question of a political nature, you might say."

"Which is — ?"

"Why dont the white men like us?"

The first Indian paused judiciously. He looked thoughtfully up at the high sky where some faint strands of white cloud were stretching to the breaking point. Such an aspect made him look wise, he knew, and he was not above a little wise-looking. As he lowered his face he took a quick peek and saw that the younger fellow was looking at the white river.

"Some of the white men like us," he said.

The second Indian swatted at a mosquito that was flitting about his leg. He knew that the action was not picturesque, but they were the only two people he had seen this morning, so he was rather relaxed in his deportment.

"Let me rephrase the question," he said. "Why is it that though some individual white men seem to tolerate us and even on occasion evince a genuine fondness for a few of us, in the main they might fairly be said to dislike us as a people?"

If I were twenty years younger I might throw him into the canyon, as a pedagogical lesson, of course, thought the first Indian.

"I will tell you," he said. "The white man in what he calls the west and we call the middle prizes action above all else. He thinks of himself as a man of action, and does not trust other men who are not. This includes most people from what he calls the east, and it includes people who read books, or engage in abstract conversation, or do not get dirty when they work."

"I do not like getting dirty when I work," said the second Indian.

"I have never had an opportunity to observe whether that is true," said the first Indian. "But you have unwittingly anticipated my next remark. The western man of action is made nervous and even angry by contemplative thought or reasoned discourse. Are these words too difficult for you?"

"Of course not, for you have been my mentor this past year."

Despite the touch of sarcasm, the first Indian was satisfied to hear that mild encomium.

"The western man of action believes that his actions are saving his country, as he calls it, from the decay of its early promise that set in when life became easy enough back east for people to make their living without getting dirty. He therefore resents people in the west who survive on the practice of quiet. He thinks that his ideal might be undermined by lawyers, bankers, teachers, writers, and the like."

"Are bankers like writers?"

"Only in the sense that they do not get dirty — I am speaking literally — when they work."

"All right. But I am wondering how you are going to get the conversation around to Indians," remarked the second Indian.

"I was, as you very well know, getting to that."

"I mean, we do get dirty when we work. I have seen Indian horse wranglers that are as dirty and sweaty as any English cowboy."

"Here I am not considering dirt, but rather thought."

"Indians think more than white men?"

The first Indian knew that in each lesson he conducted one of these moments would arrive. Sometimes he thought that they were the only reason he went on with the job. He cast his practised glance of high signification where it felt the best, right on the soul of his student.

"Some of us can manage it," he said.

The second Indian, in these situations, tried to tell himself that he offered the opportunity on purpose, to give something to the old fellow. But he knew it was not totally true.

"I do not think that Indians think more than white people do," he said. "It does not seem likely to me."

"Ah, that is not the point," said his elder. "The point is that the white man does not know how to remain still for longer than it takes to think of a curse word. But the Indian is an expert at remaining still. We can stand without moving for hours. We can sit on the ground all day without seeming to blink. It is a skill we have instituted in our way of life."

"Sometimes I wish we had not," said the second Indian. "I am not fond of sitting still. But I will learn. After the season of the mosquito, I mean."

Then he noticed that the first Indian had moved nothing but the apparatus required for speech in the past little while.

"When the western man of action sees an Indian sitting perfectly still for a while, he assumes that he is engaged in deep contemplative thought," said the first Indian. "This is what makes him dislike the Indian."

"You mean he might like us more if we were western men of action instead of sitting still from time to time?"

"Especially if he could get us to work for him like crazy for fifty cents a day," said the first Indian.

In her childhood the thing she had wanted above all else was to be good. Her mother had mentioned it every day. Her dream of constructing a world and her life in it always started and ended with the absolute idea of being good. She had had fantasies whose narrative featured a choice between happiness and being good, and she had always relished and embraced the nobility of being good. It was not that she had been aligning herself with the Church idea of the saint, not at all. It was a personal secret. Often, when she was on her way home from the tracks with her bucket, she would leave a piece of coal in front of the door of the old man who had no children.

Now she was wondering whether she was good. She had her bags packed and her saddle-roll lying with them on the bed of her room at the Nicola. The bill was paid. The food-stuffs were packed neatly in the bags that would fit Cabayo's sides like holsters on the thighs of a Johnson County gun-fighter. Now she was sitting on the windowsill, holding the pistol she had bought in Kamloops. She held the stock in her right hand and the long barrel across the palm of her left. The oil felt new.

"Do you think you can handle a Luger?" the clerk in Kamloops had asked.

"Yes, I think so," she had replied.

"Are you sure you would not like to try a U.S. revolver?" he had asked.

"I am sure about that, sir," she had said.

But she had not fired the Luger even once. She had purchased a whole carton of shells, knowing that one would not come across such ammunition just anywhere. She had kept the pistol among her effects in the room, and she had not thought of buying a holster. Now this was the first time she had laid her hands on the weapon since bringing it back from Kamloops.

Until now she had not stopped to consider whether she was good. She had heard a few people tell her that she should not be doing what she was doing. Roy Smith always mentioned the police and the law and their duty. Mr Kearns had talked to her in words that were just shy of philosophy. Before she had the gun she knew that there were religious and legal arguments against vengeance. She knew that just walking or riding past good citizens and even bad ones gave rise to their disapproval, whispered or silent.

But now that she had the pistol she had to imagine a way she could consider herself and what she was intending to be good. The most difficult battle for a person with a hand-gun is to stay on the right side of the law.

The news had come that Belle Starr was dead in the Indian Territory. In the eastern papers she was a legend, but in the Indian Territory she was dead, and many people there were relieved to know that.

Caprice tried to put her half-dreaming mind into the once-familiar path of her childhood fantasy. But the Luger was heavy in her hands.

Now the Indian Territory was Oklahoma. The land rush at noon on April 22 had closed the gap in the middle of that country, and it was filled now with people who had decided to get married and raise families and dig in the ground and be good.

Caprice tried to erase the word vengeance. It had a rhythm that reminded her of the Holy Bible. She said the word retribution aloud in her hotel room. It sounded better, but it did not erase the other word.

The trouble was thinking. The remedy was action. She was not sure that she believed it, but she got to her feet and put the Luger into its place in the saddle-bag. A minute later she was on the board-walk, carrying the bags and saddle-roll easily towards the hostler's.

A cowboy in striped trousers watched the tall red-headed woman ride at a running walk down the main street on her black horse. He saw and approved of the momentary purple ripples that appeared on the animal's black hide as its muscles moved in the bright morning sunlight.

"What the hell is that?" he said, making it sound like an oath.

"That, my friend, is Bonnie Dundee," replied the editor of the *Journal*, "and her fabulous steed."

"Dundee, eh? She the daughter of the Dundees over Chilco way?"

"Dont believe so," said Cyril Trump in his British accent. "Reckon she's more like out of this world."

"You mean she's a foreigner?"

"Well, you have seen her horse. Most cowboy's horses are sorry-looking beasts, bang-tails, hammer-heads, scruffy animals with questionable parentage. Then there is that black she is riding. I think one might make a similar comparison between the lady and most of the folks you will turn up when you lift a rock in this country."

"How come you newspaper fellows have to talk a different language than regular folks?" asked the cowboy.

The manager of the Bank of British Columbia and his fortunate wife were about to take their day's leave of one another, he in his well-pressed town suit into the temple-like edifice with its venetian blinds, she on another forlorn search through the emporia of a town that seemed larger before one took close inventory. There were manifold paths of loneliness in the west, and a banker's wife simply knew a more comfortable one than a sod-buster's wife.

The tall woman on the black horse rode by them without seeming to notice. The bank manager removed his bright shoe from the door step.

"What are you looking at, Amos?"

"Why, just a magnificent piece of horseflesh, Mother."

His wife made herself as tall as possible, lifting her nose that was really too short to make the looking down of it effective. She had some time ago ceased to make herself as thin as possible, but she could make her substantiality in her high-necked dress appear the image of municipal respectability.

"A girl with legs that long is a travesty of nature," she said.

"God works in mysterious ways, Mother."

"I do hope that she has never crossed the doorsill of your glorious bank, Amos."

"If she had, I would have been obliged to receive her custom," said he.

"Well, I am not obliged to stand here and watch you pop your eyes out at a tramp who does not even have the decency to ride a horse properly."

Caprice was now just about out of eyeshot, so the banker was again interested in the image he would present when he appeared before his employees.

"The story has it that she has ridden prodigious distances, Mother. One can not ride side-saddle fifty miles a day."

"A decent girl has no reason to ride with her legs hanging over the sides of a sweaty horse for fifty miles a day, sir," said the banker's wife, and strode away toward Foster's store.

She always uttered the last words in their conversations, except for those that he muttered when she was too far away to hear, though he half-hoped that she did hear the muttering, just so that her satisfaction would be incomplete.

The boy stepped out onto the road just before the bridge. He was not wearing his spectacles. They were probably on the ground nearby. He squinted up at her, his hand over his eyes against the high sun.

"You lightin' a shuck?"

The horse was not patient with such an early stop. He stepped up and down with his forefeet.

"I have to go," she said.

She smiled, and he did not like it. It was the first time she had treated him disingenuously. He did not smile back.

"You comin' back?"

"I might do," she said, trying to imitate his frontier lingo.

"How long'll you be gone?"

"Depends. Cant rightly say."

"How'd you get those scratches on your face?"

"Wasn't watching where I was going," she said.

The boy looked as if he could not think of anything more to say, as if he had been told by his teacher to thank somebody for something. Yet he also looked as if he were reaching for his first and last chance.

"Ma'am?"

"Yes, sir?"

"Watch real careful, will you?"

She smiled again, genuinely this time, and waved as the grateful horse dipped his rear quarters and broke into a quick pace for the bridge.

The boy found his glasses and put them on. He watched until even her dust was gone.

Come back, said the voice in his head. Come back.

The entire sweep of the great Interior Plateau is fearsome in its beauty. It is and always has been convincing in its everlasting grandeur — no single person's story could amount to much in comparison. No human being could walk or ride under that immense blue sky and remain a humanist.

In the late days of summer now or then the cows have gone up to the top of the brown rise, in among the trees, looking for something to eat. The creeks have narrowed down to a trace of inch-deep water among the round grey rocks. A pair of legs walking through tall dry couch grass will provoke thousands of chittering grasshoppers to take their crooked flight. Pine cones and dry twigs lie on carpets of red needles in the only shade to be found. Faint mirages dangle over the rounded tops of the sagebrush hills.

A human being in this place will have direct evidence of his relative insignificance, and no reasonable hope of "taming nature." A human being with a desire to be good will recognize the immense beauty all at once, and see a path into the middle of it, a way to walk or ride into her own best hope for herself.

"I hate this goddamned country," said Frank Spencer.

He had been muttering and shouting, cursing and grumbling for more than an hour. He had said more words in that time than Strange Loop Groulx had heard him speak during the whole time they had been business partners. This was because Frank Spencer was at the bottom of a bottle of rye whisky.

"Me too," said Loop. "I more'n hate it. I abominize it."

"Abominate it," said Spencer.

"Abominate the living jeezly hell out of it," said Loop. "I would like to kill this son of a bitching country."

"What do you know about hating this country?" said Spencer, his voice laced with danger.

"I would like to cloud up and rain all over this bastard country."

Spencer smashed his empty bottle on one of the rocks that contained their sagebrush camp-fire.

"I dont know why I ever came back to this god-forsaken country," he said.

Loop Groulx more or less focused his eyes on his partner. Spencer was rubbing the thumb of one hand over the blue mark on the other. If Frank Spencer did not know why he had come back to this country, who else could know? People were asking that question all up and down the valley. There was reason enough for him to stay away, that much was certain. There was still a picture of him hanging in the Provincials' station in every big town on the Thompson and the Fraser.

He looked more dangerous in real life than he looked in the photograph. When the picture had been made the subject had been angry but sober. Now he was full of rye whisky. Loop Groulx knew that Spencer had shot at least one man dead over some whisky.

"You got any more whisky?"

"No, Frank, I aint. I wish I did, but I aint. Sorry."

"Well, I got some," said Spencer, and whipped a flat bottle out of his chaps pocket.

Spencer prised the cork out with his trail knife and poured an unhealthy slug down his throat. He was walking around the camp, holding the bottle by the neck. He approached his horse that was standing hip-shot in the shade of a pine tree.

"You want a drink, you stupid dappled asshole? Well tough shit for you! Ugly horse! Ugly excuse for a horse!"

Loop would have liked a slug of whisky, but he was too smart to ask for one, and it did not look as if his partner was going to offer any.

"You know what's the ugliest thing about this country, Frenchie?"

"What's that, Frank?"

"You are, Frenchie."

Loop was not about to offer a defence of his looks. There had been times when he had laid someone on the ground for calling him Frenchie, but right now he was extraordinarily aware of the loneliness of the western landscape.

"Could be, Frank," he said.

"Could be, Frank, could be Frank," said Spencer in a grotesque whining parody.

Now Groulx decided to keep his mouth shut, hoping that silence would save his life. He sat on his saddle that was resting on his groundsheet, and pulled off one of his boots. He was hoping that it would look as if his foot had been bothered all day by a nail.

Half an hour later Spencer was lying flat on his back on the ground, snoring loudly. It was the first time Loop Groulx had seen him at a disadvantage. This seemed like just another kind of arrogance on the part of his partner or boss or whatever he was. Right now Loop could just take him and give the Provincials a nice surprise. He could do it. The whisky bottle was clear empty. He could probably find another one hidden in Spencer's saddle-gear. He could do it.

The big black horse was covered with mud. The mud was created by the mixture of dust and sweat. If Caprice had had a thermometer with her she would have been able to see that it was 96 degrees in the shade, but of course one would have to travel a good distance in the sun to get to the shade. The river was another matter. It was not very high now, and at this stretch it ambled slowly between gradual banks of sagebrush-covered soil. She did not have to urge Cabayo to step into the green water, but merely aimed his head in its direction.

The horse went for a glad swim, and the woman on his back admired the way her saddle-gear kept her effects dry. It was near the end of the afternoon, and seemed like a summer holiday. Her bruises, exposed to the beating sun, seemed to meld with the usual dull aches of riding.

Paris was a universe away. All the cities she had once strolled in seemed to retreat into fancy. Even the towns of the west could have been necessary dreams. In her bags she had a side of bacon, some flour, dried fruit, and one personal indulgence, a slab of sharp rat cheese. She could have been a range rider. She could have been working for the Lazy Eight ranch, keeping stock from drifting, checking range and water-holes, keeping her eyes open for rustlers. Writing down what she would have to remember in her tally book.

She had not written a poem since the muteness of God had stayed her pencil. She wondered whether she would return to her book after this was all over.

Now, or rather then, she thought she recognized the configuration of the hillside, the fan of shale flakes in an arrested spill from the rock abutment above to the flat sandy earth. She thought she knew the umbrella-shaped ponderosa against the sky.

She got down and took the bags and the thirty-pound saddle off the horse, and set him free to see whether he could find anything to eat. She never had to tie him, but only let the reins hang beside his head.

Then, to see whether she was correct, she took out the photograph that Minjus had given to her. It showed the two bushwhackers standing with rifles in the crooks of their arms, and in the background the alluvial fan and the umbrella. She put the picture away, walked to the railroad tracks, and followed them with her head down until she found a faint rectangle in which the pale grass was working to catch up with the neighbourhood.

Now she made camp, rigging her groundsheet as a sun-shade. In short order she had a small greasewood fire and a hot coffee can. She nibbled on cheese, and ate some of the apricots dry rather than plumping them in hot water. Occasionally she checked the skyline for movement, and looked up and down the valley. She saw a flatbed wagon drawn by four mules roiling the dust as it passed from the west to the east.

Wisdom told her that it could be a dangerous place to make camp, but she was impatient with wisdom for the time being. If those two were to show up now, at least they would be there, and something would happen. She felt as if she were in the hands of a kind of fate, and that she herself were making the moves that designed that fate. It was not the best way to operate, but she had been on the trail for a long time, and she did not know any more than did anyone else what Spencer was up to. If he had come back to the country to get her, why was he riding around sticking up stores and shooting at other people?

Had he got wind of her pursuit somewhere on the other side of the medicine line, and decided to taunt her, ride around the nearby environment and let her know that he was there for the taking if she was good enough to do it? It sounded crazy. It sounded as if either Spencer was a crazy man, or he thought he could drive her crazy.

It sounded as if he was not finished yet with the vindictiveness that had killed her brother, but wanted to tease her with it.

Wisdom told her to be more careful. Minjus had helped her. Kesselring at last had helped her. But Everyday Luigi had tried in his poor way to befriend her, and he was lying in bed with a horrible face. She should be replying to their unobliged gestures with vigilance. But that could be taken up again tomorrow. Just this one day she was going to settle in plain sight. If chance would have Spencer find her here in the open this day, it would be his one opportunity. Today her heart and her wounded body were deciding where she would be. Tomorrow, if she was still in the chase, her ears would open to wisdom and cunning.

When she had finished her coffee she left the faintly smoking fire to seek its own continued life, and carrying the coiled whip in her right hand, began to walk up the hillside.

She found nothing for a while, and then she found a boot print in the clay at the edge of a runlet, pointing toward it. Here someone had been collecting water. In the clay she also found some bear prints that were more recent. They had no effect on this day's recklessness.

She found a lot of horse buns, some decayed into drying dust, some more recent, and one of these she broke apart with a stick. There was just a trace of moistness in the centre — in this weather they would be about three days old.

She found some choke-cherry bushes, and because she did she found the little rail-tie house in the side of the bank behind them. Inside she lit a match, and because she did she found a coal-oil lamp. When she had lit the lamp she saw what she had been looking for. She knew that none of the bushwhackers' loot would be here, that they would have buried it under a rock somewhere else, probably somewhere a person could ride to from here within a half-hour.

If there had been ordinary human eyes there to see her, they would have seen grey eyes gone cold green in the lamp's mezzotint.

These looked around at the meagre furnishings of an outlaw

hide-out. There were two sleeping places made of piled and flattened brush, a cache of canned goods and boxes, empty bottles lying on their sides, and a stew kettle on an ammunition box just inside the door. There were newspapers lying here and there. Five over-ripe peaches lay on a cotton sack on top of a cracker box. A tobacco tin was standing on a shelf cut into the clay bank that served as the back wall. She went to look at it. It contained a tiny dead tortoise floating in dirty water.

She could not stand up straight in there, so what she now did she did more in fury than with the skill she had practised for the years since the end of her own settled domicile.

She uncoiled the whip as best she could in that constrained place. She slashed with it the way a person might swing a tennis racquet in a pup tent. Things were knocked over without breaking. Her ferocity was beyond any curses she might have uttered.

Finally she made one satisfying direct hit with the returning tip of the snake, and the lamp exploded, directing an instant's river of flame into one of the beds of brush. The whole inside of the cave was a flash of fire. She ducked her head and was outside, in a blanket of black smoke.

That night her little camp-fire was a lonely gleam in the immense darkness of the valley. The sky was filled with big clear stars a tall human being could reach up and nearly touch. Coyotes made their usual comments somewhere up the hillsides, something about the relationship between the moon that had disappeared and the immediate presence of a fainter light that reminded eyes of their forgotten ability.

The black horse answered them with a mutter the first few times he heard them, then remained still when they became a part of the proper night.

The second Indian could not tell by looking at him whether the older man was awake. They were both sitting cross-legged in their blankets without a fire. He spoke quietly, anyway.

"Black smoke in the day, and a fire at night. A camp that can be seen from a hawk's flight in any direction. What is she desiring?"

His small words dropped to their death and were replaced by the silence they had pierced. The old man had not moved an eyelash. This he could see in the starlight. But eventually the old man spoke in a normal voice.

"She is testing," he said.

"What?"

"Something. There is an Indian word for it, but you are not allowed to know it yet."

"Why?"

He had said this last word in a normal voice, but there was no answer, and he had developed a man's self-regard that would not allow him to say it again.

"Aint it about time we had us some fun?" asked Strange Loop Groulx. "What's the good of us having all this money if we aint going to use it?"

Frank Spencer did not say anything. He was sitting with his back to a ponderosa, cleaning the vicious-looking barrel of his Smith & Wesson .44 Russian. It was the second time Loop had ever seen the pistol. He wished that he had one.

"I mean, you said we was going to save our earnings to set us up in business, but I dont see no business. Onliest business I see you thinking about is this big woman business."

Spencer cast the fleetest of evil looks at the short, broad figure that was walking aimlessly around the desultory camp-fire.

"Come on, Frank. Being an outdoor businessman aint all there is to living. A man's got to have some enjoyment out of life. Now I know what would make you enjoy life more than anything else, but in the meantime, why dont we have some plain ordinary human being fun?"

Spencer snapped the Smith & Wesson together and aimed it at Groulx. He pressed the trigger, and smiled without showing any teeth as the loud click brought the desired result from its target.

"All right," he said, "saddle my horse."

There was music coming out the front door of the only really big saloon in Savona, music and loud laughter, and the low masculine rumble of the loud talk you hear when working men have been drinking beer and whisky together for a few hours. Once in a while a high-pitched woman's voice could be heard soaring above the general roar. On the high porch in front of the saloon you could have seen a young blonde woman in an elaborate red dress and Italian-style hair, sitting with her stockinged legs dangling from between the rails. She was dreaming of a better life or maybe a former life.

Even in the middle of its social life the frontier could be lonely. Even if you were just taking a minute's rest. Up in the room she shared with another blonde woman there was lying the latest copy of the *Illustrated News* to make it this far west. Its pages were covered with the drama of Jack the Ripper. Up in her room she dreamt while she shared a pipe of opium with her Spanish lover, a splendid count with a hundred white horses, a phantom.

But this was a truly sumptuous saloon. Most of the drinking dens in this part of the country reflected the expectation that the town would disappear like all the mining camps in the smaller valleys, so they were little more than small barns or big sheds with some tables and chairs and whisky bottles with no labels on them. But this was the pride of Savona. Here the windows were framed with dark red velvet drapes. Some of the chairs were armchairs. The bar was solid and burnished wood fashioned from a kind of tree that does not grow west of Toronto. The piano-player wore a tie and collar, and accompanied dancers and singers and the occasional reciter on a little elevated stage. Framed signs on the wall advertised Scotch whisky and French wine. You could buy champagne and drink it out of a fluted glass. Cowboys were known to brush their jackets before stepping over there for an aperitif.

Sitting at a felt-covered table a good distance from the piano was an authentic itinerant gambler. In keeping with the well-fashioned atmosphere, he had oil on his hair and no unplanned whiskers on his face. He was attired in a Prince Albert broadcloth coat in very dark brown. The game was stud or three-card draw, no rangitang wild-card entertainment. This night he was taking it easy on a lawyer he had made it his business to befriend, a dressed-up blacksmith, and a young man who was torn between careers as a newspaper reporter or a cowboy.

The only guns to be seen were a collection of rifles in the

cloakroom, where they had been checked along with spurs and hats. The management did not like spurs because they would scar the expensive furniture, and they did not like hats because they were not polite. Rifles were for shooting coyotes and snakes. Hand-guns were for leaving at the ranch.

And there were women in the room, young women. On some occasions there were even women as customers, as long as they were in groups and had come with their husbands, to celebrate a new civic project, or a large family success. But most of the women, most of the time, were single and relatively eye-pleasing. They had frolicsome voices if they knew their business, and they had the longest, whitest arms you could imagine. Some of them had the advantage of European accents.

This was a far cry from the first watering hole on the same site. Thirty years ago, long before the joyous arrival of Ontario's railroad, there had been a humble bar-room here. Dirty and tired prospectors and miners had come on weekends to quaff beer made a few hundred feet down the lake-front, and whisky that could have cut a hole in the lake ice in January. That bar had boasted a little curtained alcove that lubricated men could pay a dollar to enter. Inside was a woman's high-necked, ruffled dress affixed to a lath frame. Below it was a pair of buttoned shoes, and above it a bright red ribbon tied in a bowline. A large relative of the saloon-keeper stood ready to counsel the patrons not to touch the cloth with their dirty hands.

"How can that gambler guy wear all that stuff on a hot night in August?" asked Loop Groulx.

"Money cools his hands," said Frank Spencer.

A waiter with plaid sleeve garters approached. Loop took a step backward, not knowing what to expect.

"I am afraid there are no tables left, gentlemen. Would you care to wait for one?" asked the waiter.

"We'll stand at the bar," said Spencer.

"Very good, sir."

"Dont call me sir. I aint a banker or a politician," said Spencer.

The waiter, who had heard that line several dozen times, went away without his usual smile.

The two bushwhackers stood at the bar and drank Bourbon. In the mirror they saw themselves, two men in worn-out clothes, with money. Above the mirror was a Union Jack in a frame. Spencer looked at it with indifference. Groulx looked at it with indifferent disregard.

The stage was empty, but the piano player in the swallow-tail coat was playing loudly. The music was a medley of high points from Beethoven and Verdi, chosen for a night when the place was packed and the noise level pretty high.

"This is better than sitting around a cow-shit fire drinking my coffee, eh, Frank?"

"You wanted to have fun, so have fun," said Spencer, making it sound like a threat.

"Ah, come on, buddy, drink up, loosen up, this is our night to howl."

"Go ahead and howl, but dont do it near me," said Spencer, making it sound like an ultimatum.

His eyes were roving the crowd, looking for familiar faces, looking at the same time for faces that could belong to policemen or range detectives.

The face that showed up startled him for a second. It was a pretty female face, white and red and blue. That did not startle him, because he had been in two hundred saloons from Nogales to Williams Lake. What startled him was that the face was almost on a level with his own.

This would not have been true if the woman in the purple dress had not been wearing the highest heels west of Montreal.

"Hello, cowboy, do you want to buy me a drink?" said the woman, slowly, the way she had been taught.

"I'm not a cowboy," said Spencer, through his brown teeth.

"He's a businessman, ha-ha-ha," said Groulx. This was how to have fun.

Spencer turned and glared at him.

"You! Shut up!"

"I like businessmen just as much as cowboys," said the woman, putting her hand on Spencer's arm. "Businessmen have just as much right to have a little party as cowboys."

Spencer was using all his muscles but he was just standing still. The woman leaned her breast against his arm.

"What's your name, businessman? Mine's Clarice."

A tenth of a second later Spencer released his muscles. He shoved the woman away from him violently. She fell off her heels, backward through a table of four men, against the floor, where her head smacked loudly.

Oh, Christ, thought Loop.

Then men were all over Spencer. They jumped on him from all sides, not giving him a chance to swing one fist at them. They clobbered him and hauled him at the same time, kicking and pounding him all the way to the door. At the door they smote him between the shoulder blades, across the pate, on top of his arches, and in his kidneys. Then they rousted him across the porch and propelled him down the stairs into the dust. Horses shied and danced on both sides of him.

Loop Groulx grabbed drinks off the still upright tables on his way out. The last thing he saw was the gambler, the only man still sitting. He was peeking at his own hand, too much the gentleman to lift the corner of any other on the table.

In the early evening sun the prodigious black horse stepped to the summit of a grassy rise and stopped of his own accord, as if he wanted to take in the view. His shadow with the woman's shadow above it reached to the round edge and over into the general shadow. He was a clever horse but he did not know about staying off the horizon. The woman had had her day of recklessness, though, and now she nudged him and he began stepping downhill, something no horse greatly likes.

In front of them was a typical sod-buster home. There was a frame house made of unpainted hand-hewn lumber going silver in the weather. It squatted along with some aspens in the middle of an acre marked off by a brush fence. In twenty years, maybe, the old brush would be replaced by posts and barbed wire. Also inside the fence were two draft horses and a milk cow. No water ran through the place, but there was a pump in the yard. There was no back yard and no front yard; there was just a yard.

There were a lot more sod-busters than ranchers in the country, but there was a lot more ranch land than sod-buster land. The sod-buster was a simple man with a religion made up of equal parts work and silence. He was usually from somewhere farther east in the country, while the ranchers were usually from England or Ireland or sometimes from down south. Some of the ranches were owned by banks or other companies back east, but the sod-buster's acre was usually mortgaged to a bank in the nearest town, in this case probably Kamloops.

As the horse and the woman with red braids hanging down her back approached, he was looking at the ground to both sides, and she was looking at the pump in the yard. There was a sod-buster's grim wife washing clothes with a huge basin and a washboard. She was wearing a sun-bonnet. Beside her was a small daughter in a sun-bonnet, standing on a chopping block to pin heavy wet clothes on the clothesline. Sitting in the shade of the house was a small son, fiddling with what looked like a piece of harness. All over the place were brown chickens, scratching at the ground for snacks.

These were the people the big ranchers called a threat to range land. They were never mentioned in the romances and the dime novels. Romances had proposals of marriage at the end of them, and dime novels of the west had the threat of the hint of marriage at the end of them.

The woman with the red hair rode into the yard and sat her horse. The two faces framed by sun-bonnets looked up at her with similar squints against the sun.

I feel like saying howdy, thought Caprice.

"Good-evening," she said.

The mother was probably a young woman but one would not think of that. The girl was a very small adult. She did not seem to be the same species as the town boy with his spectacles.

"A woman's work is never done," said Caprice.

The two sun-bonnets stared at her. The boy in the shadow of the house was not even looking. He just pulled and pried at the stuff in his hands.

"Mind if I let my horse have some water?"

The woman indicated the water trough with a gesture of her hand, and then returned to scrubbing what looked like a bed-sheet over the bumps of her washboard. Caprice got down and led the black to the trough. Usually a place like this had a dog or two to come cringing or hostile to a horse's feet. A non-working dog was the only luxury a lot of such families had.

"Mind if I fill my canteen at your pump?"

The woman did not make any gesture this time, but Caprice went to the pump and filled her water bottle. The little girl sidled up to her.

"How high are you?" she said.

"Myrtle! You be polite," her mother said.

Caprice laughed, with relief more than anything.

"Five feet eleven inches, whenever I get my boots off," she said, smiling at the girl, not looking at her mother.

"My daddy's gone to the bank," said the girl. She must not have had anyone outside the family to talk to very often.

"Well, we all have to go to the bank once in a while," said Caprice.

She remembered the trouble she had had cashing a cheque back in town. Amos somebody, the fat man's name was. Without being asked his theory of finance he had announced to her that what was good for the banks was good for the country. The banker in Kamloops had probably said that to the girl's father this afternoon.

"D'you have any children?" asked the girl.

"Myrtle!"

"It's all right. No, I was never so lucky. I once had a husband who was so silly that he thought children were only a nuisance."

She turned her back while screwing the top onto the water bottle. She hung it on the cantle while the black continued to poke his face in the trough, more for the water on his face now than the water in his belly.

"Ira! You get choppin' that wood!"

There was nothing unusual here; homesteading wives usually spoke to their children in exclamations and imperatives. This was done in order to make up for the silence of the husbands, to strike a kind of medium volume of speech.

The boy did not move until his mother picked up a stone and pitched it in his direction. He did not duck, either, but eventually stood up.

"Myrt's got the choppin' block," he said.

"Do with what you find," said his mother.

She pushed a strand of brown hair back under her bonnet and looked at Caprice at last. Her look said what is such a queer-looking woman doing riding alone around here.

"Would you mind terribly if I washed my face?" asked Caprice.

The woman indicated the basin and towel outside the kitchen door. Caprice took the basin to the pump and put a little water into it, then scrubbed her face with the slippery home-made soap. When she had finished she put her hat on her head to indicate that she was ready to ride on without further imposition.

"We have to have a lot of firewood ahead of time, for the winters around here. They are short but they are fierce," said the woman.

Caprice was surprised by the sudden loquacity, but she was ready to meet it, to take her advantage of it.

"Women-folks," she said in a language she was borrowing, "have to be just as fierce as the weather around here."

"You arent just whistling," said the mother of Myrtle and Ira. "You been around this country long?"

"About a year and a bit," said Caprice.

"I could tell you was from another country by your accent in the way you talk. What country you from?"

"I came from Quebec."

"I knew you wasnt from Canada. Well, that is a fine-looking horse you got there. I can tell he is a stayer. He's not from around these parts neither."

"No, he was born in Spain."

"He's a long way from home, too."

Caprice thought she could risk taking the talk to another level. She might still be in the west where talk is ritual rather than discourse, but now she was talking to a woman's country.

"We are all a long way from home, I think."

"Well, I dont know about that," said the woman, "but I reckon I will never see Lucan, Ontario again."

"I wonder whether I will see St Foy."

The sound of chopping came finally from the small shed beside the house, then a loud curse. The mother frowned.

"I'm afraid we aint got room to put you up indoors for the night," she said with a little bitterness.

Caprice smiled with her large white teeth, and the little C-shaped scar on her cheek became a dimple.

"That's all right. My horse, as you say, has plenty of bottom, and I am sure he wont mind doing another five or six miles before the sun is gone. I would just like to ask you a question or two, if you dont mind."

Suspicion came back into the face surrounded by the sun-bonnet, bringing with it a full measure of loneliness. Caprice decided to continue anyway, as the situation had likely got as good as it would become.

"I just wanted to know whether you have seen two men in the past day or two. They are both riding brown-and-white horses. One is pretty tall and broad and the other is medium height, with a blue spot on his hand."

The woman went back to scrubbing the second bed-sheet. Caprice lifted Cabayo's ribbons from the ground and put her left boot into the stirrup, both hands on the horn.

"I never seen his hands," said the woman. "He was wearing gloves."

Caprice swung her long right leg over.

"Can you tell me which way they were going?"

"East, far as I could see."

Roy Smith was the only member of the team who carried books and magazines with him on the train when they had a road game. This year he had been reading everything he could find about the western Indians. He had formed the unusual opinion that if it was his job to teach white reading and farming to the Indians, it might also be part of his job to learn something about them. In this he stood in stark contrast to many of his fellow citizens, some area schoolteachers, and certainly other members of his team, especially the five imports from Minnesota.

"Why the hell should I be paying taxes to teach those savages how to add two and two?" was a question put to him by one landowner just a day ago. It was a question he was asked all the time because he was a teacher.

Still, it was mild compared to the letter written from General Sherman to General Grant a couple decades ago:

"We must act with vindictive earnestness against the Sioux, even to their extermination, men, women and children. Nothing less will reach the root of the case."

Roy Smith was having a late breakfast in the Star Restaurant, Chinese and Canadian Meals, and thinking about Sitting Bull. Sitting Bull had left Canada a month ago, returning to his people on the other side of the white man's medicine line. Roy Smith knew that the white people down there had a dread of the Ghost Dance. He hoped that Sitting Bull would survive their fear. He hoped that the Indians at Wounded Knee would finally be left to what was left of themselves.

He was the only man in the Star Restaurant who was cutting his sausages before putting them into his mouth. He dipped the pieces of sausage into the yolks of his eggs. As always the yolks were a little too hard. He was reading the week-old newspaper from Seattle.

I think they will probably kill him and kill them all, he told himself. A hundred years from now we will not be able to understand why they killed Indian children.

Two years ago in the Tewksbury and Graham feud in the southwest, their cowboys had killed twenty men and shot thousands of sheep. They had cut the head off an Indian man who did not hate sheep enough, and showed the Indian's head as a trophy.

Roy Smith did not know it for a certainty, but he had a conviction he could not argue himself out of: that Frank Spencer rode for the cowmen in that adventure.

"Damn the cussedness of that woman," he said out loud.

"You want more coffee?"

That was the Chinese man of indeterminate age behind the counter. Sure, yes, he nodded.

And there was himself. This afternoon he would be playing second base against the CPR nine while she was out riding toward a show-down like any Yank scalp-hunter.

Belle Starr had been killed in the Indian Territory. Already their newspapers were refashioning that whorish renegade into a beautiful female hero.

They knew that the west was becoming the past, and they needed a past that was large and noble and beautiful. Since the land rush the Indian Territory was no longer the Indian Territory, and the west was filled up with white people. They required a myth because the recent past was a bullet in the back.

Roy Smith's job was the future. He was not sure that he was doing all the right things in teaching Indian children how to add two and two, but he knew that the role assigned to them in the past, even on this side of the medicine line, would not be enough to sustain them for the future.

He had tried to argue her out of the recent past she was so silent about. You are a poet, he had said. Write a great poem about your brother. Let the police do the policing and let the poets do the poems.

I cannot write a poem now, she had said.

Sometime in the future, then. He had argued the future to her. He had argued marriage to her, proposing marriage for the future of the west.

The true western hero, said this famous poet in the Seattle paper, is the man who has completely forgotten Europe.

Roy Smith had not imagined himself a hero since the dreams of his boyhood. But she was living on drafts mailed to her from Europe. From the past. From the husband neither of them had the bad form to mention to each other.

He demonstrated his anger to the cold unbuttered toast. He hoped that he could forget it for two hours on the field this afternoon, or rather that one.

Frank Spencer and Loop Groulx were riding carefully through the Cherry Creek ranch, not looking for trouble, at least not yet, not looking to be the recipients of any trouble. They were on their way up a crude wagon road that had already climbed above the reach of the creek aspens, till there was nothing but lodgepole pine and rock outcroppings to break up the sweep of brown grass.

On one of the flattest rock faces someone had been at work with a bucket of whitewash. There was a rectangular border that framed these words: HEAVEN AND EARTH SHALL PASS AWAY: BUT MY WORDS SHALL NOT PASS AWAY.

"What does that say, Frank?"

"Just some religious horse shit," said Spencer.

Once in a while the man from Tennessee would drop his taciturnity, and Strange Loop usually probed for these times. He thought of himself as an apprentice outlaw, and the more he could learn from this expert the better. He was never without a part of his thoughts directed toward his own future. So at the camp-fire or on the trail he plied Spencer with questions of a professional nature, trying not to cross the boundary of the personal. He was interested in the personal, but he knew that he could get shot, too.

Groulx was chewing plug tobacco. The neck and mane of his horse were covered with brown spatters. He aimed for its right ear now, and just missed.

"You figger they'll get a wanted poster out on us pretty soon, Frank?"

"Already got one out on me," said the man riding in front.

"Well, yeah, I know. But you reckon they'll have one about us as a team, like?"

"Team?"

"Yeah, I mean something liked Wanted for Armed Robbery, Frank Spencer and the Savona Kid."

"Savona Kid? Who the Christ is the Savona Kid?"

"I been studyin' on a name. I mean if I am going to be an outlaw I should ought to have an outlaw name."

"How about the Fuckface Kid?" suggested Spencer.

"Why do you have to talk like that?"

"You aint no kid, Groulx. You aint been a kid for twenty years. Likely you never were a kid. You were probably a goat from the time you were dropped."

Frank Spencer did not really have a sense of humour. He always borrowed such remarks from conversations he had heard, and he never issued them except when he wanted to hurt someone.

Loop Groulx suspended his questions for about a mile. The horses were walking slowly, and the two bushwhackers had time to appreciate the beauty of the vista at this height, and the sounds of the birds who liked living among the lodgepole pines. Even outlaws like birds.

After a mile Groulx started his line of questions again.

"How long do you reckon it'll be till we are heroes, Frank?"

"What the fuck are you talking about now?" was the reply from up front.

Loop really wished that these conversations did not have to be held with the obvious scorn in the more experienced outlaw's voice.

"Well, when they get them wanted posters up everywhere, then we'll be famous, leastways in these parts, I mean in the beginning. And once we get famous folks will start to think of us as heroes. I mean like Jesse James and all. Especially the kids, eh? Kids really look up to famous outlaws."

"Not up here in this goddamned country," said Spencer. "Up here they think the goddamned Mounties are heroes. Cops!"

"No, no. You dont understand the way we are up here. I mean all that Mountie stuff. That's just the government version. That's just what some grown-ups and government people are trying to get across. I never heard of a kid yet that really thought the Mounties was heroes. No, everybody up here follows what's going on down there, 'cause that's where the books and songs comes from."

"You're reading books now, are you?"

"I know folks that can read books, Frank. I aint completely bushed."

Frank Spencer was not chewing tobacco, but he leaned over the side of his horse and spit on the miserable excuse for a road.

"I aint interested in being no hero," he said.

"What about Wild Bill Hickok?"

"A cop."

"Only part of the time."

"He's dead."

"Well, sure, but everything has to come to an end, eh? What about Wyatt Earp?"

"Another cop."

"Sure, but only when it suits him."

"A Jew."

"You know, Frank, you can be an ornery bastard when you want to be."

Spencer stopped his horse. He turned around in the saddle and gave Groulx the kind of stare that might precede a .44 bullet.

"My mother lost my father and a lot more in the war, friend. I dont appreciate what you're saying about her."

"It was only an expression, Frank."

"Say something to me, Fuckface."

"Sorry, Frank."

They rode in silence now until the mine building came into sight.

It was a typical two-by-four mining outfit, a couple of shafts in the side of the hill, and a sixteen-foot building to keep stuff in — explosives, tools, gloves, coffee, and the bright yellow pulverized metal that had made it through the little stamper. The operation seemed to have been made in heaven or somewhere, the logic was so neat.

You ride your horses uphill with empty bags, and downhill with the bags bulging and heavy. That was why they did not build shaft mines in the valleys and robbers' hideaways on the tops of mountains.

"Where is everybody?" whispered Loop.

"In a hole in the ground, stupid," whispered Spencer.

"How come there aint a guard?"

"There is. He's inside the building."

They rode their brown-and-white horses boldly up to the door of the place and dismounted. Spencer tried the door, and it gave way with just a slight protest of the imperfectly fashioned hinge. A fifteen-year-old boy was sitting at a table eating cereal and milk.

"Hands up," advised Spencer.

He claimed to have invented that robber's imperative. Later crooks would lay claim to the phrase, but there is no definitive instance of anyone's using it before 1889.

The boy's eyes opened like the peeled litchi nuts at the Canadian Cafe.

"They're up, they're up," he attested.

"See that you keep them there," said Spencer, as his eyes penetrated every corner of the room. There was one window in each wall, a precaution that would have been wise if there had been an alert guard. The only life that could be seen through them was a cluster of sorry-looking horses in a lodgepole corral.

"Hey, you're Frank Spencer, aint you?" asked the boy.

"See? You're a hero already," said Loop.

"Piss off, Frenchie!"

Spencer induced the lad to open the safe, in which rested one little poke of mineral and a paper that registered the mine claim. The robbers eyed the lad significantly, and he told them that the boss and one of his men had taken a wagon load into Kamloops the day before.

Still, it looked as if the robbery were a success, and there might be a couple hundred dollars' worth of gold in the leather sack. The two crooks trussed the youth with some reins that had been hanging on a post by the door, shoved a tea-towel into his mouth, and prepared to leave.

"Hey, Frank, look! There's a scalp on the wall."

"I told you not to mention my name when we're working."

"Ah, the kid already said it. I'm getting me that scalp."

"It aint a scalp. Cant be."

"Sure it is."

Loop Groulx seized the piece of coarse black hair from its nail on the wall and carried it with him as they rode away at a clip. Once into the trees, the two riders left the rough road and cut away through the lodgepole pines parallel to it.

"I dont know what it is about you, Groulx," said Spencer. "What do you want with an old chunk of bear hair?"

"It's kind of a trophy, I guess."

Groulx had fixed the object to the band of leather across his horse's forehead, much to the displeasure of the animal, which shook its head from side to side and rolled its eyes. Loop socked it on top of its head.

"You never wear them sleeve garters you took off the galoot in Foster's store," said Spencer.

"Ah, who the hell wears red sleeve garters?"

Gradually downhill through the spectacularly beautiful hill country they rode. For a while the only sounds were the hooves of their horses striking granite and the creak of saddle leather. But this was one of Frank Spencer's talking days, and Loop Groulx could not let the opportunity pass.

"Frank, I been wondering something."

There was no answer from the rider in front of him.

"Frank, I been auguring you for the last couple weeks, and there is something I cant figger out."

On the other hand, this was too good an opportunity for the Tennessean to pass up.

"Far as I can see," he said, "them things you cant figger out are most of the things there is."

I could shoot him from right here, thought Strange Loop. If I didnt think he might just happen to turn around while I was getting my Winchester out, I'd plug him. Well, maybe.

"I been studying on this here Cabeese woman and you. Seems like you come back up here to get rid of that botheration once and for all, but all the time you been up here you been keeping away from her. Now, that just dont make no sense to me. If it was me I would just go and plug her, and I want to remind you I got my own reasons."

Spencer just kept on riding, face forward.

"Well, I just think it's a little funny, that's all. I mean I really like being an outlaw with you, Frank. Best time I ever had in my life. But I cant figger it. Seems like you could do your outlawing just as well in Oregon, wouldnt have the Provincials and the Mounties after you and all. So it must have to do with that goddamned woman. So why the hell dont you just go and drop her?"

At last Spencer spoke up.

"I know what I'm doing, fellow. I'm just waiting to see if she cottons on to what's going to happen."

Riding east along the lake from Savona, Caprice frowned rather than smiling about the story of Spencer's ejection from the splendid saloon. It was a good story, a funny story, even comforting, one would suppose. But there was something wrong with it. She had spoken with the limping woman whom Spencer had thrown across the room, and put two and two together. But there was a secret number somewhere in the arithmetic. Arithmetic had not been her best subject at the sisters' school.

She decided to approach this problem with a trick she had often used when a poem was giving her trouble. She would push it somewhere else in her mind by fixing her attention on whatever fell before her gaze. At this moment it was cows.

She had been in this country for well over a year, so she was used to white faces and Aberdeen Anguses as part of the landscape. If there was grass there were cows, and if you rode your pony for a week there were still cows, and over the horizon there were more cows. Sometimes you were riding through the woods in the high country, with wind soughing through the needles, and you would be startled to see a half-dozen Herefords standing there.

Back home in Quebec a cow was part of the national myth. Each family was supposed to have one cow to supply milk and butter and cheese for the twelve children who dramatized the passage of this temporary residency on earth and in youth. The family cow had an amusing name, and familiar habits, and there came a time in a child's life when it was his turn to tend her, perhaps walking behind her and tapping her bony backside with a switch.

In Paris one expected a thin slice of beef blackened with

peppercorns on the outside and slippery red on the inside, and graced with a piquant sauce.

There was a cow standing up to its ankles in the lake. Its white face with lovely curls of hair on its forehead regarded her with the stupidity that would lead it eventually up a ramp and into a CPR cattle car. It had a lazy eight branded on its hip.

You try to clear your mind and look at the country, and it looks back at you without thinking at all. If paying attention only to what lies in front of your eyes really worked, cows would be better poets than Frenchmen are.

Where was she being led?

Why was she pursuing the obvious Frank Spencer eastward after he had ridden so far north?

She had ridden from the Canadian border to the Mexican border looking for him or news of him. Then she had followed the north star back, followed the faintest trail of rumours back to the valley where Pierre had died in the dirt. But Spencer had tied a twist in his path and flanked her. All the last part of summer he had had his chance to put a rifle shot into her from behind a rock, or confront her on the road. She was satisfied that the bullet in the baseball park had come from behind Loop Groulx's horse. Spencer would have fired more than one shot, and he would not likely have missed.

Roy Smith was right every time he said that she should leave Spencer to the police. But the police knew that Spencer was back now, and Spencer was not in custody. Roy Smith was right, though. The police had a better chance of coming out of this alive than she did. So why was she following this trail with no known destination? She recognized the feeling. She was writing because she was looking forward to the last stanza.

"C'est stupide," she said out loud.

In front of her she saw a little church standing alone beside the river. There were no trees around it to make it picturesque. It was just a little white clapboard building with a short spire on top. There was not another building in eyeshot, just the quiet train tracks leading away across the brown flats to their meeting place out of sight. The little building was alone, like a shrine on a forlorn road. But it was not there for the traveller's tribute. It was a building into which people would likely walk this coming Sunday.

She knew that the church in the west was a haven for those, especially women, who needed help surviving the loneliness. Families in town clothes would ride surreys and buckboards for miles over ranch roads to meet for an hour inside and a half-hour outside after the service. They would not fall to their knees as did the peasants and shop-owners in the immense cathedral where she had gone to look for a line in Paris. They did not go there to seek relief from the noise and debts of last Wednesday. They rode those miles to see whether there were still other people alive out here. When they got there they sang songs about their faith and their lord, and in their hands they held cloth-bound books printed in a big city.

Caprice did not get down and go inside as she had done the last time she passed this little church. But she led her sweating black horse to the small shade it afforded, and sat there in the saddle for a few minutes. She looked at the ground next to the white wall. It was not a lawn. It was just like the rest of the ground around here, hardened dust with a cover of sage and low cactus. About three feet from the wall she saw a brass cartridge case. It looked like a .44–.40.

☆ ☆ ☆

"I always get a little sad when I see the end of summer arriving," said the second Indian.

They were riding their homely and patient grey ponies down a dry creek bed off Dufferin Hill. Anyone watching them might think that they were dead tired and unable to keep their heads up. Any white man watching them with his ordinary eyes might think that they were lucky there were no Yankee-type massacres because these two would then be good dead Indians. Anyone who proceeded with such an opinion would have been surprised by the unfavourable result. They were tired all right, as any two men might be after the riding they had done in the last week. But they were not half asleep; they were half awake.

The first Indian, because he was nearing the age of retirement, was the more tired. But he was the more awake.

"Why do you get sad at this time of year? Remember that in a little time it will be Indian summer. You can get happy again for a couple of weeks."

"What is Indian summer?"

"It is a little something the white people cherish, a kind of second chance."

"Why do they call it Indian summer?"

"I believe it is because they think of it as the nice weather that was held in reserve."

"The Great Spirit is going to punish you, my teacher. Now you are telling white man jokes with Indian subjects."

The old man smiled with satisfaction. It was not just out of idleness that he told such stories. It was part of the tuition. His student was learning two of the last things — that living was being funny, and that the man riding with him was evolving from a teacher into a friend.

"Why are you sad when summer comes to an end?" he asked now.

"It is probably not the proper thing to confess, but I do not like to look forward to the fall hunt."

"Is this because you are an artist, and such community work does not find easy accord with your temperament?"

The younger man smiled in return.

"No," he said. "I hate to look at the deer after we have herded them over the cliff. Do not get me wrong — I love the taste of fresh venison, and I am, as you know, fond of jerked meat. But there is something about the act of inducing animals to cascade from great heights that makes me feel terrible."

"We pray to their spirits for forgiveness before and after we do it," said the first Indian. "And we as a people have done it since we came here from Asia, probably even before that."

"That I do not doubt. I am a full member of the people. Or I soon will be."

"It is what my anthropologist friend called our folkway," said the first Indian.

They had come down out of the scrub-pine country and were now on the edge of a brown grassy bench, overlooking the sweep of the valley. They could see late whitecaps that looked like horses' manes in the middle of the lake. Across the sage-dotted valley floor there were two horsemen in the middle of a big round shadow laid by the only cloud in the sky.

"Well," said the first Indian, "now that you have put your customary introductory question, perhaps you are ready to ask me the question that has been labouring to depart your breast all day."

The second Indian produced what he thought to be a rueful grin. He had been sitting up straight on his horse at the edge of the bench, trying on a pose he had seen in a magazine painting on a barber-shop wall.

"All right, wise elder. What this unworthy youth desires to know is this: why are we following those two men? Or to put it more precisely, why are we both following those two bandits and at the same time watching that woman trying to follow those two bandits?"

The first Indian's handsome lined face was inscrutable and perfectly still. If he blinked over the next minute, no one saw it. Even his horse was perfectly still, not a switch of the tail, not a quiver of the skin.

"That is a very good question," the old man said at last.

The second Indian did not know whether to be pleased at the compliment or impatient at the hedging.

"If you would rather not answer it — "

"No," said the first Indian. "It is my calling to answer your questions, unless I can manoeuvre you around to answering them yourself. What you are enquiring into is a matter of motivation."

"You could say that. It is the end of summer. Soon they will be loading their cows into trains, and we will be gathering fish by the netful and driving those unfortunate deer over a jump. This idleness has not long to run."

"Idleness? You mean education."

"Yes. Why are we following those robbers?"

The old man did up the top two buttons of his serge jacket. A crisp wind was travelling along the flat bench, carrying tumble-weeds with it.

"I believe that I once told you our survival in a smaller country filled with white people depends on learning how they think and why they do the things they do."

"Yes, sir, you did."

"Why did the one called Spencer come back across the medicine line to where he is wanted for murder?"

"Am I answering the questions now?"

"Does that question replace your former question?"

"Oh please, that is not fair. You are playing words with me. I know that you have many devious ways of leading me to knowledge, but I am suspicious about this one. I think you might be trying to put me off because you do not know the answer."

"What would that suggest?" asked the first Indian.

The second Indian put on his thoughtful face. That is, he looked patient and impenetrable, yet alert. It was something his people had added to their folkways after the white men had come into the country.

"Well, it could mean that you are weaning me away from my awe for your wisdom and higher standing in the social order because you think my learning has reached a level on which I can stand as a full member of the band."

"Yes?"

"Or it could mean that you do not have a really good notion of why we are doing all this riding."

The first Indian was looking out over the valley, toward the place where the two robbers were riding. He could not see them at all. It was time to find a path down off the bench and follow.

"When you can tell me why the Yankee came back to this country and why he is now riding away from the woman instead of toward her," he said, "then you will be able to tell me why we are following him and his friend."

He must have nudged his horse into movement, but no one could have seen him do it. The second Indian followed him. He was wondering now: did the old man know something he was not yet ready to demonstrate, or had they reached the end of the old relationship?

It would be the easiest trail just to consider the Yankee gunman crazy, he thought.

The old man was deep inside his own thoughts that were like animals watching him without great respect. Why are we doing this, he asked himself.

Roy Smith was always dropping things when she was around. At other times he was pretty graceful and secure in his power. In front of one of his classes he was not afraid to flip a pencil end over end and catch it pointed the right way. But when her tall fresh body was within fifteen feet he could not hold onto a handkerchief. He felt young, like a juvenile on the frontier. Then he had to make himself sound authoritative.

And he had to do it in his baseball uniform. The Elks were the host team for the Labour Day weekend tournament, and the city was expecting them to take the prize. For the first two days they had had no trouble, getting by the CPR on Saturday, and taking care of Ducks and Ashcroft on Sunday. Today they were idle in the morning, and scheduled for the championship against Republic in the afternoon. The Yanks had breezed through their opposition too, and had stated their view that the title game would demonstrate that the upstart Canadians had no business trying to abscond with the game that properly belonged south of the medicine line.

All over town there were men and boys in baseball uniforms. The saloons had more than their usual numbers of empty beer barrels standing beside their front doors. Horses were crammed shoulder to shoulder at the tie racks. The wooden Indian in front of the Superior Tobacconist store had a baseball hat from one of the eliminated teams on his head. There was an elevated dance floor made of aromatic new lumber in the middle of the street, and the music had commenced at nine in the morning.

Roy Smith and Caprice were not alone in the park, but they were as near to alone as they could be anywhere in Kamloops. She was standing and facing toward the river, and he was standing behind her, his arms around her waist.

"Now I suppose you are going to tell me why you are here," he said with his mouth beside her right ear.

"You know," she replied. "I came to watch a ball game."

"You rode your horse all the way here to watch a ball game? I guess that explains why you missed the first two days of the tournament."

This was, as a matter of fact, a posture they had always liked, but she was accustomed to leaning her head back against his shoulder. Now she was simply standing as she might have if he had not been there. His baseball glove was lying flat on the scuffed grass where he had dropped it.

"I'm tired," she said, "tired and I suppose cranky. I have been riding in the hot sun."

"Oh, you're used to that. You like that. You can ride to Arizona and back."

"Maybe you had better go and see whether your team needs you."

"I'm sorry," he whispered. "I — "

She did not lean her head back.

"I love you," he said.

He had her hair in his hands.

"Those are braids, not reins, Mister Smith," she said.

He let go of them. She walked away without looking anywhere but in front of her. He picked up his glove and followed her until she had stopped under the vigorous growth of a Siberian Elm. Now he did not put his arms around her, but manoeuvred so that she could look at his face if she wanted to. She did not want to.

"Roy, I wish I were in St Foy, Quebec."

He thought of making a smart remark about the lightness with which she considered his desire, but he caught sight of a tremble in her chin, a tiny movement that ceased so quickly that he wondered whether he might have been mistaken.

"Go to the school," he said. "Tell them I want them to take care of you till I get there."

"No."

"I will come with you."

"You have a game, stupid." She lifted her head and attempted what turned out to be a transparent bravado.

Then she leaned into him. He put his arms around her, and this time the baseball glove was flat against her back. He held her in the park until a pack of boys came by and began calling wise cracks. His schoolteacher's instinct told him to take one step backward.

"Will you be at the game?" he asked.

Her eyes were grey like winter's sky in Quebec.

"I 'low as to how I will, podnuh."

Whenever they felt the need to extricate themselves from their most common disagreement, she would try on the kind of western language found in Ned Buntline stories. This time her voice nearly failed before she could finish her sentence.

"Will you come to the victory party after we demolish the Yanks?"

They were both embarrassed by the silence that cut between them, but no words would come that were not worse. She smiled with all parts of her face except her eyes, and walked across the dusty grass toward the noise.

The sun always rolls with what human beings designate as pride right through the valley from horizon to horizon on Labour Day. On this Labour Day, or that one, children sprinted from place to place, the boys trying to get as dirty and ragged as they could for the last day in their old summer clothes. When the east-bound train clanked and squealed down the main street, shooting steam at passing drunks, it did so in a dress of red, white and blue bunting. On Labour Day people in western Canadian towns felt as if they were Yanks, and wished they had six-shooters to go with their ice cream and fireworks and barking dogs.

The Provincial Police smiled this one day of the year, as cowboys and railroad workers carried their foaming steins of beer along the boardwalk or into the street. Once in a while they would find two men struggling to hurt each other, and rap one or both of them across the small of the back with their sticks. They smiled too at the saloon ladies who were with the men, their gaudy face-paint cracking in the bright sun of outdoors.

In the field where the championship baseball game would draw most of the celebrants later in the afternoon, men and boys and women were flinging horseshoes at railroad spikes. A poet who was more interested in social life than in private death would have liked the symbolism of an amusement that married metal belonging to the two lives of the Mainline country. Other people were interested because they were placing bets on the games, laughing loudly when they won, laughing pretty loudly when they lost.

There were lots of Indians in town for the weekend. If there was one thing the white men did that made sense it was Labour Day. On Labour Day a white man would throw his arm around your shoulder and say You're okeh with me, Harry Charlie, which was supportable because then he would insist that you have a swig out of his pocket bottle of rye whisky. In the middle of the evening on Labour Day you would not be surprised to see a train-man wearing an Indian neck-piece, and an Indian wearing a CPR hat.

You would not be surprised to see a half-naked young man lying in the horse-trough in front of Yessler's horse hotel. He was not injured and he was not asleep. He was just cooling off to show that this was just as much his idea as it was the idea of his friends from the ranch where animals were identified with the sign III.

As Caprice walked her horse by the trough on her way to the big arched door of the livery barn, this young man spoke to her from his repose in the water.

"Lady, you are a sight for sore eyes, and let me tell you, I have the sorest eyes you ever saw."

She had undone the belly-cinch and reached to jerk the thirty-pound saddle from the damp blanket on Cabayo's back, when she saw a rifle pointed at her. She dropped to the hay-strewn floor and rolled even as she heard the report of the Winchester. There was a second shot. Her mind raced to fix the particulars. The gunman had made his first try from across the street, and the second from halfway across the street.

Now the legs collapsed from under the black horse and he fell with an enormous crash, his heavy head landing on her legs. She looked up and saw the man in the light of the arched door. Her left hand dived into a saddle-bag and came out with the Luger. The rifleman's third shot skipped off the saddle and smashed something behind her. She did three things at once: she transferred the Luger to her right hand, released the safety, and threw the dying horse's head off her legs.

The rifleman was on one knee now, and she knew that his eyes were going to adjust to the indoor light. She executed a somersault, arriving on her toes and running bent over to any shelter she could find. It was another horse. A bullet snatched the heel off her left boot, and she flipped over and fell to the hay. There she pointed the German pistol and fired at the shape in the doorway. The gun almost flew from her hand, and she would have a bruise there tomorrow. She grabbed the pistol in both hands and fired again, but the shape was gone from the doorway.

The shooting was over but there was no silence in the barn. Horses thumped the floor and screamed. The sharp scent of gunsmoke made her head snap back, and her eyes squeezed shut with quick pain.

Then she moved again. The side door opened into a wide lane. There was no one there. The sound of the shooting would bring people eventually, unless it was considered part of the holiday noise. She walked as close to the wall as she could. Her dark red hair passed a painted sign that offered something for twenty-five cents.

There he was, in a doorway. Beside the doorway was a vertical sign that declared the availability of room and board. She could not shoot into the doorway, because there might be a woman on the other side of the door.

But he moved now, out of the shadow and across a shaft of sunlight. It was Groulx.

She did not fire yet. She raised the gun slowly to shoulder level and waited.

"You're crow bait, Groulx!"

He turned, the rifle barrel trying to find the source of her hard female voice. She squeezed the trigger. The Winchester flew from the bandit's hands, end over end into the dirt of the street. Groulx stared in amazement for one second, then turned and ran.

"Merde," she said.

She ran after him, and nearly pitched into the dirt because of her uneven boots. Around the corner she looked without care, and had to throw herself back against the rooming-house wall, as Groulx's brown-and-white horse thundered by her. In the flash of that instant she saw his right arm hanging beside him, a bright red stain all down the white sleeve of his shirt.

She raised the Luger and fired again at the retreating form, but the bullet only disappeared.

Then the people started to arrive.

"You are a total asshole, Frenchie," said Spencer.

He was holding a handful of currency and watching horseshoes flying through the air. In the past hour he had broken even, and he did not like breaking even. He figured they had about broken even on the mine robbery, and he had come to the Labour Day horseshoe pitching with the hope of winning or losing. This asshole with the bloody sleeve was not helping matters.

"Frank, we got to get out of here. There are enough bulls in town anyway, what with the goddamned weekend, and now they got something to do."

Spencer admired a ringer that deprived him of twenty dollars. He was also, on further consideration, not entirely displeased with the turn of events. He paid out the money with a coyote grin to a banker in a straw hat, and clasped Groulx on the injured bicep. Loop cried out and his partner smiled with satisfaction.

"Good work, faithful companion. Now we will do what you have suggested. Can you fork a bronc?"

"What?"

"Can you sit a horse, man?"

"Sure I can. We got to find a doctor out of town."

"That's my brave Kid Fuckface," said Spencer. "Now, we will pick up a bottle or two of whisky for your arm and my contentment, and then we will commence our ride to the Elsie."

"The what?"

"The Campbell ranch. I want to show you where this all started."

Loop Groulx was completely out of his depth, and the shock in his arm was turning to thick bone pain.

"Show me? What, show me?"

"Show her."

Caprice was not at the field when the ball game started. First she had stripped the dead Cabayo of their appurtenances. Then she had paid the hostler more than he was used to for a grave. Today, she had said, yes I know it is Labour Day, all right then, tonight. Then she had paid him some more money to rent an ordinary buckskin mare with no beauty but with what the hostler promised to be extraordinary bottom and fair speed.

"She's corn-fed and mountain-bred," the man told her.

"How does she react to the sound of gun-fire?" she asked him.

"Probably a hell of a lot better than I do, pardon my French," the man said, lowering his face and shaking his head.

"I dont know how long I will be wanting her," she said. "I will give you two weeks in advance."

"Not necessary," said the man, partly in response to her penned-up grief, and partly because he had looked into her grey eyes and could not hold back a memory of love. He felt his foolishness and his age.

Then she tried to track down a cobbler to fix her boot, but if there is anyone who wants to drop his tools and have a year's worth of fun on Labour Day, it is a cobbler. So she went back to the livery barn and knocked off her other heel with a hammer and chisel. Now she was under six feet tall. And at last her heart was not pounding.

But it was caught in something. There was something that would not let it expand as it wanted to.

As it had one day in an orange grove in Spain. There was a lot of the colour orange in the air, and in front of it was a horse's black head.

Now her left hand flicked at the left leg of her trousers, flicked at something that was either gone by now or deep in the fabric.

She could not feel her right hand properly. She flexed her fingers, knowing that she was going to use them. Hoping.

Strange Loop's brown-and-white horse followed the white-and-brown horse, because he was accustomed to do so. Loop had savaged his flanks with his spurs on mounting because of the difficulty of getting into the saddle without the use of his right hand. Spencer had watched the awkward and painful ascent, then stepped directly off the hotel porch into his stirrup. That had made Loop madder than anything. He rowelled his horse, but his horse was accustomed to it.

Now they were riding down the street that would take them past the livery barn.

"Frank, are you going to tell me this is the shortest way out of town?"

Spencer turned his head a quarter of the way around, finding the edge between haughtiness and practicality.

"It is the shortest way to something," he said.

As they passed the big arched doorway of the barn, they both peered into the darkness, not confident that they were seen.

Just in case, Spencer gave out a long low wolf whistle.

At the baseball field they were in the second inning, and Roy Smith was standing on third base, gulping air after having raced there with a triple.

In the livery barn the old man's son, who was supposed to be plying his shovel and broom, was carrying a small greenish-grey book, open in the middle.

"Hey, Dad, what the heck does this mean?"

"What," asked the distracted father.

> "What! shall the poet squander then away,
> For thy poor purposes, himself, his mind,
> Profane the gift, which Nature, when she gave
> To him, to him entrusted for mankind,
> — Their birthright — thy poor bidding to obey . . ."

"Where did you get that?" asked the old man.

"It was laying on the floor, Dad. I just swept it up with the other stuff."

☆ ☆ ☆

The two bushwhackers rode their mounts at a fast walk along the good wagon road to the Campbell spread. Loop Groulx had no idea why they were riding into the high range country north-west of Kamloops. His right arm was numb now, the deep pain having been replaced by an absence. He did his best to flex the thick hairy fingers of his right hand from time to time. Putting the best light on the situation, he figured that his business partner knew a sawbones who would work on gunshot wounds without being too meticulous about reporting them to the authorities.

"How far we going, Frank?"

"Dont worry, Frenchie, our place of destiny is just fifteen miles from town," said Spencer, sounding amused.

"Sweet Jesus, Frank, I hope to hell you know what you're doing. My arm is killing me."

"Everything is going to turn out fine, pilgrim."

Spencer reached into his saddle-bag and extracted a bottle of whisky. He pulled the cork with his teeth and spat it out on the ground. After taking a long pull from the bottle, he offered it to Loop. Loop wanted a drink badly, but he had a terrible time taking one. His right hand could not grasp the bottle or the reins, and he could not drink with the reins in his teeth. Finally he looped the reins around his saddle-horn, and had a good slug of the high quality whisky.

It was the first time Spencer had been on this road since the night he had shot Pete Foster. The choke-cherry bushes along the sides of the road were covered with dust. The northern slopes of the rumpled brown hills were covered with bright sunflowers. Along one straight stretch they met a flatbed wagon driven by a Chinese man in an immense cowboy hat. Only Spencer raised his arm in greeting as the wagon passed, leaving the two riders in a snarl of dust. Spencer had a big toothy smile on his face when he looked back at the disappearing wagon. Groulx was more persuaded than ever that his partner was coony.

They stopped on a small promontory and sat their saddles for a spell. Groulx knew that they were not blowing the horses. They had been walking them most of the way, as if Spencer were savouring this expedition. The Tennessean was scanning the road behind them with his dangerous eyes.

"What you lookin' for Frank? You reckon as to how the police are doggin' us?"

"Nope."

"Then what are you lookin' for?"

"Good lord, you are a stupid man, Groulx. I dont know why they call you Strange Loop. They oughta call you Stupid Loop."

"Damnit, Frank, if my arm wasnt killing me — "

"If a bull had tits it would be a cow," said Spencer, and wheeled his horse about, inducing the beast into a nimble trot.

The road seemed flat for most of the way, but it rose slowly and inexorably to the higher country. The alders gave way to pines, and the sharp blue mountains came into view behind the closer brown humps. Groulx's arm responded to the quicker pace of the horses, a rhythmic ache running up and down from shoulder to elbow. Once he reached with his other hand, bent over so that he would not let go of the reins, and he thought he could feel the bullet in there. It was the bullet or a piece of bone. Whatever it was, he did not probe it again because he did not want to faint and drop out of the saddle.

In the western half of the North American continent it was immediately apparent that human beings had a close relationship with animals. The natives of that gigantic area had a spiritual relationship with them, wearing the same clothes and taking their names. The immigrants from the east made them work or fed them so that people in the east could eat them. Thus they too shared their condition. But a man never realized how fully he was like an animal until he had a hole in his flesh, till he could see that he was made of meat.

Loop Groulx, never a greatly complicated man, now felt his personal horizons shrinking toward each other. He was becoming fixated on pain and the desire to escape it. If he had thought of putting a bottle of whisky in his own saddle-bags, he would have finished it by now.

"Can I have another slug of that licker, Frank?"

Spencer drew his parti-coloured mount to a halt and reached down.

"We'll both have a little slug. One. Because right past that little clump of sorrel is the Campbell buildings."

Loop had a short look, but he didnt know what sorrel was. He didnt care, either. He was just glad that he was going to have a slug of whisky. He tried for three glugs of the bottle's neck, but Spencer nipped the bottle away, spilling a little whisky down Loop's blouse.

"You are looking a little puny, partner," said Spencer.

"Just get me to that sawbones," said Groulx, his voice coming from a throat with tightened muscles.

But they did not move right away. Spencer walked his horse to the top of an upthrust rock and looked back at the long even rise they had negotiated. Apparently he did not see what he had been looking for.

"We left sign that a tin-horn easterner could cut," he complained.

"So let's get on to the ranch," suggested Groulx.

Spencer got down and flexed his saddle-stiff legs. Groulx decided to sit where he was. For a while they stayed still like that, resembling a sentimental painting such as one was likely to find in an Alberta hotel lobby.

"Here's the way it's going to go," said Spencer at last.

Oh shit, thought Groulx.

"Here's the way it's going to go," said Spencer. "I am going to set right here for a spell, and you are going to ride on into the ranch.

Soon as I see what I am hoping to see, I will come on in. Meanwhile I want you to scout around there and see if there's anyone didnt go to town for the Labour Day crap. You got it? There might be an old Chinaman and maybe a woman. You check it out. But dont go busting in. Go in careful. They dont know you, but if they seen that wanted poster you been hungering for, they might figger out who you are. What I mean is, make sure you see whoever's there before they see you. Savvy?"

"Who's going to fix my arm?" asked Groulx.

"Ask the old Chinaman," said Spencer, an unkind grin on his face.

So through the lengthening shadows Loop Groulx walked his horse in the direction suggested by the wagon road. High in the air in front of him he saw a little bird chasing a big bird in an erratic course.

Less than an hour later he was back. Spencer heard the triple-thump of a galloping horse, and had his .44 Russian in his hand when Loop Groulx came into sight. He was looking past Groulx and up the road as Groulx came to a clumsy stop. There was sweat on Groulx's face and something other than pain in his eyes.

"Old Chinaman!"

"What? Talk to me, boy."

"Old Chinaman! Maybe a woman! You want to know who's at the Fucking Campbell Ranch?"

Spencer's eyes were checking out the road upward and the road downward.

"You better tell me quick or I'll drop you right here," said Spencer. His playful cruelty was gone now, and replaced by straight danger.

"There's Provincials there, that's what. At least four of them, and one of them is our old buddy, Constable Burr."

"Son of a bitch. That weasel's smarter than I thought."

It was not pure admiration that characterized Spencer's words. It was a spooky kind of excitement, a mixture of astonishment and anticipation. Groulx did not like it one bit. His horizons were getting very close to each other, and it looked as if Spencer was thinking of something new.

"Frank, I could use a touch of that whisky," he said.

"You're in luck, Frenchie. There's one shot left."

He tossed the nearly empty bottle to Groulx, and Groulx tried to catch it with his right hand. The bottle fell to the ground under the belly of his horse. But it was unbroken. Spencer did not even look at him as he got down awkwardly and kneeled on the brown grass among the restless legs.

"Actually we are both in luck," said Spencer. "There she is now. She aint as smart as Burr, but she is persistent."

He had been looking down the slope, and now he picked up the reins hanging in front of his animal's nose and hoisted himself into the saddle. In about five times as long Groulx got up too.

"You're not planning on the ranch, are you?" asked Loop.

"No, sir."

"Where are we going?"

"West."

"We came from west."

"We are going west, making sure we leave good sign. You know about west, dont you, Frenchie? It's called freedom and opportunity."

So they rode on an angle away from the wagon road, westward. The fabled island of Atlantis, the Fountain of Youth, El Dorado, the Oregon Trail, the North-West Passage, the Lost Something Mine, that had all at one time been waiting for someone with the heart to go westward. Even Loop Groulx had once heeded the call of the west. Right now he just wanted a white bed. He didnt care what direction it was in.

The two Indian observers had it both ways. They were sitting their ponies on the edge of a cliff, sitting perfectly still, so they would appear picturesque and what some people termed romantic. But they were sitting their horses in the shadows of a clump of rock-clinging ponderosas, so nobody with ordinary eyes would be likely to see them. If they had been a few hundred miles to the south and east, and fifteen years earlier, they might be two scouts for Red Cloud, looking down on some illegal white gold-seekers and planning sudden demise of those immigrants.

The first Indian had heard Red Cloud speak at a convention long ago, and he had come back to his own hills filled with a mixture of envy that his own life could not be so dramatic, and gratitude that he did not have to slap paint on his face and ride to highly likely death in a skirmish with white treaty-breakers. It was part of his pedagogical method that he never told his young charge about his meeting with Red Cloud. Or the Oglala woman who wanted him to seek his future in the Black Hills.

It was enough to be an old source of mystery in a land that was being crossed with steel rails and wagon roads and telegraph wires. Those things had introduced time-tables to the world. It was enough to be someone who could come and go according to irrational time. If a white man asked him how old he was he always replied: many moons. They liked that.

So he was really interested in this story he had been reading in the soft ground along the creek bed, and in the open country between the river and the hills. This woman with the light spots on her face, and this man who should have stayed on the other side of the medicine line. They were both crazy. So they were both riding outside the boundary of the white man's time and into Indian territory.

"Why are we watching these insane people?" asked the second Indian. "I understand that history demands my understanding the ways of the white immigrants, but this is not history. This is a spook story."

"This is your graduation exercise," said the first Indian.

"I am glad of that," said the second Indian. "I will be one happy graduate in another month — "

"Another moon."

"Another moon, when the red salmon with the big noses come up the river. I am going to eat salmon till my skin is covered with scales."

"So, you do not like to make deer jump off the bluff, but you will gladly put a spear through the flesh of a fish that is only trying to raise a family."

"I dont want to talk about this. I want to talk about these crazy people chasing each other up and down the valley. If I have to observe them anyway, I might as well know what I am looking at."

"Or you could forebear talking altogether, and just observe," said the first Indian. "Many whites think that is the Indian way."

The young man smiled ruefully. He was a young man, so he could afford to be generous. He could gracefully accept the bright remarks of his elder. He smiled in a companionable way and reached his hand into his cedar-root game bag.

"What is this?" asked the first Indian.

The young man was holding some field glasses in his outstretched hand.

"I got these in Kamloops. For you. Take them."

"No."

"A gift from a grateful graduate."

"I do not need them."

"I will never tell anyone."

The old man snatched the glasses out of the hand, and put them around his neck.

"Go ahead, have a look. Look down there, just past that clump of cedar."

The old man trained the glasses inexpertly at first, unable to pick up anything but a blur of sagebrush.

"Do you see the cedar?" asked the student.

"It is all just a blur brought closer."

"Turn that round part."

Then the blur resolved itself into a sharpness of outline the old man had not seen in years. All at once four horsemen rode with eerie silence into the circle. One of them sat his mount like an Englishman.

"Constable Burr," said the first Indian.

"Not constable blur?"

"That is terrible," said the first Indian. "That is the worst one I have ever heard you try. I think that you had better be one of those famous silent Indians."

Thus did the second Indian know that his gift was accepted.

"Of course," said the second Indian, "it is with Indian eyes that you look through the white man's glasses. The glasses mean that once more you have the advantage over him."

The first Indian was ranging over the whole vista now that he had the hang of the gadget.

"They mean that now my Indian eyes can see what my head has for some time been thinking," said the now younger older man. "These immigrants are staging some kind of parade. It is as if they have all together come to understand what is happening."

"Do we?"

"Oh, yes. But we understand it as a narrative of fate, and we have always understood it. They have been late in understanding it because they have been trying to understand it in terms they are accustomed to. They have their peculiar notion that such actions can be explained by looking into the individual heart and head. It is what my anthropologist friend called motivation."

"You are fooling me," said the second Indian.

"No. They have this word motivation, which means the reason a single person is moved to do something unusual."

"Even after a cow-woman or whatever you call her has ridden to the end of the world and back again? Even after a hunted man comes back into the hunting grounds of the hunters? I thought that you said I was ready for graduation. I think I do understand what is happening now, but I do not understand why the white man thinks he understands. Motive nation? Crazy."

"Sane."

"What?"

"It is we who are crazy. That is our hope for survival," said the first Indian.

He was still sitting with a straight back on his pony, the field glasses held to his eyes. Once in a while he would pull them to a side and check the terrain without them.

The young man sat absolutely still. The ponies did not switch a tail or make a grunt. The September wind announced its tidings through the ponderosas' clumpy needles along the line of the cliff's edge.

The old man let the glasses hang against his deer-hide blouse.

"Eight."

"At least eight," said the second Indian. "The two renegades. The red-hair woman. The four pony police. The schoolteacher. Mayhem, theft and murder."

"Excuse me?"

"Something I heard their medicine man say."

The old man looked out over the hazy valley with his own eyes.

"I thought the picture-maker would be following them, too," he said.

Caprice was not stupid. She knew that she was cutting the two dry-gulchers' sign because they wanted her to. Or rather that Spencer wanted her to. She had given up trying to understand why he had come all the way up here and then commenced to ride away from her. She knew that something was supposed to happen at the ranch and that something had changed his mind. Now he was leading her northward, up the Deadman River valley.

Deadman River used to be known to fur-hunters as Rivière des Défunts, and to local roustabouts as Knife River. All three names were left there after 1815, when a clerk for the North West Fur Company post in Kamloops went riding with a client up the side of the trickling stream one day in early autumn. The two men disagreed about the best place to set up camp, and the loser of the argument was Antoine Charette, the unfortunate clerk. The loss of the argument was indicated by a knife in the possession of the other man. Antoine Charette had often thought that he would like to leave his surname on some local topographical feature, as several other Quebeckers had done. The closest he was to come to his dream was to leave his final condition as a colourful designation for a sometimes fugitive waterway. Luckier, perhaps, was a man named Vidette, whose name remained on a lovely lake forty miles up the Rivière des Défunts.

Caprice was not thinking of history and geography now, though. She was thinking of fate.

She was looking at the new prints of two horses she guessed were brown-and-white, prints left in the dusty parts of the gravel-strewn bench land that formed the first miles of the ride up the valley. The warm afternoon wind smelled of sage, and some of the small clumpy cactuses still offered their yellow flowers. The buckskin mare plodded without particular grace over rock and couch grass. Caprice was used to looking at the brown surface of the earth past the magnificent black Spanish head of her own horse, and now the ride was only on an animal anyone could have ridden. Now the ride was bitter. The Luger was in her hand once an hour.

An hour up the Valley she rode through a small Indian village made of scattered lodgepole houses and a newly painted church. At the base of a blood-red rock bluff she saw the mound of a new grave with wild flowers laid on it. She did not see a living Indian.

In another hour she saw the five hoodoos. Halfway up the eastern slope of the valley the light brown pillars stood free of the ordinary earth. They were forty feet tall, and wore stone caps that reminded her of some soldiers she had danced with on Bastille Day on another continent. She threw the memory to the ground behind her. She did not want to remember anything that happened before last year. She wanted to gather a year's memory and let it strengthen her long right arm for the close future. She did not want to imagine a future beyond the next day.

The earth here was memory itself. The cliffs along the west wall were inlaid with petrified wood. The shapes of sea creatures hid beneath slabs of stone speckled with jasper and agate. A few years ago Caprice had worn expensive rings on both hands. Now she wore gloves that were strong enough to hold a whipstock and tight enough to hold a pistol.

The valley was becoming slowly more narrow, the walls a little higher. Other creeks fed their scant water to the river. Frugal Criss Creek murmured a little. Barricade Creek spoke for a moment. The tall woman on the ordinary horse followed a dusty road north, feeling a cooling of the air as the hills came closer and the sagebrush disappeared, to be replaced by forest. The river could be heard splashing now as it fell between rocks. Then the valley opened out again, and she saw below her a flash of water.

By the time she reached the lake the sun had fallen too. The east slope of the valley was still bright, but shadows were filling the valley floor. The road followed the east side of the lake. She swung to her left, looking for a place with trees dense enough to keep her camp out of view.

First she unsaddled the buckskin and rubbed her down well with a few handfuls of bunch grass. Then she laid out the bedroll and the weapons. This night would be cool with the onset of fall at this altitude, but she was not going to take a chance on a fire. She had to be satisfied with hard rations and water from the lake. When darkness fell it was nearly complete. She could see stars reflected in the surface of the lake. She thought they were the only other eyes there.

In the morning she ate cheese and raisins while she was riding, and she was back on the narrow road before the sun reached the east side of the lake. North she went, the road climbing again and becoming all the while more narrow. It was as if she were being conducted through an enormous natural loading pen toward her last journey. That was not memory so she allowed the thought. She passed another lake and then another, water with Indian names now. Beside one of them rose a giant white castle, and memory tried to get on the horse again. But this castle was two hundred feet tall, and made of sand. There were no defenders on its parapets, and she was not on a course to lay siege to a castle.

But the earth was a place to read. It was not easy for a former poet to resist the opportunity to read. She chose, though, to read the writing on the thin road. She did not imagine that she was leaving a story for others.

Now she saw Vidette Lake, the last lake on the valley floor. It was probably filled with trout that would soon lie still in the high sun. She stopped and looked at the quiet water and fought down an insistent wish. She took the Luger out of her war bag and pointed it at a dead tree that stood uselessly with its roots half out of a nub of rock.

Then she followed the road that was now only a horse trail as it twisted up to the right around a hillside and at last onto a plateau. She could see for miles now, past rolling treeless grassland to the blue mountains on every side but the south. Stands of alder and cottonwood dotted the range country. In an hour of riding she came to a creek bed that had more water than rock in it. Here the trail split and followed the creek bed in both directions. She decided that she had come far enough north, and took the right fork. A few hundred yards later she came to a silvery old lodgepole bridge. The buckskin stopped and gave her head a shake. Caprice nudged her with her knees. The buckskin moved to the other side of the bridge and stopped again, ears stiff and turning. Then Caprice listened, and came back from wherever she had been. She could hear the roar of a waterfall.

She got down and led the animal, wishing now that she had Cabayo with her. The sound of the water became louder as they followed the creek. If she had been here in the spring the roar would have been deafening. If the late winter had not brought so much snow there would be no sound at all.

Then she saw Deadman Falls. The water slipped over hanging moss on sheer rock and spilled through its own spray a hundred and fifty feet to the river canyon below. Short brave pine trees stood on the edge of the chasm. The buckskin resisted her hold on the reins, leaning away from the drop. Caprice felt as giddy as she had felt on watching the new tower being built in Paris. Memory went through her like a knife she could not feel.

Then she saw the two men. They were sitting their horses near the edge of the precipice among the trees. Then the two men saw her.

There could be no more searching and no more following. The plummetting skein of water spoke without variation, as if it had been turned on by electricity for a tableau.

Strange Loop Groulx heard the noise as if it were a part of his bone-ripping headache. Feel my forehead, Frank, I think I got a fever. There she is, Frank, can we get this over and go home? Get me to Doctor Trump.

The logical thing would be to pull Campbell's Winchester out of the scabbard and get down, sight it over the saddle and put five or six shots into her. But Spencer did not want the Winchester. He did not want to do it with the Winchester. She was just about six feet tall, taller than her brother was. He did not come all this distance to do it with a rifle. You could do it with a rifle on the open range.

With Cabayo she could have simply looped the reins around the saddle-horn, but she had known this horse less than three days. She tied the lines firmly around the narrow trunk of a small tree. Then she took down her whip and pulled the Luger out of the bag. She left the box of shells where it was. There would be no use for reloading today, no use and no time. Maybe the mare would die in a few days, tied to a tree. Someone would find an unfinished poem in the saddle-bags. She rummaged for a moment till she found the notebook. Then without hesitating she walked as close as she dared to the edge of the vertical rock, and holding the big pistol in her gloved left hand, used the other to throw the notebook into the air over the gorge.

She was just about sick with the giddiness. It was stupid — she could ride a horse at speed over a dark trail into the muzzle of a gun, but a cliff with music threatened to distract her mind just when her heart had reached the day it desired. One hundred and fifty feet below there was a roiling pool filled with boulders that had a thousand years ago snapped off the face of the high wall.

The late morning sun was turning the cliff face white. It was as hot as the middle of the summer even at this altitude, but that did not matter. Her mouth was dry even as the water spoke going down the cascade, but that did not matter either. Her eyes caught a glint of light high up among the trees, but now that today had arrived that did not matter. She began to walk around the precipice edge that was the same shape as the scar on her cheekbone.

The two men began to walk their horses around the edge toward her. If they all continued at their present paces they would meet where the Deadman fell. I was right to throw the poem down, she thought.

They are not using their rifles this time, she thought.

The two brown-and-white horses were picking their way no faster than a human being would walk upon the uneven surface next to the lip of the gorge. Their feet came down one at a time on good solid rock with a trace of moss.

Then there was nothing but movement under their feet. Without disturbing the speech of the water, a broad slab of stone with two horses unfortunately riding it gave up its place at the top of the wall and slid straight down for twenty feet. Then it struck a ledge and bounced out into the unsustaining air. Caprice halted her steps to watch, and saw the two horses, black against the white, their legs stretched out stupidly beneath them as they dropped. One hundred and fifty feet below, one of them smacked soundlessly against a rock and disappeared a second later into the water. The other just disappeared. A horse's head showed for a moment in the white, then was gone.

She began running as well as she could to the place where they had stood, her boots serving her better than they would have with heels. Where the surface sloped she skidded toward the edge, but kept moving, grabbing with her hands when she had to. There was no pistol in either hand now. She had no idea whether she would need it. She heard a yell that was made of no words in any language.

Loop Groulx was hanging onto the root of a small tree that had until today been a few yards from the edge. As she approached him, trying to balance speed with a satisfactory grip on the earth, she saw that there was blood all over his sleeve and shirt front. He looked up at her with ferocious desire and then let go. She could not see his descent, and if he made a sound during those four seconds it was not as loud as the sound of the water.

Lying on the ground now, Caprice could hear nothing else, not even the quick breath coming from her lungs.

But without words a question formed somewhere inside or outside her. Where was Frank Spencer?

For a half-second she entertained the idea that there had never been a Frank Spencer. She had seen the horses falling plainly, but no men. She had not even seen Groulx fall, only his eager face disappearing.

Had Spencer managed to leap from his horse just before the rock gave way? She got up and walked among the small trees, looking for a shape. He could be aiming a barrel at her back right now. She could not focus her attention properly — it was as if she were just partly here, walking unsteadily and without aim among the small trees, the sound of the water like the blood inside her skull. Had she imagined Spencer?

She recalled the constant argument of Roy Smith. Maybe she should just get on her horse and ride away. Let the Provincials go about the business of looking for the killer, if he was in the country.

Maybe his body was lying in the water below, turning with the ceaseless life of the river trying to get free. Maybe he had been on the other side of his horse when it fell, cut off from her view.

Approaching the edge of the fresh rock, she felt the dizziness again, and got onto her belly to look down at death. She saw Spencer's face looking up at her.

He was standing on the narrow ledge that the huge slab of rock had bounced from, his chest flattened against the rock wall, and his .44 Russian in his free hand. His face was about ten feet from hers, and it was formed out of a deep hatred that must have been shaped in Tennessee before anyone was born.

Now her giddiness was gone entirely. Now she was totally alive and here. She stood up straight so that she was nearly six feet tall in her flat boots, and from where he was clinging she must have been half the sky.

He was going to shoot. But he waited. Again he waited.

The whip stock was familiar in her hand. She shook the length out behind her in a space between the small trees. Her eyes looking down saw both the white water between the boulders and the upraised pistol in the murderer's hand.

Now he was going to shoot, and kill them both. He was going to make sure. He was finished waiting.

Quicker than death the whip went down, and Spencer's .44 flashed in the sun as it flipped end over end up into the air and then vanished into the braided descent of Deadman Falls. She did not know whether it fired.

Once more. One more snap of the arm.

She looked at Spencer alone on the rock face. He never took his eyes off her. The only one to say anything was the creek jumping to its life.

Then she lowered the whip, holding it two feet from the end, letting the other end touch Spencer's face, gently, like a spider on a sleeping man's forehead.

For a few minutes, while thousands of gallons of fresh mountain water fell over the brink into the gorge, Frank Spencer stood resolutely still, his eyes never leaving those grey eyes above him. Then he grasped the whip with one hand. If he moved his other hand from the rock to the whip he would be committed. Caprice braced herself as best she could, one boot finding a crack in the rock. If the solid earth had given way once what was there to stop it from going again? Spencer grabbed the whip with his other hand.

His face was bright with hatred, the invisible sanity that nobody understood. He would still kill them both. She refused every thought that tried to enter. But he weighed more than she did.

"Let me help you with that," said Constable Burr.

Caprice would have had to look into what she thought of as the future to see the death of Frank Spencer. Ten months after the bright day at Deadman Falls, the bad story that had begun thirty-six years earlier in Tennessee ended in the jail yard at Kamloops.

As if it were just any other summer morning in the brown valley, the sun jumped up and the air became hot an hour later. Frank Spencer was hobbling back and forth across the eight feet of his cell floor as he had done all through the darkness of the night. Now the morning light was descending the west wall of that last room, and the prisoner had consumed the only breakfast he could imagine getting into his stomach, a pot of British tea.

His body jerked when he heard the steel key in the steel lock. His last visitors were here, two men in the service of the silent personage they called God, and a jailer with a chisel and hammer in his hands. All of them waited in an embarrassed speechlessness while the steel rang and the leg irons were carried away. Then the prisoner had a few minutes to talk about last things with the men in robes. The scent of new lumber drifted into the room.

On the wall was a yellowed clipping from the *Inland Sentinel.* In pencil someone had underlined the words: "yet comparatively speaking, a young man. He does not present the appearance of a man who would commit so serious a crime as that with which he is charged."

"Can I have a pair of slippers?" Spencer quietly asked.

"What?"

"I made a promise I would not have my boots on when I died."

In the slippers he walked between Sheriff Pemberton and

Constable Burr to the bright new lumber in the yard, the two robed figures walking with heads lowered at the end of the procession. Spencer proceeded resolutely up the steps and stepped onto the trap. He shook hands with the sheriff and the policeman and the two spiritual advisers, ignoring the man in the hood.

He felt the rope brush his face before the noose was adjusted behind his ear. If his hands had been free he might have grasped the rope first with one hand, then with both.

A white cloth was fitted over his head.

He mumbled a prayer that could not be heard nearby.

He was seen to be trembling.

☆ ☆ ☆

Arpad Kesselring helped her off with her sheepskin jacket and hung it neatly over the back of her chair. Soo Woo himself, and two of his relatives bustled around the table, arranging napkins and cutlery for the fifth time. The tablecloth still had creases in it, and the glasses sparkled from having been rubbed inside and out. Soon the steaming dishes were being paraded out of the kitchen and fighting for space on the table. The men jostled one another for a chance to assist their guest.

"Try the barbecued pork, it is scrumptious," said Mr Trump, the editor of the *Journal.*

"Thank you," she said.

"Leave some room for the shrimp balls," suggested Mr Minjus, the photographer for the CPR.

"They smell nice and garlicky," she said.

"Can you tell us how you felt when that revolver was pointed at you?" inquired the Middle European journalist.

"Not yet, not yet," said Doc Trump. "This is a dinner first and foremost, gentlemen. If our guest and benefactress wishes to recount her experiences for your profit, let it be later while we consume cordials in my offices."

Still the dishes kept coming. Soo Woo was not wearing his usual plaid shirt and apron, but a two-piece green silk outfit bearing illustrations of complex dragons. No one had seen it before, but all were glad to see it now. It seemed to provide a proper ceremoniousness for the occasion.

The food kept coming. The diners felt that their only recourse was to eat it as fast as they could. Caprice did not lag behind any of the rest, though she was the only one among them who was using chopsticks.

Her new boot heels sounded good on the boardwalk as they all marched past the Nicola Hotel, past the B.C. Express Company office, past the funny window display in the barber-shop.

"It seems to me," said Caprice, "that if we are going to the doctor's office for liqueurs, we are going the long way round."

The four men were smiling, and so was Addie the afternoon bartender, who had thrown aside his apron and joined them as they were passing his establishment.

"Well, yes. But we have to make one stop on the way. Yes," said Mr Minjus, "and, well, here we are."

They had stopped in front of the wide arched door of the hostler's stable.

"After you, miss," said Herr Kesselring, with a perhaps exaggerated Continental bow.

Inside, it took only a few seconds for their eyes to adjust to the shadows and yellow light. Her eyes picked out a number of brightly coloured dresses, one of which was being worn by Gert the Whore.

"Your bruise is all gone," said Gert.

"The exterior one, anyway," said Caprice. "What are you doing in a stable, Gert?"

Gert's smile was perhaps not larger than any of the others, but it was the most pleasant to look at. She took Caprice's hand and turned her so that she was looking toward stall number one. Out of it came the boy with spectacles, his hand clutching the end of a length of rope, and of necessity following him stepped a big white creature that turned out to be a stallion.

"Oh my," said Caprice.

"That's right," said a man's voice.

This was a white-haired gentleman in a black broadcloth suit with an iridescent blue-black vest. He was Mr H.P. Cornwall of the Manor, someone generally more spoken of than seen in the town of which he possessed a considerable portion.

The boy put the hackamore lead into her hand. She reached out her other hand and touched the white horse's muzzle, then she pulled her hand back.

"What?"

Some of the people laughed. They were all enjoying this more than she was so far.

"This, well, lady, spoke earnestly to everybody in town just about, and came to my stables with a good story and a bag full of assorted currency," said Cornwall in his British accent.

"He gave the horse to me for a lot less than it's worth," said Gert.

"The horse is not as valuable as what you have done for this community," said Cornwall.

Caprice had a flash of memory, of walking along the boardwalk in early summer, listening to the buzz of commentary behind her.

"You are giving this horse to me?"

The boy spoke up.

"His name is Hiss — "

"Hisan," said Cornwall. "He was foaled in Arabia."

She walked around the animal now, patting his hide here and there. Hisan shivered, and if the assorted company had been watching closely enough they would have noticed the faint red hairs on her forearm lift.

"I dont know what to say," she whispered.

"How about trying 'giddyap,' " suggested Doc Trump.

Everyday Luigi was sitting in a wicker armchair in the ward. He was still in pyjamas and a robe, and he still had a cumbersome bandage around the bottom half of his head, but he was wearing bright high moccasins stitched with tiny bloodstones, and he had his pyjama legs rolled up so that one could see them.

The two Indians sat on straight wooden chairs facing the brave Triestino. There had been some discussion as to whether they should rather have been sitting cross-legged on the floor, but the first Indian would have nothing of it.

Caprice stopped at the door to watch. First the Indians would move their arms and hands in an interesting pattern. Then Luigi would wave his in an Italian approximation.

"No," said the first Indian, "you just called me an uncooked porcupine. Try it again, and keep that elbow up."

"He *is* an old uncooked porcupine, you know," said the second Indian.

"You may be a full member of the people now," said the first Indian, "but I still have to make my report to the council."

Everyday Luigi looked at the younger Indian and made a quick gesture with the fingers of one hand and the wrist joint of the other.

"Exactly," said the first Indian.

They all turned to watch when the tall woman with red braids and brand new boots advanced between the empty iron beds.

"How," she said.

"Oh, we say the words and then we make the signs," said the second Indian. "Then we get him to try it."

Luigi made a slow gesture with one hand pointing toward his breast.

"He says he feels pretty good to see you," said the second Indian.

Caprice shook hands with the two native men, then kissed Luigi on top of his head.

"Imagine," she said. "You can understand seven languages now, even if you can speak only one. You could be a great poet."

The white stallion walked beside a sorrel fellow, his breath visible in the grey light of the false dawn. On their backs rode Caprice and the schoolteacher Roy Smith, hand in hand.

It had been a short night but they had filled it with the disputing of their wills and the moist adoration of their bodies. Now they were riding through the empty streets of Kamloops. Even the town dogs were curled at doorways. The townspeople's horses, picketed in yards and vacant lots, stood with their heads down, free of insects, given to absence.

But someone somewhere was playing a guitar. The notes must have been coming from an open window or a porch. The tune was perhaps Spanish and then perhaps Irish. The accompaniment was the echoed clopping of the horses' feet.

"All right," said Roy Smith, "if you will not tell me where you are going, it doesnt matter. I will go with you."

"No, teacher. You have just begun the school year. Your place is already made."

They rode, hand in hand, to the eastern edge of the town. There she made the slightest move of the rein, and the great horse took one more step and halted.

"Are you going to come back?" asked Roy Smith.

She let go his hand and lifted her braids from her chest and let them fall to her back. Then she put on her tight gloves.

"That is for history to tell," she said.

"This is not history," he said. "This is our lives. This is my sanity."

She leaned from her saddle and put her large gloved hands on either side of his head. While she was kissing him the enormous white sun lifted from its rest and swept the valley through. The mist on the river did not have long to live.

"Couple, adieu; je vais voir l'ombre que tu devins," she said.

Then she performed the slightest pressure of her long thighs, and the white horse stepped off. Roy Smith stayed where he was for an hour, watching Caprice ride into the sunrise, consoling himself with the shortness of life.

She rode eastward through the west that was becoming nearly as narrow as her trail.